EVERY MAN ALSO

ROBERT WINSHIP

Texas Review Press
Huntsville, TX

Printed in the United States of America

**Permissions
Texas Review Press
English Department
Sam Houston State University
Huntsville, TX 77341**

Library of Congress Cataloging-in-Publication Data

Winship, Robert, 1930-
    Every man also / Robert Winship
        p.   cm.
    ISBN 1-881515-19-2 (paper)
    I. Title
    PS3573.I53234E94   1999
    813'.54--dc21   98-43485
                                                 CIP

In memory of

Jess Neely

and

Joe Davis

EVERY MAN ALSO

Every man also to whom God hath given riches and wealth, and hath given him power to eat thereof, and to take his portion, and to rejoice in his labor; this is the gift of God.

—*Ecclesiastes*

One

The first of them came in too early and too fast and, because of the gloom of the hour and their unfamiliarity, jarred their frames at the front gate where a dip had been figured into the street. Then they cruised through and back out again, grimy with the grit of the open road, aflutter, and went down the street to Basil's.

There were eighteen of them at Basil's then, before seven-thirty, and they ordered coffee and scrambled eggs and sausage and toast. Several were unsteady, and it was these that got a rhythm going with their heads at the tables and began to yell and chant with the rhythm, until Basil came out of the kitchen and stood smiling at them with a slow look in his eyes, and then they quit.

"Go out to the parking lot," he told them. "It's too early."

One of the unsteady ones belched. He could do it anytime he wanted. Basil stood at the door until the laughter died down, and until they all stopped looking at the belcher and at him, and were instead looking at things on the tables before them, then he went back into the kitchen. Soon he was back with a fresh pot of coffee.

"Welcome," he told them. He moved about, pouring. The slow look was gone from his eyes, now, and he was smiling, and as he poured the coffee they looked at his furry arms and shapeless hands.

"You will need the noise this afternoon," he told them.

The belch sounded again, and then everyone was laughing some more. Basil went back to the kitchen and left them to the waitress, who moved in with six warm plates held fanwise before her and to the side.

When they were through and had had more coffee they went outside again to the cars. There were by this time other people in the place already and more entering, and the newcomers had seen the cars in the front, and looked at the group as they went out. Six of the group were girls. They went to the restroom together and were the last to go outside.

One of the unsteady ones had some new crepe which he was distributing to replace old, tattered crepe. It was blue and gold.

"You can let your top down now, Flea. It's not going to rain," said the unsteady one with the fresh crepe.

"I get to ride in the convertible," one of the girls said.

"Me too!" another squealed.

"You better leave the top up, Flea," one of the other boys said. "It's going to rain for sure."

Flea laughed. He was slight, and happy, and had brown eyes.

"The top goes down," he said. "The girls can all ride with me!"

When they were re-creped and loaded and the engines were started, the four cars had to wait in line to get out onto the street because the traffic was heavy now.

A white car that was sailing by on the street honked nine times in rapid succession and the driver stuck his left hand high out the window and above his roofline, making an uncomplimentary gesture.

Some of the girls shrieked back at him.

"Yea Bears!" they yelled. "State Bears!"

One of the other drivers stuck his head out his window and yelled at Flea, who had all the girls now.

"Let me go first. This ain't a parade!"

Flea nodded. He braked his convertible. He had lost magnitude now because the six girls were sitting high on the back of the seats and he was nothing but a chauffeur. The girls looked a little strange sitting like that under the gloomy sky. They would get cold.

The driver who had yelled at Flea slid down out of the parking lot and into the street, picking up speed. The slow breeze whipped and popped the streamers on his car, making it appear to scud along.

"We'll get stopped for sure if the girls go first," he said. "Some ballplayer or somebody would step out in front and stop the car. Nothing like a car full of girls for getting stopped on a campus."

"Right," said one of the unsteady ones. He lay down in the back seat, which he had all to himself.

"Let's make a run through," said the unsteady one who was now very steady in his reclining position, "and then go find a good bowling alley somewhere so we can sit down in the soft seats and wait." He closed his eyes.

"What about the girls?" asked the third one, who was in front.

"Hell with 'em. Flea's got 'em now. When they're around you can't relax anyway. Jake, let's find a bowling alley."

Jake did not answer. He was leading the way.

The four cars braked carefully past the dip at the front gate, then eased up the long, evergreen-shrouded promenade to the first building. The convertible was third in line; the girls yelled and waved to the few students on the sidewalks.

"Yea Bears!" they screamed.

And that was all there was to it.

The campus was a big one, with bare trees that were black near the ground with recent rain, and red buildings with arches, and sidewalks with clumps of sweatered students who stopped to compete with stares. Some of the students answered back.

"Yea Warriors," they yelled.

Some threw small things that did not matter.

And at nine-thirty the driver of the dingy blue Oldsmobile whose name was Jake consulted his watch, made a wrong turn to get away from the others, and sped away to find a quiet bowling alley with a snack bar and soft seats, for the waiting. Flea could have the girls.

He was a big man who was so full of years now that he knew it was not healthy to be so big, but he leaned into the steps and climbed them as he had done thirty years ago, when he was scouting other teams.

That was one thing: about the heart. No one in his family had ever had heart trouble. No one. And now at fifty-three he could stand sideways before a mirror with his clothes off and suck in his stomach and press his legs together and see that his thigh was as wide as his waist, from the side . . . .

He opened the heavy overcoat so his knees could work. He went all the way to the press box without stopping. But this time he did not enter the press box; he went instead to the exact middle of the top row and sat down and leaned against the cold concrete rise of the box behind and above him. He got a yellow ticket out of his pocket, looked at the number, then leaned forward and looked at the stamped number between his feet. He settled, breathing hard.

The field spread far below in the sun like a grilled pool table, and the goal posts, pepperminted now with red and gray on the right and blue and gold on the left, held the streamer-ends of their crepe wrappings out in the breeze: skinny, licking flags, rattling and popping like tiny artillery in the empty stadium.

He shivered a little in the thin sunlight and then got out his field glasses and began to glass the field.

"Hello, Mr. Mason!"

He took the glasses away and looked to his left, where a tall young man was climbing.

"Won't you be in the box today?"

"No," he said. "Not today." He had raised one finger in greeting.

He put the glasses to his eyes again and after awhile sneaked a look and saw that the young man was no longer there.

That was another thing. The young man was a fourth or fifth-string guard. In his day he had suited everybody out for the games, and had sent a student manager up to spot for the radio. But not any more. They did not do it that way any more. Now the coaches were all young and had charm so they could go out and recruit the boys in the first place, and they had squads so big that they had to suit out three teams and maybe an extra punter and an extra place-kicker and that was all; everybody else sat in the stands in street clothes.

His mouth was a straight line beneath the glasses.

At one o'clock people began to come into the stadium. He watched them through the binoculars: colorfully-dressed people— the early ones, the real fans—not filing as yet from the aisle openings in the upper deck across the way, but sauntering, pausing in small groups on the concrete stairs to talk and shout and enjoy themselves. He could hear the women now and then from across the field.

Charlie and Benjie and Ace walked out on the field from the ramp and he saw them and put the glasses on them. They walked out to the fifty-yard line and scuffed at the turf with their shoes as if they were testing it.

He smiled under the glasses. They were killing time, trying to hide nervousness by playing at being busy. He understood, remembering.

In the glasses he could see the red and gray ticket hanging from a coat button on each man's front: their passes to the sideline, to the Warriors' bench. The glasses made them look closer together than they really were, as if they were afraid.

"You'd better be, Charlie," he said. Then he smiled a little.

He watched them look at the ground and scuff at it and try to think of things to say. Benjie was grinning. Benjie was the end coach; he was always grinning, except rarely when one of his boys got blocked in or dropped the ball.

Soon they grew tired of sampling their own field and headed back toward the ramp and the Warrior dressing room. He watched them go. In the glasses they were too close together and seemed to be leaning a little as they walked without making much headway. The glasses made them look like they were climbing a green hill, crowded together for protection.

He smiled, putting down the glasses beside him.

The sky was high on this perfect afternoon, and clear the way a dirty windowpane is clear, with no real blue and yet no clouds, either, except a few translucent traces that appeared not to move; and the breeze was constant but not gusty, steady as if the whole stadium were moving against a mass of still, cold air, toward the north.

He watched the people come into the stadium, in streams now. He saw that they were all happy.

He thought: happy. Be happy while you can. You won't be happy for long and I know which ones will be sad when it's over and it's the ones with red and gray corsages on their women.

Then he looked at the far corners of the upper deck across the field and saw clumps of people sitting there and he knew that very shortly the stadium would be filled to capacity. But he had known about the sellout crowd for several days now, since Novak, his business manager, had told him.

"Sellout, Mase," Novak had said a week ago. "We can't miss it."

"Good," he had said.

"When State comes we always draw good," Novak had said.

"Especially this year."

"Right, Mase. A sellout. Can we take the game?"

"We're the Warriors," he had said, not looking at Novak.

Now he saw the Warrior cheerleaders along the sideline in front of him, carrying their red and gray bullhorns which they stacked upright, side by side on the end of the midfield stripe. He picked up his binoculars again and looked for one of them: a girl with light brown hair. He found her quickly—there were only four.

He thought again: I wonder if she would need a pillow. No, I bet she would not.

Someone back in Mason's past had needed a pillow under her hips but he could not remember who it was. He was indeed getting old. Someone had needed a pillow and had fussed at him about it; not griping, actually, but looking forward with hope to the day when the mechanics would change, somehow, and everything would be all right—without the pillow. Had it been Martha? He could not remember.

But the thought of Martha made him look at his watch, and then he got to his feet and began to descend the steps, much slower than he had come up.

Martha was his wife, and she had once been very beautiful but now was too heavy and had lines around her mouth which prompted the nervous habit of moving her mouth around in an effort to take up the slack.

He found her at Gate Four. They started back upstairs.

"I don't know why you insist on sitting outside today," she said.

He could not tell her that it was because he wanted to be sure nobody watched his face during the game.

"And the Goodsons. They wondered why you weren't at their buffet just now and I didn't know what to tell them except that you said you had to be at the stadium early, and they practically insisted that we sit in their box and all I could say was that you had said we couldn't . . . ."

"Save your breath, Hon. It's a long haul."

"Can't we go sit in the Goodson's box?" Her voice was reedy.

"No."

"They've invited us. Lem thinks it would be nice to have the athletic director in his very own box."

"Save your breath, Hon. We'll enjoy the change."

She sighed and began to take the steps, slowly, with her husband behind her.

When they were seated on the top row and he was holding Martha's hand in some sort of payment for having caused her to lose her breath, the Warrior band began to play a march below them.

"Listen at that!" he said, feigning exuberance. "Isn't that better? Now, if we were in the press box we'd be listening to it on the radio!"

"Not really," she told him, between breaths.

"Really," he told her. "Really, Hon."

He thought of asking Martha about the pillow, but then he decided that it was not the proper time to ask. Maybe it would never be.

The stadium filled. People came up the steps in long, packed queues, now, and he was surprised to see how many of them were smiling. It was not because they loved football or because they loved the Warriors, but because they loved anticipation. They loved feeling the fact warm and close that now, here, were the Warriors and the Bears, finally: Tech and State. And they loved holding the feeling close with both hands and knowing that they were to be a part of it.

When the teams came out on the field to warm up he had several thoughts among the new noise. He saw that it was overcast now; that the colors were not bright on the field and the stands across from him looked like a great tweed fabric . . . unwavering because the moving parts were too small to see without the glasses. And another thought he had. He thought of something he had read about World War II. A lieutenant from a Middle-Eastern nation and his men had some prisoners out on the Iranian sand. And they presented the prisoners one by one and drew a line in the sand with a foot twenty feet away, then placed bets. A fire was going nearby, with stove-lids in it, and tongs for handling the lids. They cut off a man's head and applied a red-hot stove-lid to the spurting stump of his neck with the tongs, and saw how far he could run toward the drawn line before he fell. Then they settled the bets before the next man ran.

They were bickering, laughing. He shivered. No doubt it was sport.

He felt Martha snuggle against him.

"Oh, it'll be such a good game, Mase," she said.

Sport.

He did not answer her. He picked up his glasses instead.

Both squads lined up in checkerboards at their respective ends of the field and ran through calisthenics, watching their captains lead them. All motions were neat and perfect; hands clapped and feet swung.

Long ago Mase had often said that you could watch the teams warm up and pick the winner; but he had had to concede later that he had been wrong about that . . . or maybe it was he that had lost the ability to predict. He could not predict anything about the game anymore. In a contact sport in which mental attitude counted for so much, he had seen lackadaisical teams go out and play a perfect game; and he had seen teams so fired up that they threatened the very dressing room walls in getting to the field, only to go out and lay a collective egg. The young coaches still could predict, they thought . . . .

He smiled thinly. But he could pick the winner today, boy. Yes, sir, boy. But he found that he did not want to think about it.

The squads broke apart, then, with the linemen going to one side to charge on the snapped ball, the backs and receivers to another going down under passes, and the punters and place-kickers practicing their specialties. The Warriors had a Number 26 who could punt seventy yards at will. He began drawing a crowd noise with each kick.

The crowd today was a vibrant one: he could feel it breathing around him. Today was different . . . everything was poised, waiting.

Both sets of cheerleaders began to work while the squads were still warming up; the yells they drew were great voluble coughs of sound, loaded with enthusiasm.

Mase put the glasses on Charlie, the Warrior's head coach, who was standing near the holder as his boy kicked field goals from thirty yards out. He saw that Charlie was moving his feet over the turf in empathy, never still, and he watched him take something from his pocket and pop it into his mouth. Aspirin. It would be aspirin, where Charlie was concerned. Mase grinned a little.

Then, just before the squads went in, the Warrior cheerleaders stacked their bullhorns and took a breather, and an impromptu yell came out of the red and gray section. Mase heard every word of it, because of his interest. He had heard it before . . . .

Hit 'em on the helmet!

Hit 'em on the socks!

Hell, yes! Hell, yes!

Go, Tech jocks!

Fifty people yelled it from the Warrior section, in perfect unison and without the cheerleaders . . . who watched with grins that were apparent to Mason even without the glasses.

This was something else. Mason did not smile. He listened to the wave of titters following the yell and was glad when it swelled to a heavier sound as the Warriors trotted off the field.

The Bears followed, then, looking brighter and faster in their blue and gold that contrasted with the midday gray.

He had seen it grow and flex in thirty years, this idea that the students had of the athletes. And in years past he had tried to talk to people about it. But not anymore.

He remembered when it had begun at Tech a long time ago. Two of the trustees who had had big handshakes and loud voices had brought in twenty football players who did not care if the sun came up . . . and the crowds had swelled, and the dollars. Then later when good players were paid, and then later than that, when cars were to be had through excellence . . . until the leagues and the conferences and the athletic associations had set up stiff rules of amateur status and stiffer fines, and never looked the other way anymore. He remembered the easy courses for athletes.

And now . . . .

Hit 'em on the helmet!
Hit 'em on the socks!
Hell, yes! Hell, yes!
Go, Tech jocks!

He almost liked it, in a way. In a way it was cute. The cheerleaders had tried to make it official. But mothers had written in.

He had tried to tell people. Now the athletes were as smart as anybody else, but they found an image and a way of acting all set up and ready for them when they entered school and they followed it—most of them—out of necessity; out of loneliness. And the thing was fed and kept alive by the other male students, knowing and unknowing, in competing for the girls. It had become a real stigma. Speeches had been made. And Mason had seen athletes who were good students cry with the frustration. And nobody knew. He had tried to tell people, in years past. He had tried to tell of what he knew: of offensive linemen changing the whole line's blocking pattern at the line of scrimmage a count ahead of the snap of the ball, of the complexities and mental gymnastics which had to be mastered by every player, of studies which had shown, or championship teams, that the best players were superior students, on the average . . . .

Go, Tech jocks! Our jocks are better than your jocks!

He had told people of the time during Christmas holidays one year when the president of the school had gone into every male student's room to see what the rooms would show in the absence of the tenants, and had found bodybuilding equipment in three of every four, and of his surprise . . . .

At least the term was a backhanded compliment: jock. An athlete's first piece of clothing when he dressed . . . the masculine image for sure!

And the students. They jeered at the athletes on the campus, behind their backs. Oh, yes! Behind their backs, for sure. And they set up a stigma of the girls so that anyone who went with an athlete was suspect. These same students who had each lost the girl, in high school, to a football player . . . . But they all had weights hidden in their rooms. And they all came to the games, and cheered mightily, when their very own jocks defended their own honor. *Go, Tech jocks. Win, jocks.*

Mase knew that grades are a matter of interest, and that football demands high interest and leaves less room for other interest, so that a top player who can command top grades is a superman. He knew that the game demands aggression. Once he had told people these things, but not anymore.

"Mason," they had said, "it's time for you to step down. You will be athletic director only."

And Charlie did not know about the things. Charlie talked a good game, and did not know.

Mason sneered. Then he saw that Martha was looking at him. "What, Hon?"

"I said, aren't you excited?"

"Sure. Sure I am."

"You don't seem to be." She moved her mouth around.

He picked up his glasses so he would not have to see her.

Mason had stopped trying to tell people of what he knew. He had given up. Perhaps he had been wrong. Charlie had not spoken of these things, and Charlie had had success—more success.

And now in his heart Mason knew above all that he hated Charlie not because he had taken his job but because he had done so well at it. Mason could not predict any more; all his answers had become wrong answers.

But he could predict this one!

Mason smiled a crooked smile under the glasses.

And Charlie, not knowing the things about the athletes that Mason had tried to tell, having heard Mason himself say them but not believing and so forgetting a long time ago, did not discipline his boys. So there were episodes, and people remembered them, and the image and the stigma lived on.

Mase had given up. He did not even know whether he believed the things any more. And after today it certainly would not make any difference what he believed about the game or the players. After today when people asked his opinion about the sport he would give it and turn away, or not give it. He had never been able to face a man without looking into his eyes. Or probably he would change the subject.

Mason put the glasses down. He had been looking through them at nothing, anyway. He sighed, then, and shifted his shoulders a little. The Tech Athletic Director was ready.

When the people were up all around him and Martha, lips parted, eyes staring, frowning a little to get noise ready inside, and he heard the cheer begin down near the ramp like a faraway crashing sound, drawn out and growing like a coming surf, he got up and helped her with his hand under her arm, gently. Oddly he remembered a talk he had had with the engineer when the stadium was going up, fifteen years before.

"You don't build to hold sixty thousand, Coach. You build to seat sixty thousand and to hold a hundred thousand. And why is it like that? Well, it's because when you have a long run or when the teams come out and everyone jumps to his feet your sixty thousand stadium will fall down, that's why, because there's a lot more weight with everyone getting up at once, so we have to stress it high."

And he had thought at the time that crowds do not jump to their feet at once when the teams come out. They get up in small groups and they straggle, and the yelling is in pieces and not all at once.

But not today. Today the teams appeared simultaneously out of the ramp; and not trotting, either. Running.

And no one wanted to sit down to await the kickoff.

Mason looked at Martha.

"Want to sit down, Hon?"

She moved her mouth, glancing at him. Then she looked back to the field.

Both squads were packed in great circles, heads bowed. They were praying. This was something else that Mason knew about; after today he would not want to think about it anymore.

All the seniors walked to the middle of the field abreast, then, for the coin toss. Coaches called for this when a special effort was indicated; it often occurred during the State-Tech game. Twenty-one boys faced each other and watched the man in stripes bow this way and that, shouting.

The Warriors won and elected to receive. The crowd still had not sat, and the roar that sounded might have been that following a touchdown.

Twenty-one boys ran to opposite sidelines, then twenty-two ran back, strapping helmets, clapping hands. Mason could tell from the way they all stood in position, shifting their weight and lifting first one foot then the other, that tension was high on the field. He knew already that it was high in the stands.

The whistle sounded, the blue line advanced, picked up speed, and the ball took off, tumbling in the air. And the tension came to fruition, then sucked back as the ball was caught on the five-yard line, and then the cheering began—spotty and involuntary, in shrieks until the ball carrier was piled up in a skidding, pounding heap at the twenty-yard line. And then a great sigh, and people sat once again, shuffling, watching.

Go, Tech jocks. From the students.

Go, Tech Warriors. From the fans.

Except that now with the heat of battle upon them and with something of themselves that was so very important out there on the field somewhere between the two bucking, heaving lines, the Tech student body forgot all about the jock part, and it was Warriors throughout and *Warriors go*, now. The jock part had died. It would live again on the campus at eight o'clock Monday morning, win or lose.

Mason smiled, wanly. He licked his lips.

The Warriors ran left guard for one, then off tackle left for three, then passed incomplete to the tight end on a button hook with three blue and gold Bears slapping the ball before it skittered to the grass; and with the grunt of crowd empathy at the incompletion came a large silence on the part of Warrior fans and a swell of gusto from the Bears.

Mason smiled again, but grimly. He could hear his heart in his ears. And he sensed that Martha was looking at him.

"What, Hon?"

She did not reply. She moved her mouth instead.

After a while she said: "You didn't lean, Mase. You didn't lean with the Warriors. Usually you push me the way they are going when they run a play."

And he could sense that she was studying him.

He thought: already. Already after one series of downs and she has noticed it.

"I don't know what you mean, Hon."

He saw that she was watching the punt, moving her mouth around to take up the slack in her lips that early age had made.

It was a good punt. Mason saw the Tech right end get knocked off his feet five yards from the line of scrimmage, and he saw a little Number 15 for the Bears field the punt on his own thirty-yard line, dodge the first two men in faking to his right, then sail forty yards down the field to his left, to be shoved out of bounds on the Tech thirty. The stands around them were quiet. They could hear the enthusiasm on the other side and they could see it, from far away, like individual little whitecaps on a pitching sea under a pending hurricane, already blowing.

Suddenly Mase did not want to see any more. He stood, aware that Martha was watching him.

After a time he made as if he had risen to stretch and adjust his coat, then sat again.

The Bears were in their huddle, he saw.

He did not want to think of it, but there was no way, now, that he could keep the words out of his head: a chain of words: his own words: "They will start with a wide-tackle six defense. The right tackle is slow to the inside in this setup, so you can bump him with the left end from outside and leave him and have the end circle and get the linebacker. Fake a pitchout right then give to your left halfback on a delayed dive. He will run by the tackle . . . ."

The Bears ran an unusual play, a delayed halfback dive left, and their Number 37 ran past the Warrior right tackle who was off-balance to his outside, and the linebacker who was on the ground, and made sixteen yards straight down the field.

Mason sighed. His hands were tingling.

"Martha, I'll go get some cigarettes."

She regarded him with some of the sharp disfavor that adversity brings to any communication.

"Don't be silly. You haven't smoked in years!"

"This is a good time."

He was up and walking down the steps, hearing the ebb and surge of noise from across the field. It was funny, he thought, but every time the noise picks up, the voices you hear leading it are the women. He wondered if it were because the voices were shrill and that only; then he decided no, that it is because when they are in the mood to yell they yell at everything.

He bought cigarettes and lit one, then stood around a little until he saw several people that he knew, coming grimly after the extra point to buy things, then he went into a telephone booth, sat down, and unfolded the door closed.

Mason sat there, smoking. Soon he dropped the cigarette on the floor and crushed it with his toe because his legs were cramped and the heel would not come down.

More words ran through his head and he could not stop them.

"The quarterback, McRath, puts his left foot back if he is going to his left, and his right foot back if he is going to his right, and he begins to do this about the beginning of the second quarter or earlier if he's hit hard a couple of times . . . . The starting left guard has a tendency to lean back when he is going to pull. You can blitz a fast linebacker over him when he does this and catch the play behind the line of scrimmage . . . ."

He lit another cigarette, forgetting that he hated cigarette smoke in a closed place.

"When they send a man in motion they never come back outside tackle to the weak side, so you can crash the weak side end and sack the quarterback from his blind side when he passes . . . ."

He had written the words, printing with a soft pencil with his wrong hand, his left hand, on three sheets of wrapping paper, then had lost his nerve and had made a telephone call from another city instead, from a pay telephone using the name Asa Covington, and had read the printed letter, then destroyed it.

Why Asa Covington? It had popped into his head; that was all.

Mason saw now that a small young man was waiting to use the booth, and was beginning to peer inside with some concern.

He got up and stepped out.

"Are you all right, sir?"

Mason did not answer. He had not heard the young man at all.

When he got back upstairs he saw that the score was still seven to nothing, the first quarter was almost over, and the Warriors had the ball at midfield. They had just made their first first down.

He lit a cigarette and sat down, sensing that Martha was studying him, moving her mouth around, pursing it.

The Warriors came out in a little spread formation, with an end and a halfback set out together wide on the left.

"They have cooked up a shotgun formation for you . . . two receivers out wide together. They have never used it before . . . ."

The Bears covered the two men with a single cornerback. At the snap of the ball the two men split, the wide receiver going deep outside and the defensive back taking him and the offensive Warrior halfback hooking to the inside. The pass was on target to him, but another Bear back had sprinted in after the snap, before the ball was thrown, cut inside the receiver, fielded the ball out of his grasp, and juggled and swatted it for ten yards only to drop it, accompanied by a dying roar from the Bears fans and a great grunt of relief from the Warriors.

"And the spread formation is only to see if you will cover with two men. If you cover outside with one man, then run another one in, man for man at the snap, you can intercept and score . . . and they will drop the spread. They don't have many plays from it. Do this or cover with two men from the outset and they will go back to their standard formation."

He remembered the voice on the telephone, in Chicago—a man whom he had never met—and he remembered his own surprise when a feminine voice had stopped him, halfway through his reading and had asked him to repeat a phrase. A stenographer, on conference hook-up . . . .

There had been much more. It had been the greatest scouting job of his life.

Mason clenched a fist. He would have to relax. It was amusing, in a way; he had thought that he would be enjoying it. But he had to admit that he was not.

And he did not know how the man in Chicago had relayed the information on to the State coach. Perhaps directly, by telephone; maybe they had done this before. He did not know. He knew only that if State beat Tech by more than seven points or maybe by more than ten, now, after the man in Chicago had placed his bets—he, Mase Mason, would be richer by an even hundred thousand dollars. Tax free.

"Mase," Martha was saying, "the Warriors are not doing too well."

He felt a tide of compassion, and took her hand, smiling.

"I know, Hon."

"State is favored, aren't they?"

"By seven points."

"That's funny. That's exactly the difference, now."

He thought: but there will be more. There must be more.

And there was. Eight times without doubt and four more by hunch he saw his own hand in the game.

The final score was twenty-eight to nothing. The State Bears were the conference champion. They carried their coach from the field.

"Go," murmured Mase Mason with a sigh, as they started down, "go, Tech jocks."

"What? What did you say?"

"Nothing. It's all over."

Since he had quit coaching, stepping into the dressing room after a game had always seemed to Mason like going back in history to the misty scene of a battle that he had read about: everything was steamy and close with the dying heat of action. A historian knows certain things about a certain battle. Being there and being a part of the aftermath make every written point vanish; everything is different. The important points that everybody talks about later do not exist, have not existed. Hidden things are important. He had never understood this feeling.

Dr. Bechtol let him in. He was drunk.

That was all right. He was always drunk at the games. Staley Jergens, the team trainer, had often said don't ever let Bechtol sew on you if he is sober. Sober he is horrible, but drunk he is a great man with a stick-tie.

"Let 'em in," rasped Dr. Bechtol. "Let 'em all in!" He waved his arms.

"No," Mason said.

"Hello, Mase," said Dr. Bechtol. He left, then, for a back room.

The bare and baring bodies were steaming and muddy, and almost everybody was crying. These were other things that Mason had never understood about the game: how it is that with a good, fast turf the players can get muddy under their uniforms, when you can go back to the field after the game and not see bare ground anywhere. And the crying: usually after a losing game a half-dozen players cry. After a very important game that has been lost the number who cry is proportional to the degree of frustration and this involves many things. Mason himself could not remember ever crying after a game. Someone had told him once that it is the manliest and most masculine who cry. He had looked for it and had decided that maybe it was true: maybe it was because these had tried hardest and had less left within them to inhibit crying when it was over. He thought: maybe it's the cowards who don't cry. The cowards and the traitors. But everything is relative . . . .

He caught sight of his own face in a mirror, studied it, and saw that it was properly stern. He felt good, oddly good, and relaxed; it had been easy, and was getting easier. He was surprised.

One unusual thing about such a dressing room is that almost all the players have hair, and most of it is cropped close. This makes them look young but the thin mud and the crying makes them look older. It is a strange thing.

Benjie, the end coach, brought in a big cardboard box that was smoking cold with dry ice. He set it on a table in the middle of the room and ripped the top off. Inside were rows and layers of Eskimo Pies, ice cream on sticks. Naked players passed by and helped themselves. Strangely, it slowed most of the crying. Nobody could cry and eat ice cream at the same time.

The showers were going full now and players trooped to and from. Hot water vapor came out, and wet tracks made the concrete floor slippery.

Benjie bit off a big chunk of ice cream and mouthed it, with his jaws ajar. He tried to grin at Mason through the rank humidity.

"Next year, Mase," he slurred.

Mason nodded, accepting an Eskimo Pie.

"Where is Charlie?"

Benjie waved to the conference room, off to one side, where a battered door was closed.

"Wait till he comes out, Mase. He's taking it hard."

Mason nodded, turning away.

A tall tackle whose name was Drobisch was still half-dressed in his uniform and was wandering about asking a question. He had been knocked senseless during a goal-line stand and nobody was taking care of him. He could not remember anything.

He stopped a guard who was returning, glistening and steaming, from the showers.

"What happened?" he demanded, for the twentieth time.

The clown of the team walked by going to the showers. He had red hair and had just composed himself from the crying.

"Get your shirt back on, Moose," he said to Drobisch. "We got to go get 'em this last half!"

"God damn . . . ." Moose turned, groping, eyes wide. He tightened the drawstring on his shoulder pads.

There was a laughter. It made those who had heard feel better; after all, the season was over.

"What happened?" Moose Drobisch demanded of another shower returnee, stopping him with a great hand flat against the chest.

"Somebody hit you with a Coke bottle from the stands, Moose, while you were on the bench."

There was more laughter.

"Yeah. Oh, yeah . . . . But what happened?"

After a time another lineman led Drobisch to his stall and began to help him get undressed. Mason could see them talking: the one gesticulating, demanding; the other naked, calm, nodding, going about the undressing with a dirty face.

Long ago Mase Mason had told people of the greatness of the game. There is a victory in defeat, he had said to them. You put forth a great effort. You win. You lose. They have in common the great effort, and a great effort stands alone and succeeds alone. Winning and losing and the difference between them are something apart from the great effort, which has a success all its own, win or lose. So, he had said, go hard and you can't help but win, partly; go hard and there is victory even in defeat . . . .

Where had he lost it? Had he lost it along with his bit about the jocks? He realized that he had not told anyone of either in a long, long time, since he had been deposed as head coach, since he had stepped down.

He stood there, lipping his ice cream and trying to keep it away from his teeth, watching the shorter lineman undress Drobisch and lead him to the shower.

After a while he went to a back room and he saw the quarterback, McRath, still in his uniform, lying on his back on the table. He was lying very still, with his right hand clenched and in repose on his chest; and Mason had a worried thought, but saw eyelids clenched, also, and knew that he was all right. Dr. Bechtol was sewing his left hand, where he had been stepped on: cleated and torn down the meaty part of the palm near the little finger.

Mason moved close. He got ready to speak. McRath had taken a terrific beating. He had been sacked six times.

But then Mason realized that when he spoke McRath's eyes would open, he would smile with dry and crusted lips, and try to sit up, and would speak to him with respect and call him "sir." And suddenly he knew that he would not be able to take it . . . .

He went back into the main room.

Some of the boys were dressed now. All were silent. They would leave quietly, in a hurry; they would shoulder through the sparse crowd outside without speaking, perhaps looking for a girl. Then, later, they would smile again, trying it out. The season was over. And, after all, they had finished second in an eight team league. They would talk about how many boys would be back next year, and so on. Their worlds would continue. The idea made Mason feel better.

He still had not seen Charlie. Not that he wanted to see Charlie, at all; but he always had, after the games.

Two doors opened, then, simultaneously: the battered door where Charlie was, and the outside door to the ramp; and Charlie stepped from his door with his hands in his pockets, leaving the door open, and Wilson of the *Sentinel* came in from outside. His door closed of its own accord.

Good old Wilson. The other sports writers were still in the State dressing room. Most of them would stay there.

Wilson took it for granted that Charlie had been there all along, for he saw him and headed for him; Mason was nearby so he moved in also.

"Mase . . . ," Charlie said, throwing his head to one side in the helpless gesture, leaving his palms in his back pockets. His face was white and thin and shiny, his eyes puffed. There were great sweat circles at his armpits; his tie was loose and wilted.

"Coach," Wilson said. He was small, fiery, but now subdued. He held a cigarette that was wet and limp but burning.

"Coach . . . ."

"It's all right, Charlie," Mason heard himself saying. He had meant to glower, to be stern. He put a hand on Charlie's shoulder, hating the hand.

"What was the turning point of the game, Coach?" Wilson asked, getting ready to write on a pad.

"When we took the field. You know that!"

Wilson snickered. He had gray teeth, and when he grinned he showed at least ten teeth, and they all looked exactly the same.

"Was there anything special that you noticed . . . I mean . . . anything special?"

Charlie stared at the sports writer, then managed a thin smile at Mason.

"I thought Carey played a good game," Wilson said, waiting. Charlie frowned.

"They all tried," he murmured. He was frowning. "You can put that down. I think we got a good effort from everybody . . . ."

The coach picked up enthusiasm, then, speaking, frowning hard: "Yes. We had a good effort. Yes, there was something special that I noticed . . . It was like . . . ."

Wilson stared. Mason stared.

Many moments went by. So many moments went by while Charlie stared at Mason that Mason felt something drop inside him.

"It was like . . . ," Wilson reminded.

One of the players stopped on his way out and handed Charlie an ice cream bar.

"It was like we were out-coached," Charlie muttered. He looked at his ice cream bar, seeing how he could bite it.

"No," Mason heard himself say.

"No? Hell, Mase, nothing worked! Not a God-damned thing worked! If I didn't know better I'd say our workouts were scouted . . . don't quote that, Wilson. But I know that that could not be because we worked out all week in the stadium. You saw! We worked out all week in secret in the stadium and I had sentries posted with field glasses and they watched the tall buildings . . . and . . . ."

Later he sighed. He began to eat the ice cream.

"Out-coached, Wilson. Print it if you want to." Charlie's voice was hoarse, played out.

"That's all there was to it. We tried. Nothing went right."

"Don't print it, Wilson," Mason heard himself saying. It was not what he had meant to say at all.

"Just one of those things," Mason said. His voice was strong. He saw that both men were grateful to him.

"Say they have a great team," Charlie said, then. "Say that I said don't take anything away from them. They were a great team out there today."

The pencil scribbled, and all three stood listening to the noise it made.

"Any injuries, Coach?"

"What difference does it make? No! Don't say that. Say no bad injuries. We'll plan for next year."

McRath came through, then, going naked to the shower, and the three of them watched him go.

"I'll say McRath was glorious in defeat and McRath is back next year!"

"You do that," Charlie said.

They separated, then. Wilson went to talk to the few boys who were left. Charlie folded his arms and ate his ice cream bar, then lit a cigarette and got it wet with his fingers. Mason stood around, watching the last movements in the dressing room.

He thought: easy. It was easy.

But he knew deep down that a crime is always easy so long as the heat of the action is still about. It is later that it becomes hard, when the sweat has gone.

He thought: go Tech jocks, You God-damned jocks, you P. E. jocks.

And you son of a bitch, Charlie.

Mason began to tremble. He walked out of the dressing room, saw that there was no crowd at all left at the ramp entrance, and strode toward Gate Four to find Martha.

Later that night a strange thing happened. Mason went into his bathroom to brush his teeth, and had to open the door to the medicine cabinet before he approached the lavatory, so he would not see his face in the mirror. It was a juvenile stunt. But then he saw how the toothpaste was striped and he spent his time thinking about how ridiculous it was to be using striped toothpaste; and this was not a juvenile stunt at all . . . .

Monday morning brought the first real norther of the season, and the wind had a severe and steady weight to it. Mason, patting his hat down securely and holding the flaps on his blue overcoat from inside, left his car in the lot and walked past the tennis courts to the field house and his office. The icy air sang and hummed with a disturbing note in the chicken wire fence around the courts; one had to almost believe again in spirits. It was a strange effect on so bright a morning. The wire did not show the push of the wind, either. Perhaps that was the disturbing thing about the sound: there was nothing to see, though the air was clean and clear.

Inside the great building he was struck by the quiet which he had come to associate each year with the sudden end of the football season, and in his new sense of vacancy the song of the chicken wire in the wind kept going in his head.

He stood by his big desk taking off his coat and his hat, reflecting as he hung them about the paper on the desk: how in years past there had been much paper and then how he had shuffled it off, thinking that to have smaller amounts of paper on one's desk was better, and then, later, how the paper had not been there anymore, so that he had kept dead paper around so he would have something—anything— showing; and how now the few papers he had on his desk were ri- diculous because he had had them all there for six weeks at least and had shuffled them around into different positions everyday to give effect . . . .

And all the while the spirit song of the chicken wire was going in his head. Going until he knew what it was. It was herald and embodiment of an idea which he had but had not realized until now: the idea that someone must suspect something. Of those who were there who saw the game, someone must know. Someone must have realized that the Bears had had advance knowledge of things . . . to be otherwise was unthinkable. The chicken wire said it to him, sing- ing in his head.

He sat at the desk for a time, looking at the few ridiculous pieces of paper. Then he got up and went to get coffee.

When he got back with the plastic cup that burned his fingers he sat again, and, as he toyed with the dead paper on his desk, was glad all over again that he would soon be leaving.

On impulse, then, he swept everything on his desk into his bat- tered and flattened wastebasket, which he held in his right hand below the edge of the desk. Then he returned to the coffee.

Someone must know. They could not all be that stupid: that nobody should have seen.

The chicken wire sang it in his head.

He studied the idea as he sipped, and as he studied it he realized that if anyone thought that something had been amiss and thought that Mase Mason was involved, that person would come by his office sometime today to test him. Today, while the effects of treason would still be fresh and virulent on his face and before he had practiced covering them . . . .

Mason smiled at the coffee.

He had learned something about treason these last few days. He had found that, while he did not like to look at his face in the mirror, he had been able to rest easy—there had been no haunting feelings.

And he believed that he had figured it out.

The shame of the traitor is merely the shame of the half-breed, but in a brighter light. That was it. Keep from getting your feelings of love and hate mixed up and you can do anything without regretting it. He had learned that he who betrays and who has also hatred is safe; and the more hatred the safer; it is the traitor-through-weakness or through-luck who suffers. The personal tragedy of Judas was not that he had hated but that he had loved: not enough and yet too much, too, and so had done the thing without the hatred which would have made him a real alien and a perfect enemy; and so he must have had guilt already before he did the thing or else a plan in his head which failed.

And Mason had the proper hatred, enough so that he could let it show on his face in absence of guilt, and people who doubted would see the open hatred and mistake it for grimness at having lost the game and so would go away satisfied.

Mason smiled into his cooling coffee cup.

He thought: you son of a bitch, Charlie. And you Tech jocks. Go, jocks.

He did nothing in his office for a whole hour, and at the end of that time Staley Jergens, the trainer, walked in. He was short to a fault, and always wore a ridiculous red baseball cap which had the effect of rounding his head and making him appear even shorter. When he walked in, Mason's mind went back again to something he had heard someone—he had forgotten who—say on the practice field one day while watching Jergens pad about, some distance away: "Look at that Jergens. He's the only man in the world who has to cuff his Bermuda shorts."

"Mase."

"Staley."

He sat down in an old straight chair by the door and put the soles of his shoes together with the feet barely on the floor as a child might, and looked at them. Maybe he was one who suspected something.

"Glad it's over, Staley?"

The little man sighed. He leaned back, relaxing.

"This is the first Monday morning in a long time that the training room has been empty, Mase. It's nice."

"No injuries?"

"Not that. They're just sick of coming for treatment. Like, 'Hell with Jergens. I'll let it get well slow, like it's supposed to.'"

He laughed, running the sound together like a goat.

Mason laughed with him. He leaned back, and they looked at each other.

After a while Mason said: "Kind of hard to finish up on a note like that, though . . . ."

"Right. Glad it's over but I think we're good enough to have gone to a bowl."

Mason imagined that the trainer was extra serious, that he was staring and at the same time trying not to stare.

Mason sighed. He put his hands behind his head and interlocked the fingers, looking at the frosted glass of his closed windows and imagining that he could feel the cold of them and see the sweat that he knew was there on them.

"Did you notice how quick they went into a defense for Charlie's new spread, Staley?"

He had not meant to say it. It had been farthest from his mind, but had popped out. So he swung around and glared at the minute trainer.

Several moments went by. Jergens watched his hands, then looked up.

"Well, no," he said. "I didn't. I guess I don't notice such things. Did they?"

"Oh, I don't know. Maybe not. Maybe it was because they did everything so well. I guess I was just looking for things."

After awhile the trainer blurted: "Mase, I never saw boys try so hard, and . . . ."

"I know. That's the way it was, wasn't it?"

"It seemed that way to me. But I was busy."

"Yeah, I noticed. Nobody got anything bad? No bad injuries?"

"I don't think so," murmured Staley Jergens.

Later he said, with the inflection of question in his voice: "About the deer hunt . . . ."

Mason looked at him anew, smiling, now, genuinely.

He thought: that's it. Of course. The deer hunt.

Every year after the last regularly scheduled game Mase Mason had gone deer hunting. It had always been a celebration. In the old days most of the athletic staff had gone with him; then, after he had stepped down, only Jergens and one or two of the assistant coaches had gone. He remembered the contortions which he had gone through to keep from inviting Charlie in recent years. And now Jergens was reminding him that he had not been invited.

Mason sighed. He leaned forward suddenly and picked up his thin plastic coffee cup, tossing it off, sucking it dry by a quick and grand inhalation, then he threw the cup into the waste basket.

"I believe the hunts are over, Staley." It was a lie, grandly given, and he did not look at the little trainer.

"Not this year," he said.

"Not this year."

"No."

Later, then, after they had talked enough about things that did not matter, the little trainer walked out of the office.

All morning he sat there, leaning with his elbows on his desk, waiting, measuring the hatred within and finding it high and recognizing safety in it: safety from the others and safety from himself; thinking about the game and remembering how it had started as all games start with a great pageantry of rattling crepe and cavorting cheerleaders and color and noise, and how the pageantry had changed into moments of truth that tested everyone there, and how the moments of truth had then caused by their results a thing very different from a pageantry: a realization that life is hard and basic and pageantry a necessary mask, an opiate, needed to dress brutal fact. Nobody came.

He remembered the contact man, whom he had suspected of being a lawyer: young, personable, shrewd, who had given a name but no representation, and who had surprised him by telling about point spreads and so on and then had listened to Mason himself talk before he had made the pitch. Mason had told him about the jocks. He had told him that college athletics were doomed. And the man— he had called himself Johnson—had agreed and then had gone right into his proposal. It had been done in a reasonably loud voice and with a smile, and there had been frequent but not-too-frequent allusions to the coach, not flattering. Mason was to await directions, he had said. The game would receive national attention, he had said. And Mason would receive one hundred thousand dollars for merely insuring the point spread; not for fixing the game . . . no one could do that but the players . . . and such a thing would then be dishonest, he had said. He had also said what Mason had known all along: that Tech could not win anyway.

He wondered, now.

And nobody came.

He thought: and they sure had me pegged. I wonder how they knew about the hatred and I wonder if it stuck out as much as the hatred in Julius and Ethel Rosenberg and it must have stuck out more because the Russians had to court them and remind them that they were Jews and oppressed, and this guy who called himself Johnson didn't even buy my lunch.

Then it was noon, and still nobody else had come to his office. He saw that it was twelve o'clock and he relaxed.

Mason leaned back again in his chair, looking at his translucent windows, locking fingers behind his head. Nobody had come by and that meant that nobody suspected anything. There would follow, he mused, several days during which one of the coaches might figure something out, especially after tomorrow—Tuesday—when they would view the film. He would have to maintain himself past that period; but it would be easy. Nobody would really peruse the film as they would had it been in mid-season. Especially Charlie, who was no doubt already making plans for a short vacation and relaxation. That was another thing. The son of a bitch never consulted him about pleasure trips. He considered himself above Mason. Mason was a has-been, a hanger-on, an old dog whose teeth were gone.

Mason allowed himself a slow smile.

He thought: I showed you, son of a bitch. I almost wish you knew it.

He remembered, then, his parting conversation with Johnson, a month ago. Johnson had been ready to leave, and had already given his handshake with its tricky bastard warmth, and Mason had thought of one crucial point.

He arose now and reached for his coat, then his hat, getting ready to go to lunch.

"Johnson," he had said, marvelling that both of them had the nerve to conduct the talk in his office; marvelling more that that was apparently the place for it, "how do I get paid? You don't send a man down here with one hundred thousand dollars, and you sure as hell don't send it in the mail!"

He remembered that the smile on Johnson's face had crippled and then had soured completely and died. And that Johnson had sat down again.

"Your choice," he had said, after a time.

Now Mason had on the coat and hat.

"I go deer hunting on a man's ranch every year after the last game," he had said. Glibly he had said it, then, and proudly. "And he has many acres and cabins, and he caters to hunting by the day also. You can send a man there with the money. I'll meet him there." It had sounded like a reasonable thing.

Johnson had jumped up again, offering the bastard hand.

"Great!" he had said. "Perfect. Name the place in your scouting report, and the time. Tell him how to get there. And our man will be there with the money. If anything is amiss and you are not fully satisfied, you have my address."

It had seemed easy, and proper. Mason had done it.

Mason left his office and went alone to lunch.

He returned to the office at two o'clock and sat for two hours as he had before, doing nothing, waiting, seeing and gloating that no one came to test him; that no one came at all except Novak, and he only to pass idle moments and to fish in his ridiculous way without ever getting to the point for an invitation to go deer hunting—as he had fished every year for the last five without success and without any bait, either, really. The subject never arose.

That night at home he was quiet, and he saw that Martha was watching him. She had caught him holding the newspaper and staring at something—nothing—beyond it.

He sighed and looked anew at the paper, thinking of things to say and trying to get ready to answer her question before she asked it. This was the part of marriage that was hard for him. But he had thought that maybe it was a good thing: it meant that they had a rapport of sorts and that she loved him.

He saw now that she was moving her pursed lips a little, studying the crocheting that she was doing, holding it out from her and looking at it, patting and kneading it a little into flatness. Her arms were soft and flat near the shoulders of her sleeveless gown. Soft round arms are better, he thought.

"Hon."

"Yes?"

"What would you say if I retired? I'm ready, too."

"No. The job . . . ."

He saw that she was shocked and then he regretted it. He had meant to go to the deer camp and then to come home with the announcement, as if he had gone to think and had come home with the conclusion, honestly built, perfectly arrived at, objectively contrived . . . .

She stared at him over her glasses that had bottoms only for the close work, and no tops: half-glasses that had caused him to tease her and to call her Grandma when she had got them. She had never been called Grandma before. She never would again, except in a tease.

"Why . . . why, Mase?"

"Why not? We have enough."

She moved her mouth a little, then took off the glasses and stared.

"But you're only fifty-three. You have a dozen years left."

Silence reigned for a time.

"I'm sorry, Hon. Forget it." And he took up the paper again. It was an abrupt manner of changing the subject which he had learned and had adopted some time before when she was going through the menopause, to keep her from crying.

"No. No, Mase . . . ," she called the paper down again. He rustled it with impatience.

"College athletics . . . ." He stopped and groped for words, then he got up and crumpled the paper where he had sat and walked out to the middle of their den where they were sitting.

"I mean . . . you remember how I used to come home and tell you about the boys and the professors . . . how I used to say I told the professors that they didn't treat the boys right because they set them apart and let them know that they expected them to be sorry students even though in some cases they never said it . . . and then sometimes they were sorry students and I used to tell the professors that when this happened that it was their—the professors'—fault as much as anybody's . . . and how they used to look at me sideways when I said it . . . I told you!"

"Martha, they were right! The professors were right! And the other students! Now the alumni are trying to make graduate athletes wear a different ring! And the boys walk around in a group on the campus and everybody stops and stares at them and it wasn't that way when you and I were in school but it's that way now and it'll never get better. It will get worse! And I want out of it! It's all over!"

"Why, Mason. Don't yell at me. What will you do?"

"I'll decide. I'm going to deer camp in a week. And I'll decide."

He walked out of the room to get away, going to the kitchen where he opened the refrigerator and stared inside for a long while and then closed it without taking anything out.

Later he went back to the paper and saw that she was very quiet with the crocheting, pursing her lips and moving the creases out first on one side, then on the other; and the air in the room was different. It was colder.

So this was the only way in which guilt showed up for him; not in worry at all, but hiding in the hatred and in the rejection of all that he had formerly stood for. In this way he repressed feelings of being a traitor and he did not realize it.

The next day he thought constantly and with joy of the day when he would walk out of his office for the last time. He sat with Benjie and Ace and waited for Benjie to set up the VCR. He had come in of his own accord to the viewing room, where there were forty empty desks.

"Where's Charlie?" he asked.

Neither answered for a moment.

Then Ace said: "I don't know."

Benjie cleared his throat, then went for the light switch on the wall.

"I think he has business downtown today," he muttered.

"Or fishing. Or corking off," Mason said. He wondered if he should show displeasure, then decided against it. He felt too good now to show dishonest displeasure; it would cheapen his mood. He thought: the son of a bitch.

It was amazing, then, that they missed the things in the film. It was like a simple riddle that no one can answer who does not already know the answer, like crushing one end of a hard-boiled egg to make it stand or like putting it in salt to make it stand.

The moving splash of greens, reds and blues on the screen made an eerie light in the darkness. The red and the blue figures bunched, separated, bunched, separated on the screen, and in the half-light the faces of Benjie and Ace were stolid, almost pouting. Mason studied them as they watched. He knew how they felt. They had put so much into a winning effort and with such enthusiasm toward victory that the defeat had left them with a sullen surprise that still lingered. And still they could not read the sellout. Mason saw all the keys in the film; with surprise he noted that neither Benjie nor Ace stopped the tape a single time to run a play again.

And when the little spread formation appeared and the Bear defensive back began to run in to intercept a pass before the ball was snapped, even, Mason had to bite his tongue to keep from saying something. He found himself wondering if the two coaches were competent.

"One big wax job!" Benjie announced when the film was done.

Ace sighed. He yawned grandly, and stretched.

Mason sighed also. He got to his feet, feeling great.

"Time to play, boys," he said.

Ace said: "Win, play. Lose, play. It's all over."

He arose and walked out of the room lighting a cigarette as Benjie began the faster process of rewinding the film.

"What did we lack, Mase?" Benjie murmured when the lights were on again.

Mason studied. "You tell me," he said.

"The boys, I guess. Maybe it's passing the buck. I don't know. Maybe we were out-coached. But when something like this happens after what we put into it, I remember what somebody said: 'I'll give you the good coaches and you give me the good boys and I'll beat you every time!'" His voice was droning, a monotone.

Mason snorted. "Recruit!" he said. "Go out and get the good boys, then Charlie will be a good coach!" He walked out of the room.

When he left to go home that afternoon he took three things with him that had been a part of his office since he could remember. He took a brass bulldog, four inches high, that he had used as a paperweight and which had fallen to the floor twenty years ago and had crimped an ear that had never been straightened out. Straighten a bulldog's ear? He used to tell people about the reason he had never straightened the ear back, but no one had asked in years.

He took his old book of plays which he had used when he coached. It was soft and feathery with age. It was dead.

And he took an old team picture, faded and ochred, in which the players all had arms crossed and long hair—some still parted in the middle—and the uniforms were drab, skimpy affairs from the waist up with leather sewed in at the elbows. The man seated in the front row, center, with a ball cradled in his lap, was designated in yellowed once-white ink as R. F. Mason.

He walked out feeling good, full, and a little sad. The bulldog was in his left coat pocket, and he could feel it banging against his leg. He would go deer hunting, as he had each year, right on schedule, and when he returned it would be during the Christmas holidays so that his announcement that he was retiring would fall upon skeleton ears only, insofar as the school was concerned, and there would be no rush of people to his office because people would learn of it in ones, twos and threes . . . and now he could begin to remove the few things that he wanted to have so that after the announcement he would not need to show up at all.

In his car and homeward bound in light traffic he reflected upon the last few days. He smiled. He twisted the rear view mirror down so he could glance one time at the smile, and he saw that it was a real smile, a satisfied smile. It was indeed all over, and he was home free.

The film had proved that he was home free. It held no proof at all of wrongdoing on anyone's part, and he had verified this by sitting through it with two coaches whom he knew to be astute students of the game, and he had watched them pass upon it. It made him wonder, now, about smart men. Maybe they only memorize things that others tell them, and show them. Maybe real insight is a myth, he thought.

Mason smiled all the way home. He was smiling because he knew that Charlie would probably never see the film. Benjie or Ace would tell him about it in flat terms and he would not want to look at it. Mase Mason was indeed home free, with a hundred thousand dollars. And in five days he would be in deer camp, and could sit by himself and feel the comforting cool warmth of the hundred thousand dollars.

Mason had no regrets.

That evening he and Martha spoke in short words and shorter sentences of their meal, of the weather, of the news on the front page of the *Sentinel*, and she was in bed and asleep at nine o'clock and he at eleven, as always.

At three o'clock Mason awoke. He was gasping. He threw the covers back and swung his bare feet to the floor in the total darkness, sat on the edge of the bed and sucked for air, trying to think, trying to remember something . . . . He knew there was something that he should remember. There had been something like an explosion in his chest while he was asleep just now, and as he sat there realizing that his eyes were sandy and rolling, his being coming to him swiftly now from a long way off, he drew wind gustily and tried to think.

He thought: the heart. It's not the heart . . . there is no pain. Maybe I ought to awaken Martha and tell her . . . tell her what?

His pulse was hammering, shaking the bed. After awhile he got up and stood there in the darkness. The room seemed absolutely quiet beyond the pounding.

He shuffled out of the bedroom, feeling for things. He groped his way into the living room with care, trying to remember, trying to think. At the living room window, then, he stopped and looked out at two street lights, one close, one far away and troubled by tossing limbs. With satisfaction he noted that the heartbeat was slowing and was calming . . . .

Outside on the street he saw a skinny dog, trotting. He saw it stop and sit as if to scratch fleas, but instead it made strange motions with its forepaws, like a kitten swatting at a swarm of gnats. Then it arose and trotted on into darkness. Mason listened for the wind, which he could see, but he could not hear it. He sat down in an easy chair to wait, watching.

It came to him, then, from the first, so that he had to build it again in his mind, not knowing what it was yet, going through it again.

He had been dreaming.

He saw it again, now. It was a man with a rifle: a hunter. The hunter was climbing with unsure feet downward, across loose rocks of all sizes which might roll at any moment if he were careless. The hunter was peering as he went, stalking something.

Then a crashing sound: a shot. But the hunter's gun was not the one; it pitched down and clattered on the rocks, picking up chalky streaks and bending the scope; and the hunter himself dived after the gun but turned over in midair so he came down on the back of his head on the rocks and Mason could see the face contorted and the eyes staring up and the mouth trying to speak or to bite. Then he saw the heavy shoes kick twice together and then shudder separately, loosening a few small rocks that rolled down. One rock rolled against the man's cheek and the man made no motion to push it away, but stared quietly past it at the sky. Later there was a red stain on some of the rocks but Mason could not tell where it was. He was interested in the man's face. It was his own face.

Slowly then it came to him, so slowly that he sank back into the chair in the dark living room and tried to feel the comfort and the cool through his pajamas but could not, realizing stupidly that the heart was coming on again and he was beginning to draw deeply for air once more.

Outside the limbs, which he could see, whipped back and forth in a dark wind, which he could not hear.

The realization struck him squarely: any man who might be picked to deliver a hundred thousand dollars would look upon a hunting camp as a godsend. Any man who might be picked to deliver a hundred thousand illicit dollars would be a courier, a lackey, a cheap hood; and he could shoot the man who was to receive the money, call it a hunting accident, and go home free with the money for himself. No one would know the motive because no one would know the story. And the man in Chicago would, if he ever learned of it, laugh and slap his leg and mark up one for the courier and promote him as a thinking man. And no one would know. No one. There would be no motive to find.

After a long time Mason's pulse calmed again and he stared out at the dark street and began to think. He thought for a long, long time. He heard the clock in the den strike three-thirty, then four o'clock, and he remembered that it was due for a winding. The four strokes had come too slowly: tolling.

Early in his thinking he saw his only way out. He thought and thought for a better one, but came to none other, because he knew that the game was over now and the bets were won and any extreme action which he might perform would only cause him to be empty-handed. He had no recourse. But he felt deeply that the man in Chicago would pay off. The money would be there if he did not do something amiss.

So he knew that he would have to have someone with him at the deer camp: someone whom the courier, who would be a cheap hood, would suspect as being in Mason's confidence. And Mason knew that renegade athletic directors and traitors do not confide in men, where money is concerned. In women? Yes, but not in men.

And he could not take a chance on Martha's seeing the money.

When he heard the clock strike four-thirty Mason got up and went back to bed. He did not even remember to wind the clock. Or maybe he remembered, but felt it unimportant.

Two

The young man asked, "Another one?"

"Yes. Another one!"

"The whole litter?"

"Yes." The woman, who was older than the young man, had just emptied a covered dustpan into a garbage can. Now she removed the top of the can again, in afterthought, and threw in the paper which she had used to cover the dustpan.

"Let's go get coffee," the young man said.

"We just got back."

"That's all right. Celebrate the litter."

She grimaced at him, not smiling where a smile would have been in order.

"You disappoint me," she said. Her voice was low and husky for a woman, her face attractive.

"Don't I always?"

"Stop it. Now, don't you say that again."

He snickered, a little sadly.

They were outside in the cold air behind the Hall of Life Sciences, an old red building with character on the Tech campus, and the woman had just come out of a little wooden building which stood in the midday shadow of the greater brick structure. No one else was in sight.

"Come on, Frieda. Let's go get coffee and eat. I'll buy you a hamburger."

After awhile she said: "All right. You're on." She was standing there looking at the row of six covered garbage cans. Then she shuddered, visibly.

"Come on," she said, taking the young man's arm.

"Not that," he said, drawing away.

"You disappoint me," she teased.

Together they went into the back door of the Hall of Life Sciences, up worn marble steps, across a dim hallway then down worn marble steps and through the front door to the sidewalk in front of the building. Here the sunlight greeted them with welcome warmth. They walked together along the sidewalk in the bright sunlight.

The woman was forty, perhaps, the young man maybe twenty-five. They made a handsome couple, walking, except that she wore a white lab technician's robe that made her seem too committed to something to be walking with the young man.

"You know, Frieda," he said, nasally, "you're cheating. You're supposed to let them be eaten, first." He was obviously teasing.

"Stop it."

"No. I mean it. The program is supposed to be completely void of outside intervention. Hands off except for food and water."

"Let's talk about something else, Vern. I know my own experiment."

"Okay."

But at that they stopped talking completely. And, walking along, they seemed more in accord with the way things should be when they did not talk.

Buzzers sounded in the buildings around them then, shortly, and all together so that they could hear the sound but could not tell exactly where it was coming from; and at once the sidewalk and other sidewalks were loading with students, hurrying, singly mostly because it was the noon hour and there were lines to be formed and tables to be claimed. A noise picked up on the campus: a quiet noise of impatience, almost of rustling hunger.

"Behavioral sink," the young man muttered.

"Stop it. It's not, either."

Vern laughed at her then, walking along and watching her, teasing. "Ah, ha, ha!" he said.

The December sun was unusually bright this noon, though not overhead in the summer fashion, and it made furtive shadows that hung up in the branches of the evergreens and spilled out long to the north on the ground beneath them, causing the hurrying students to squint as they walked along. The grass was crisp and browning, though still basically green, as the campus held with a loosening grip to the verdancy that was its legacy through dual blessings of care and a long growing season. And a few brown leaves were about. Some of these rocked a little beneath the hedges as the thin air blew at them, swirling at them with cool, constant nagging.

Most of the students were heading for the cafeteria in the student center, some to their dormitories. Vern and Frieda were enough ahead of the rush that they went instead to the coffee bar in the basement of the school library. Here they would be able to sit at a table and be served. Most of the staff and many of the graduate students came here every day.

They seated themselves at once at a round table with a polished black top near the concrete wall that was painted green and that really was the inside of the exterior wall of the building basement, and they waited for A. John. A. John was the black waiter, a young card, *bon vivant*, everybody's friend. He came soon because they were among the first.

"Burgers, coffee, and fries, A. John."

"Ain't it!"

He was gone again.

The place filled. It was a quieter crowd than would be filling just now in the cafeteria.

"What's on for the weekend, Frieda? Let's go to the bay."

"I'll work, Vern. Thanks." She did not look at him.

Later she reached out and clasped his hand once, hard, then removed her hand again to her lap. She was watching the people in the room.

"Second fiddle to your beloved rats, again," he threatened, smirking a little.

"Not beloved, Vern."

"But second fiddle."

"No. I've got to get finished." Then she looked at him and smiled, letting warmth cover him for a moment, sweetly, genuinely.

"Oh, Vern," she murmured, "I'm ready to get away!"

"I'll bet!"

"I am!" The smile died as she looked away again. It drooped off her face strangely, going in a surge of sadness that was quickly wiped away in turn.

"Look," she began, then, calling his attention away, "there's Mason."

"Who?"

"The athletic director. Don't you know Mason? At that table over there." She smiled and waved briefly at Mason, who had nodded.

Vern had twisted with little interest. He now returned to her with his eyes. "No," he said.

"Don't you go to the games, Vern?"

"No."

"I do. I am very dignified. I scream and yell."

"Who do you go with?"

"Whom do you go with. No. With whom do you go."

"OK. *Whom?*"

She did not answer him, nor did she look at him. She was a

strangely beautiful woman, a little masculine in a voluptuous way that defied description but that did invite study; her voice was the voice of a housewife-turning-whiskey-and-cigarette-matron, but she was not married, nor did she smoke. There were those who knew that she drank upon occasion, but most of these kept the information to themselves as proprietary knowledge. She had blue eyes and almost blonde hair, and a nice figure that the white muslin robe hindered but could not hide entirely.

There was noise in the room now, and quiet noontide gaiety, but of an introverted sort: conversation judiciously given to discussion without real feeling—or real awareness—a luncheon type noise befitting a college maturity.

Vern sighed for her benefit, looking juvenile for the moment but failing to excite her attention.

"Well, I guess I'll have to get someone else to go to the bay with me," he threatened.

"I have to work, Vern."

"Hell, you've already done the experiment once! And you're supposed to leave them strictly alone, anyway. A day and a night wouldn't matter!" There was a pleading in the young man's voice that spoke strangely of something . . . some sort of strong attachment, with real feeling.

"I'm sorry." She would not look at him. Her eyes were still moving about the room.

Abruptly, then, he turned and studied Mason. Then the hamburgers came.

When A. John was gone again, Vern took a bite and tried to get something started around it.

"I like niggers," he said.

Frieda Colbein stared at him, then had to watch him grin with the hamburger in his mouth.

"That's the answer, Frieda. I've got the secret. You say 'I like niggers,' and this makes you a member of both sides and a member of neither. You're safe, you see. Both sides think you belong to them and secretly both hate you for being an individual. Not 'Negroes'. Or 'blacks'. It's 'I like niggers'! That's the answer. Nobody can argue with you when you say that!"

"Dirty pool, Vern. I can argue with you."

"Dirty pool?" He was eating and talking at the same time, and grinning triumphantly along with it.

"Dirty pool why?" he demanded. "Dirty pool because you have to join one side or the other, when the truth is in between?"

"No. The words are wrong."

"They are not wrong. They make it. I like niggers. This makes me a member of the radical middle . . . how about that?"

But she was eating. Suddenly she looked as if she were about to cry, and this caused Vern to eat in silence for a long time, watching her. He saw that when she opened her mouth to the size necessary for the hamburger, lines appeared in her neck, along the jawline. They ate without speaking for a long while, raising heads from the biting to chew and to watch and hear the scene about them: the clatter and the chatter, the calm hubbub.

"Let's don't go back right away, Vern. Okay?"

She had said it abruptly, looking at him, and he saw that her eyes were large the way a little girl's eyes would be large in a strange place. For a moment then he thought the words might be an invitation to something, but as he watched her he quietly decided that such was not the case. And he wondered at her.

When they were through they had more coffee and then when that was gone the crowd had thinned and most of the tables were empty except for the mess on them. A. John paused in his clearing of the tables—he had the rest of the afternoon for that—to show some students at the bar the old trick about getting a peeled, hard-boiled egg into a milk bottle without tearing it apart. He produced the props from somewhere in the kitchen, lighted the paper, and they watched the egg suck inward and into the bottle as the paper fumed and went out.

"How about it?" A. John demanded.

But it was an old trick and everyone had seen it before.

"Now," A. John demanded, setting his stage, "can anybody git it out?"

"I can," a boy said.

The bottle was swept to him along the bar.

Frieda, watching, said to Vern: "He should be in lab somewhere. It's one-thirty."

The boy tilted the bottle up, shook it so the egg nestled neatly in the neck, then covered the bottle mouth with his own mouth and blew hard. The idea was to blow air past the egg so the increased pressure in the bottle would force the egg out, slowly.

He blew too hard.

The egg disappeared from view and the boy was up and choking.

Then, amid tears of his own and laughter from everybody else, he spat out the intact egg which he had almost swallowed whole.

A. John crackled. He slapped the bar with clumsy, flat pink palms.

"Hoo, boy!" he yelled. "That's rate! That's the way!"

When the laughter had subsided, the waiter had another one for them.

"Now who bets," he asked, "that I can't do it with the shell on the egg and not break the shell? Another egg?"

There were no takers. Some fun was made of this but no one would bet; and Frieda and Vern found themselves studying each other. Vern shook his head.

"Boil the egg in vinegar," whispered Frieda. "It softens the shell. Go tell him."

"No."

"Go on. Tell him you know. Tell him you like niggers."

"No." Later he smirked at her like a little boy.

The egg tricks died, then, and the waiter began to clean the tables once again after the students had left.

"Ready, Frieda?"

"Let's have some more coffee."

"Well, I've . . . all right."

"After all, it's supposed to be hands off the rats. You said so yourself."

"Right. Let's go to the bay."

But she only smiled and did not look at him.

By the time nearly all the luncheoners were gone and just before the afternoon coffee-breakers would begin to come in, Vern had decided that he would leave, with or without Frieda Colbein. He was preparing to scrape his chair back, had hands pushing in readiness with elbows cocked, at the table edge, and was about to ask her once again if she were ready, when he caught her warning glance.

"Look here, Singer," boomed a voice behind him. "Here's someone you must meet."

Vern got up and faced two middle-aged men in overcoats who had just come in.

"Doctor Elliot Singer, Doctor Frieda Colbein and Vernon Hobson, both of my department."

Vern shook hands a bit spastically with the short, smiling, bouncy stranger. Frieda nodded, smiling thinly.

"Singer is visiting from California," said Dr. Balch, showing his teeth as he always did. Balch was head of the department of psychology, and knowledge of this fact seemed to force itself on Vern, who appeared to be studying ways that he might get away gracefully.

"We're proud of this girl, Singer," Balch went on. He turned and removed his coat, motioning his guest to do likewise, then took them both and draped them across a nearby chair. Then the two sat at the table with Frieda and Vern without asking. Balch waved his hand in the air without looking back for a round of coffee, and Vern, who still had not sat again, moistened his lips to make them work smoothly for him as he begged his getaway. Then he saw Frieda's eyes on him, calm and yet with something in them for him that should not have been there, and he sat down again.

"Frieda is duplicating John Calhoun's experiment on overcrowding among rats, Singer. She's been at it . . . a year and a half?"

He had raised eyebrows, then, for Frieda.

"About," she murmured, unscientifically.

"Perhaps you saw the paper, in *Scientific American,* I believe," Balch went on, "early in 1992, or thereabouts."

Singer looked doubtful, but interested. He was staring at Frieda through glasses of a thickness that made his eyes appear small and dead, and he had crossed his arms on the table.

"Most important work, Singer!" Balch was booming again, enthusiastic.

"What with the world faced with overcrowding, the experiment has become a classic example of what can happen with plenty of food in a limited space . . . a study in pathological togetherness, you might say." He paused to laugh abruptly, then leaned to get a pipe out of his pocket and began to fill it with rough-cut tobacco from a worn leather pouch.

Vern fidgeted.

"You know about adrenal stress, of course," Balch went on, "and how populations stabilize and begin to die off when they run out of space. The Calhoun experiment gives some insight into how the overcrowding works, and what happens with plenty of food and no disease. A most important work!"

When A. John had set the coffee around, Dr. Singer leaned closer to stir.

"Singer is a biologist," Balch said, into and through and with his new smoke, richly, watching his billowing pipe in near cross-eyed fashion.

"I'll slosh!" Vern blurted.

"What happened?" Singer wanted to know in a high voice of Frieda.

"Horrible things happen, Doctor Singer . . . ."

"Tell me some of them. "

She sighed to get ready and only Vern could tell that the air she exhaled came in pieces. He saw that her fingers were clenched into white fists, and that she was trying to hide them beneath the table edge.

"I'll positively slosh!" he said again, hearing something beginning to sing in his head, knowing that it was not the thing to say. He glanced quickly at Dr. Balch.

"Do we have a self-corrective for the population explosion?" Singer was smiling, prompting.

She smiled a little.

"Believe me, Doctor Singer, we don't want it . . . ." Frieda's voice was not strong.

Balch cleared his throat. He removed his pipe and took a slurp of his black coffee, as a cowboy might, squatting by a campfire.

"I'll have rats in four interconnected pens six feet square," she began bravely. "Two are not connected together so they represent the ends . . . and the other two in the middle receive the most traffic because they are each connected on both sides by stairs . . . ."

She faltered, took time to fumble with her coffee, and saw that Singer was nodding that he understood.

"Go on," he murmured.

"Pens one and four have only one stair each, you see, and pens two and three in the middle have two stairs each . . . ."

"Go on."

"The stairs . . . the stairs . . . ."

Vern saw as in a fog that she was faltering. He saw beads of perspiration on a brow that was otherwise ladylike, and suddenly he saw hopeless blue eyes full of terror upon him, and a trembling mouth.

Vern Hobson sloshed to his feet.

"Gentlemen," he croaked, "Doctor Colbein is not feeling well. You will excuse us, please. You will have to visit the lab, Doctor Singer, and see the experiment." Then he said, "In person." It was a ridiculous thing to say. And as he helped her to her feet he realized numbly that Balch's eyes were popping, his mouth agape.

"You will excuse us," Vern said.

They walked out. As they went to the door, without paying for the meal, Vern saw that only Mason was in the room, sitting at his table, watching.

Outside she began to cry. They stopped in the concrete stairwell and he held her to him for a long moment, then they began to walk up the rough stairs.

Out on the sidewalk again, she separated herself from him.

"I'm sorry. Oh, I'm sorry! What must they think of me! Whatever must they think of me?"

"Okay, Baby. It's okay. It's the rats. It's okay."

Later he said: "You need to get away. Come go to the bay with me this weekend."

"No, Vern. I'm sorry. No." She was still crying as she walked, making a regular, very small sound with the sobs.

When Mason left the coffee bar after three o'clock he went back to his office, where he sat for a long time, staring and cracking his knuckles. Nobody came into the office.

Now for the first time in his life Mason regretted that he was not a great lover. But this was not the form that the thought took in his head because he, like every man, had always secretly in the innermost considered himself a great lover, knowing instinctively as every man knows who has been faithful to his wife the unlettered truth that the really great lovers of the world are not the suave and the gilt and the calculating, mustached lecherous but rather the virile faithful domesticated to whom years add honest stature and pride in children; this worth like the value of pure water in a cocktail lounge being reality only from a higher viewpoint that sees water as the base of all life through eyes of a greater scope, and failing as water fails across the bar because the hazard of having is boredom and loss of scope, and the price of success and its symbol being bored and showing a campaign against it . . . .

So he had considered himself in vanity also a great lover, nonpracticing now in the popular lesser view, having taken to heart such things in the past as the admonition of Satchel Paige—which admonition he had clipped out of a newspaper once in glee and had carried for a long time crimped and yellowing in his wallet because as a sportsman himself he had wanted to recognize the genius— "Avoid carrying on in society. The social ramble ain't restful . . . ."

Until now. Now the scope had changed somewhat. Now he was a traitor; now it would be nice if he had a special lady friend. Now he had need of one.

Sitting there in his office at his old desk, Mason was frightened. And the thoughts he had about women and how one went about a proposition were thoughts designed and cast in the light of real fear for his life; and this made them important. He would have to be crafty. The scope had indeed changed.

Faces paraded for him in his mind's eye: young, youngish, his own age; pretty and plain; laughing and sad; loud and quiet; with bleached hair and with discreet hair; all of his acquaintance and all having attachments of his acquaintance and all possible candidates except for one critical element: time. He had three days. And with three days and three days only, one had to be a lover of reknown and with standing proven or he was reduced to offering money . . . .

But as he thought of the women and looked at them in his thoughts and tried hopelessly to look beyond their faces, he returned time and again in his thoughts to the sequence that he had watched just this afternoon in the library coffee lounge. He had left the place confused and he was still confused; a hunch told him that something had been there that was headless and nameless but that was his staunch ally now.

He remembered Frieda Colbein. He had met her years ago. She had not seemed fast at all when he had met her, but he remembered that when she had come on campus for the first time ten years ago as a post-doctoral instructor she had occupied most of the time and quite a bit of the energy of one of the freshman coaches—a young man whom he himself had later fired because of some indiscretion — he had forgotten. And he remembered that whenever he had passed her on the campus he had said, "Hello, Frieda," and that she had returned, "Hello, Coach". . . smiling.

So this constituted friendship. And now his whole being balked at beginning with anything else. He would not take a whore. He would go by himself first. He knew that he must have someone with him whom he could trust a little, or at least believe in, a little.

And then there was the thing—headless, faceless, nameless— that he had seen in her today. Maybe . . . just maybe . . . .

Mason had always believed in strong hunches. He had always played them. As a coach, it had paid off in the past more often than not.

Now he cracked his knuckles and felt foolish.

At five-thirty he called Martha and told her that he would be reviewing the university film with Charlie until eight, then he went to Basil's and ate oysters. After that he got in a telephone booth and looked up Frieda's number and address in a light that was too dim, and called her.

She was friendly. Strangely, she seemed too friendly. But that was what he wanted; he told her that he was coming to her place, giving no reason and taking no time to try to assess her too-friendliness.

The street lights were dim in the gloaming, the shrub bushes large. He found her name by the upstairs bell at a walk-up in an old, sedate brick home, and he went to the top of the wooden stairs that made sagging noises, and tapped lightly three times on the door.

She opened it. She was smiling. That was odd. He had expected a white, drawn face, and concern. Then he saw that he was indeed with a friend, and that concern was indeed there under the smile— and wonder at his coming—but that she knew who Mason was, and had respect for the image, and something else that was strong within her covered the concern.

"Hello, Frieda." He made the smile warm. And he thought that by shaking hands with her he could dispel any doubts she might have. He was right. The roué does not shake hands with prey.

"Hello, Coach. Come in."

She was in beige slacks and he saw the long roundness of her and then left that to look at the room: tastefully decorated in interesting things—black and gray conversation pieces on the walls, books, paintings, and so on. Mason was impressed.

"Nice," he told her.

"Thank you. Sit down."

Softness was in the room. It was comfortable.

He wondered how to begin. But he knew that there would have to be conversation first.

He wanted to say: "You have watched me and admired me. Here I am." And he wondered what her reaction would be.

Instead, he said: "Nice place, Frieda. Nice place."

"Thank you," she murmured again, after he had sat on the sofa.

He saw that she was still smiling, seemingly genuinely pleased at his presence, and somewhat honored. Honored?

There was a time during which neither said anything, when Mason stretched, sighed, and looked happy, with her watching with her real smile.

He did not feel like an old lover. He felt like a young lover. He laughed.

"Perhaps you've wondered why I've called you together," he said.

She laughed gaily at that. It was the right thing to say, and he grinned with the success, feeling a little foolish and like a schoolboy.

"Could I get you something, Coach?"

"Mason."

"Mason?"

"Anything. Please!"

She went into her little kitchen, which he could partly see.

"You surprised me!" she called out from the drainboard.

It was a good beginning, a bold beginning, and somewhere in the depths of his hidden fear and worry he blessed her for the boldness of it.

"I'll surprise you some more," he called back. And he heard her laugh gaily again, though she had moved out of his sight.

Good. Good. We can't miss, now, he thought.

After a short while she came with tall drinks and he took his and sipped it without knowing what it was but realizing that it was good and not too sweet.

"I was sad after the game, Mason. The last game. I was very sad. I was quite sure that we had a better team than that!"

"I was sad too, Frieda . . . ."

"But it all looked so easy! I was really disappointed."

Mason sipped his drink, looking at it.

"Do you go to the games?" he asked. "Most of them?"

"All of them. I love it!" Frieda Colbein was putting herself into the visit with gusto.

"This is not the usual Ph.D. reaction . . . ."

"I know. Some don't like it, some distrust it, and some are not honest with themselves."

"It's the fashion," he said, still studying his drink.

"Yes. It's the fashion." She said it with resignation.

After awhile he asked: "How's your work, Frieda?"

"Fine, but let's not talk about it. My work is successful at the present time but at the present time I've had it up to here." She indicated her throat. Her voice was a little ragged now. "In fact, I'm almost through with a project and will be thinking about a short vacation soon. Ready to get away, and all that." She spoke as if she were hurriedly describing something distasteful.

"How's your drink?" she asked him, obviously to change the subject because he was only half through.

But he took the excuse and drained the glass, then handed it to her, thinking that it would not do to get high and make a pass at her because he wanted to assure her in his proposition that such as that would not be a factor . . . .

As she came close to take his glass, carrying her own which had also been emptied just now, Mason saw that her eyes were puffy: eyes puffy, the bitch's look of the upper lid which comes from a too-narrow plucking of brows and which can also come from crying, as if the eyes themselves had seen something or maybe nothing, either, and that the problem: the cold breath of awareness one has sometimes and the sudden conviction that it is a short, short visit and then one will be away a long, long time so it is necessary to take time to smell the roses and one looks for roses to smell and does not see any and then one thinks back and does not remember any, either . . . .

"You've been crying, Frieda."

"You saw me. This afternoon."

"What is the matter?"

But she was gone with the two glasses.

While he watched her in the kitchen he realized that the drinking would be ahead of the conversation very shortly, so he had better begin to talk and see if he could work into his pitch, smoothly, adroitly, though he knew that the question when he asked it would be blunt—as subtle as—he remembered something he had heard years ago: a moose in the bathtub . . . .

"You spoke of a vacation," he began when he had his second drink in his hand; "It's time for mine. Every year after the season is over I go deer hunting on a friend's place. Have for years."

"You enjoy it?"

"Yes. Of course. The man's name is Raleigh Jones and he has two thousand acres in the hill country . . . we used to go together, the staff and I, but this year I'll have to go it alone . . . ."

He was watching his drink, hoping that he was not being too obvious yet, listening for something from her and hearing nothing.

"Deer hunting," she murmured, after a long while.

"Yes. Oh, it's a man's game, of course. I've never taken Martha along. Tried to several times to no avail, so Raleigh knows I'm married but has never met my wife . . . ." The voice trailed off and he cleared his throat to get rid of the weak sound.

Mason stopped for a time and occupied himself with sipping. The drinks were beginning to hum to him a little in his head while warming his stomach. He wondered if he were being smooth, or if she already saw it coming.

"Deer hunting," she murmured again, huskily.

He felt a little desire, then, and spent several moments shedding it.

"Yes."

"I'd like . . . ."

"What?"

"Oh, nothing. It's just that I've often thought that I'd enjoy that sort of thing."

Could he believe that she had said it coyly? He realized that the drinks had damaged his sensibilities. He could not tell. It would have to be blunt, now, because the sophistication was almost gone.

"Well, you said you wanted a vacation!"

She watched him, uncertain, and her eyes were very large and steady.

He thought: you fool. Mason you fool. She is way ahead of you because this gal is nobody's fool. Go ahead and spit it out.

But he said nothing, realizing now that she was in step with him. He watched her thinking.

"Raleigh Jones," she murmured. "And how far away is Mr. Raleigh Jones?" Her voice was husky and with a timbre to it, and he felt desire again and struggled against it.

"Four hundred miles," he told her.

She nodded. Then he saw that she was waiting. He was uncovered at last.

"Well?" he blurted, finally.

She opened her mouth and looked at him, waiting.

"It's to my advantage to have you along, Frieda. I apologize for the implications, and I swear to you that I don't like them, and all.

And I can't tell you why but it is to my advantage to have you along and I swear to you some more that I will not touch . . . ."

But she was on the couch with him now and her hand was warm over his mouth while her other hand was cold on her glass, and he saw that she was beginning to cry and that it was beginning strongly, with a warped mouth.

"I'll go, Mason. Yes! Yes! Oh, please, yes! Don't say any more and leave that part to me . . . ."

Then he was petting her, awkardly because they were both holding glasses and because she was crying genuinely, gratefully and yet with force.

Later he got away without having made love to her, according to plan. He had told her to be ready in three days, then he had refused a third drink, had kissed her hand quickly with the advisement that he would call her again on the telephone within a day's time, then he walked down the stairs and got in his car.

Mason felt great. His brain sang to him now. Before he started the engine he looked at his face in his rear view mirror, holding the door open so the dome light was on.

"You cutter," he said. "She likes you. You cutter. You'll have to be careful."

Then he started the engine and drove away, thinking: hell with that. He tried not to realize that she probably would have agreed to go with anyone, so strong was the wild something in her to get away.

Three

It was blackest night above the lights and a small snow was falling into the one street, and the few people there were considering it a lark that it was snowing. Some of the younger ones stood out in the street with faces upturned to sample the flakes, and there was a happy noise of a minute Mardi Gras, though the time and the place were all wrong. The snow was the thing.

A few cars were parked along the two-block part of the one street that had street lights, and the cars were all angled into the curb in the very small town tradition. There was no traffic and it was quiet except for the few shouts at the snow and except for now and then when somebody opened the cafe door and let the noise of the juke-box out for a brief run while the door closed.

The snowflakes glowed briefly on the cartops, reflecting blues and greens from the neon signs, then paled and disappeared at once into wet cartop nothingness. It was cold enough but the flakes were small and too sparse and a light rain had wet everything earlier.

The one street was really a highway, and there was no traffic because the town was too far away from everywhere. Great cliffs that hunkered unseen in the total darkness near in upon the town at either end of the one street made it a ranching community instead of a farming one, and that made the people fewer . . . .

On the north side of the west end of the lit two-block part was a poor movie house where the lights were brightest on the sidewalk. The theater was claiming itself to be the Majestic, in foot-high orange letters with plain white lights behind the letters; in summertime the bugs gave the letters quite a time. Now somebody had tied a pet raccoon in a little black harness to the old hitching rail in front of the theater, and the raccoon was getting snow on his fur. He sat upon the sidewalk and washed his face like a kitten, and jerked his paws in the air like a kitten, too, and the flakes made a high, light frosting on his back and tail. Wind came down the street now and then and blew the raccoon's fur a little, making his tail roll to one side on the wet concrete as he sat.

Three young men who had been drinking trooped together up to the theater, where they stood beneath the lights and looked at the posters, which showed tiny chariots with matched horses turning a corner around a great, kneeling statue that must have been a hundred feet high. *Ben Hur* was showing. The sound track could be heard from inside, now and then: making music that was indeed majestic like the sign said, though scratchy and far away.

The three young men wore jackets of different drab colors and shapes, but their pants were exactly alike: faded blue Levi's that were too small for them and had apparently been too small for a long time because of the areas on knees and seats that were worn powdery white, and cuffless at the bottoms over and in one or two cases of the six into cowboy boots that were without real shape or color.

One of the young men draped himself over the hitching rail and looked down at the raccoon.

"Rover," he said. "You son of a bitch. Where is he? No. I know where he is but when will he be out?"

And the raccoon stood for him like a tiny, humped, long-legged bear, black nose up and sharp, pointing in little this-way-and-that movements.

"Hooooee!" The young man yelled. He rolled once against the rail so his back was against it, his elbows propped comfortably. He blew out his breath two or three times hard and shook his head as if to clear his eyes of something.

The other two walked to the hitching rail, then, and also leaned back against it.

"Fifteen minutes," one of them said. "We got fifteen minutes. That's time for another one. Let's go back for another one."

"No," the first one said. His coat collar had a fat wool lining that was coming apart.

"Come on."

"No. I got to drive back."

"We'll let Junior drive back."

"No we won't. Not my car. Rover maybe, but not Junior."

The other two laughed and one of them looked down at the raccoon. He squared himself away with much lost motion and swung a foot as if to kick the animal. He laughed some more, shortly because Rover had paid no attention to the threat.

The three young men became bored quickly with waiting for the show to be over, and they began to move around a little to keep warm. The wind picked up, the snowflakes grew larger and more numerous, and some of them splashed minutely on the sidewalk.

The one with the fat wool collar spotted the girl in the glass cage ticket window and began to whistle at her. Gaining purpose, he squared himself away on the sidewalk fifteen feet away from her and directly in front, plunged his fists into his cramped pockets, rocked back and forth slowly on worn heels, and leered.

"Pssssst!" he called, and when she looked up he winked, using his whole face and contorting his mouth with the inertia of it. Hearing his two friends laugh, he kept it up, reeling in place, leering.

"Pssssst!" he called. "Pssssst!"

The face behind the glass was a pretty one, rosy now with confusion; his own face was not pretty. He had obviously not come to town to be with girls at all, because a wispy reddish stubble covered his chin and made it dirty, the nose was shapeless as if a hurried job had been done with dry clay, and the eyes were puffy and pig-like.

"Pssssst!" he said.

There was nothing the girl could do. She could not leave because the last feature had not yet begun, she could not turn away because the chair was cramped; she tried staring him down for a time but lost that game in a hurry because she had not the experience for it, so she looked down and blushed. Once or twice she smirked a little, and this was the wrong thing to do even in uncertainty because it encouraged him to greater efforts.

"You fool," her lips said once when he looked up, trying to show anger.

The three whooped at this and soon the other two were joining in the act, rocking, leering, making the catcall. A passerby, had there been a passerby, would have been appalled. Rover took no notice. He moved to and fro in the falling snow like a tiny high-pockets bear.

For five minutes by the clock they kept the foolishness going, acting like the adolescents which they were not any more but which the alcohol had recalled for them by the expedient of covering up their most recent learning and unshackling their most recent desires, which were the free acts of absolutely irresponsible youth, seeing her using the phone and then slamming it down but not appreciating it either, whooping, yelling, giving the catcall with voice, now, instead of the mere sibilant air which had begun the thing, until several things happened at once.

"I'd kiss!" roared the first one with the fat collar. "I'd kiss!" He kissed his closed fist at the unsympathetic plaster ceiling, and then stopped his noise and stared stupidly, still reeling, at the man who had appeared on the sidewalk and who had taken his elbow in his hand.

He jerked the elbow away. Then he saw that the man wore

khakis, an immaculate white cowboy hat, and a neat chrome-plated revolver that adhered, close and tight beneath the jacket edge, to his right hip. And at that exact moment the few people who had been watching the first showing of *Ben Hur* this night began to walk out of the theater with crimped and straining eyes, and the first one out was a young man the same age as the revelers or a little younger and dressed in the same fashion except for a forty-dollar jacket and a clean-shaven face, who went first to the raccoon and lifted him high, untying the cord that had bound him to the hitching rail.

Rover nuzzled the young man happily. The cord was loosed and folded away into a jacket pocket.

"Come on, Junior," the first one with the fat collar said, "let's go home!"

"Just a minute," said the man with the revolver. "Just a damn minute!"

Junior cuddled his raccoon and stared. He moved closer. He had an innocent face, unusually clear and serene for a male in his twenties, with the look of one who is awaiting his opportunity to speak.

"What's going on?" he asked, evenly.

"Let's go home," said the fat collar. But his elbow would not come free.

The movie manager was there with them, then, a nothing little man with a habit of blinking, and most of the twenty or thirty people who had been in the movie had seen the action now and had formed a distant circle to watch, some of them standing in the thin slush at the edge of the street. There was no traffic.

"Just a damn minute!" shouted the man with the hat and revolver, asserting himself for the people watching.

"Let me go!" shouted the fat collar. He pulled loose with a magnificent jerk. He was a strong, bullish young man, however drunk.

The deputy sheriff was young, himself. Now at the jerking away by force he reacted as he had weeks ago while refereeing high school football games and made the unconscious motion to his rear pocket for the red handkerchief, to throw it on the ground; but then he caught himself and grinned, perhaps realizing that the people—who had cringed a bit—had thought he was reaching for his gun.

"Don't you resist me!"

"We wud'n doin' nothin'!"

"Disturbing the peace! Resisting arrest! Now you come with me!"

He had the elbow again and again it was jerking.

"Come on!" The deputy looked back at the young man with the

raccoon.

"You, too, Raleigh! This is your bunch! Your dad's bunch! Come on!"

The five of them walked slowly, with some struggling and shuffling, down the darkened sidewalk; and the people stood and watched them go. There were fat women in the little crowd, and thin men with red, creased necks. They began to disperse, some laughing a little, the men explaining to the women.

The girl had her face in her hands, in the glass cage; and the manager was patting her shoulder, grinning but nervous, blinking. "It was nothing," he told her. "Forget it. You did all right. I'm proud of you. It was nothing."

The jail was three blocks away on the edge of town, in the dark: a two-story stone building that had crouched there in somber threat for eighty years; a light shone through cracked and smutty window-panes from the downstairs office. And the door, when they entered, creaked and squalled appropriately enough on blacksmith hinges that had known grease but had never learned to accept it . . . .

"Call your dad, Raleigh."

"Okay, Mr. Beck." Raleigh Junior was very pale.

"We wud'n doin' nothin!" shouted the fat collar.

One of the others sought to soothe the fat collar. He had seen him do unreasonable things when least expected, in the past; and now, in a situation which was not serious and which all of them would want to laugh at tomorrow: a comedy of no import involving five people who had all known each other in friendship for years, he sought to calm.

"Come on, Smitty," he mumbled.

"Come on, Smitty," the other one said.

Smitty ground his teeth squarely above the misshapen wool collar, seeming to get drunker by the minute. Then he clicked the teeth together and shuddered, making fists.

"Smitty," the first one said, drawing it out. "Easy, now. Every-thing's all right."

Raleigh Junior had been dialing, then mumbling into the telephone, and now he raised his face with its cheek-line as clear as a nun's, took the raccoon in both arms before him like a baby, and watched to see what would happen with eyes that showed wide fright and at the same time an odd, dreamy detachment, as if he were at that time somehow far away.

Beck was shuffling on his desk top, leaning over it with a pencil stub already located and in one hand, pawing through paper looking for a pad, or something. The others could not see that he was laughing, struggling with himself for silence.

"Smitty!"

It was a shriek, honestly given and in warning, but too late.

The kick caught the deputy full on the seat, delivered with the instep instead of the toe and with a full arc of inertia behind it and a force of considerable rage; and Beck for a brief moment was floundering on the tabletop, causing things to fall to the floor, rocking forward so that his face dipped down against a dirty coffee pot near the wall and sent it clattering in pieces.

Smitty's friends sighed. It could be heard very loudly in the room, had anyone been listening.

The upshot of the farce was that, at nearly eleven o'clock, Smitty was secure and snug in his quarters for the night, fat wool collar and all, his car keys were in Beck's pocket, and the three others—Joe, Jim and Raleigh Junior—were handed a flashlight and told to walk home.

"And I want that flashlight back tomorrow!" the deputy sheriff thundered at them out the door.

"Yes, sir," Jim said. He was the wiry one, and now he was shivering, though the snow had ceased. The wind had backed around into due north, and was now raw and steady.

They walked through the brief town and out of it, turning on the flashlight at the long bridge to the south and east, and by the time they were off the bridge and trudging up the hill that was longer by far than the bridge and steeper than any other hill anywhere near, Jim and Joe were feeling the returning soft edge of their drunkenness and were hailing its welcome warmth against the cold by being relieved. They began to laugh and to talk in bits and pieces between still shivering teeth. Raleigh walked silently, carrying himself upright, holding the raccoon, which was now a dozing bulge under his jacket.

"Did you see that?" Joe demanded. "Did you see that Smitty?" The two of them laughed.

"Junior, did you see that Smitty?"

He smiled for them a little, though they could not see it.

"Boy," he said. "Boy, he got arrested, didn't he? And will spend the night in jail."

"Case he won't!" Jim shouted.

"Smitty got arrested," Raleigh Junior said. Later he tried to laugh a little in keeping with the others, but his laughter was small and had wonder in it, and a little fear.

At the top of the hill, Joe said: "June, I'll carry Rover awhile if he's heavy."

"No. No, thanks. He's asleep."

They were walking now with quick, jerky strides along the rear edge of the oval of light that swung a little to either side as Jim's arm moved with the walking, much faster than they would have walked in daylight. Moist gravel that was polished white and angular crunched beneath their feet at the asphalt's edge and the wind blew behind then, pushing them on.

Beyond the shoulder of the highway was a shallow ditch and then a running ridged series of little hillocks left by the grader long ago, covered with dry clumps of rangeland grass that was without color in the dim light and here and there tall enough to be whipped by the wind; and beyond that was higher ground and a wire fence and then more grass and trees, irregular and scrubby and moving with beefy, restricted cedar jerks in the norther.

They had nine miles to go, but that did not matter. And because Joe and Jim worked for Raleigh Jones and spent most of their time with sheep and goats instead of cattle, they were used to walking and their boots were old and comfortable in the act of walking and so they gave it no thought. Joe in fact wandered a little out to the side as they went along, into the weeds and grass at the edge of the light, then he tried walking along the little ridge that the grader had made long ago and that was hard, now, and proper rocky turf, though narrow. He balanced along like a small boy on a rail.

"Oh, I am so drunk!" he yelled. "Oh, I am so plowed!" Then he tripped and went down in a heap in the rocks and grass, and lay there for a while, laughing. He was not really that drunk.

"Kicked his rind!" he exulted anew. "He kicked Beck right in the rind!" Jim stopped and went over to Joe and they giggled together for awhile, then Jim helped Joe to his feet and they went on.

Later Jim hugged Raleigh Junior as they walked, using his left arm.

"What do you think of that Smitty, June?" He was laughing happily still. "What do you think of Smitty now?"

Joe said: "How about it, June?"

"I think Smitty is in jail," he said.

"I wonder if he's asleep, yet?" Joe wanted to know.

"Hell, yes." Jim said it as if he were disgusted, which he really was not, and spat on the ground.

The wind had blown some of the cloud cover away now, as the front moved through, and overhead they could see the dark indefinite shapes of mist scudding and stars peeping through here and there, briefly.

When they were almost halfway, Raleigh Junior made a high crying sound in his closed throat and began to run. He ran down the road away from them, in the right direction, holding his raccoon bulge before him with both arms as a woman eight months gone with child might try to do, but higher. And he ran with speed.

The other two stopped and watched him go, with Jim holding the light on him.

"Junior!" screamed Joe.

"Let him go," Jim murmured above the wind. "Let him go. It's light enough. He'll be all right."

Later, when they were walking again, Jim said: "This is my beloved son, with whom I'm very proud." He said it as if he were quoting.

"Of whom," Joe said, almost reverently.

"What the hell."

"In whom?" Joe almost decided.

They were quieter now, and the levity was gone. They walked as if they were sober, which in fact they were, and made a job of the walking.

Raleigh Jones, Senior, put his *Time* magazine down, got up, and looked at his mantle clock again. It said twelve-twenty.

He was a handsome man, with age in his neck which the sun had helped put there, but nowhere else. The hair was pure white and thick, and was combed without oil which would have made it yellow—and as he paced now in the big room he moved like a virile man of thirty might have moved, with size and yet with grace and real strength. Again he looked at the clock.

Twenty-five years ago Raleigh Jones had lived in the city and he had discovered suddenly one day that he was a liar and a cheat. It had happened very simply: he had been a sales executive for a manufacturing concern, and had talked a customer into trying a new piece of equipment, experimental and yet almost exactly like the old piece which had given trouble. The customer was a manufacturer himself, and so had listened and had agreed. The price of the new piece, Raleigh Jones had told the man, would be the same as the old price, because no new processes or material would be involved. Then when the piece, made of rubber and metal almost like the old one, had proved successful, Raleigh's boss had said, "We'll raise the price. We've been needing to for some time and this will give us the opportunity which we have wanted . . . ." And the customer had told Raleigh that he was a liar and a cheat. And the customer is always right, especially when he says things like that. Raleigh had watched himself, then, and had found other real examples of cheating.

He had already inherited a thousand and fifty acres of hill country land from his father; when he had made the discovery he had quit his job and moved here into the old house which early had had scorpions and rats and some larger animals in it, and had begun to work. The realization had hit him that he did not have to be a liar and a cheat in the competitive situation when he owned a hundred thousand dollar's worth of land, especially since the things that made him a liar and a cheat happened every day, such as faking the expense account and saying doubtful things to customers in order to obtain an advantage.

His wife had died shortly thereafter, leaving one small, dreamy son; but she had been very unhappy anyway, having found that she had been happier in the city even though her husband had become a liar and a cheat from spending all his time striving for a business advantage, because she had been able to ignore it.

Now, as the years added themselves to his already substantial number, he sometimes wondered if he had had a right to leave the competitive situation when so many of his friends who were also liars and cheats could not and the only advantage that he had had in being able to leave was inherited wealth. Could a man leave his own small wrong behind him so that it was a part of a place and a situation when they had been responsible, as if the small wrong had always belonged there, not to follow him in guilt but washed off, left behind? Was it playing fair, had it been playing fair to leave because of the advantage of wealth and thus wash off the wrong when the others did not have this advantage and could not leave the competitive rat race? If a man could leave because of money and play fair, Raleigh had decided, then by his leaving the wrong behind where it had spawned he had proved that money does have a moral value apart from economics. Sometimes. Money can be and do all other things; why can it not then have a moral value?

It still puzzled him.

In twenty-five years he had doubled the size of his place. And now, ultra-sensitive and introspective and conscious of what is right and what is wrong, he had built into his beloved son his own moral beliefs. With pride. And he had seen them take hold in the boy, who was now a man, and he had proved that it can be done. Nowhere before had he ever seen a person who had never done a hateful thing; but Raleigh Junior was such a person. Raleigh Jones often wondered at his success.

At twelve-thirty he felt an impulse, put on his coat, opened the back door and then closed it behind him, got in his car in the dark cold, and started the engine.

He moved over big gravel that was tight beneath the tires, across the yard and down the dirt road to the gate, which was a quarter-mile from the house. Here he stopped, got out, opened the swinging green gate, got back in, drove through, and then without getting out again to close the gate swung the new Chrysler out upon the highway, feeling it rock grandly as it mounted the smooth asphalt. Then he braked at once. Something was coming toward him, far ahead in the edge of the lights.

Raleigh Jones peered ahead, sitting there in semidarkness with the tiny dash lights white and red under his face and the road lights fanning out into the distance before him. Abruptly he killed the engine and got out, leaving the headlights on.

Raleigh Junior staggered into the light. He was still running, or still trying to. His eyes were slits because the gasping mouth was demanding all the room in his face; his arms were flailing and falling limp at his sides, to rise from the shoulders to flail again, and he was making the fierce masculine sounds of oxygen lack and exhaustion: "Ahhh! Ahhh! Ahhh!"

And on his head, perched and clenched with frightened balance, wild with eyes that shot bold, emerald-green reflections back at the Chrysler's headlights, having ridden for miles in abject fear of falling into an unknown, clawing in absolute panic with the loss of security which his pet upbringing had not prepared him for and which his wild instincts had answered with claws and clinging, was the raccoon. And blood was everywhere below Raleigh Junior's hairline, running and dripping from long and short claw gashes in his forehead, his neck, his cheeks, trickling into the creases of his eyes, down along his nose to pool in the corners of his mouth, stringing down the brown jacket front, forming black splotches . . . .

"God, son! Good God!"

They collapsed together in the realism of the Chrysler's headlights and the cold, moving air.

Raleigh Jones had knocked Rover to the road when father and son came together. And after a long while of gasping and of con-fusion he picked the grown boy up in his arms like a child and took him to the car.

"Smitty's in jail!"

"That's all right. That's all right. God. You . . . ."

It was a stark mutter.

After a while they drove back up to the house. The green gate was left open against the north wind, swaying a little in the darkness with the fickle strength of it, bumping now and then against a post.

When the sun was riding quietly and unfelt on the hill to the east, and the wind had died and ice was three inches thick and rounded on top in the chicken trough, Mrs. Waskom had almost finished rattling her skillets and pans in the kitchen. Her husband, older by far than anyone on the place, had let the chickens out and had gone already to the oat field half a mile away to open the gate and let the sheep in. His breath hung out before him now and then in the cold, still air.

At the big round table, which someone had painted white years ago and which now showed oak through worn places in the old paint, Jim and Joe were quiet and docile until they saw that Raleigh Jones was not angry at them about the night before, then they came alive and ate with deep relish. There was a great platter piled with scrambled eggs on the table, another with fat brown discs of sausage still sputtering at the edges, high biscuits, snowy and light and browned dark on top and bottom, strawberry preserves, and enough scalding coffee to go around three times.

Raleigh Jones ate with his knife always in his left hand, as a landowner should. He kept his head down when he ate and had little to say; this meant that when he thought of something to say and said it, everybody looked up and listened.

"Sunday," he told them in his deep voice, quietly. "The men in the new cabin will be leaving early this afternoon. I want it cleaned up: Jim, Joe."

"Smitty's in jail, Dad," Raleigh Junior said.

"Smitty can stay in jail. If he's not back here by Tuesday I'll go in and see if he needs bond money."

That was that. Of his three young hired hands, Raleigh Jones liked Smitty the most because he was the most dependable, but he was hardest on him when something went wrong.

"I want the cabin spic and span. An old friend and his wife will be in it tonight or early tomorrow."

Later he said: "Joe, get the eggs off your mouth."

He watched for things to which he could call attention in the eating habits of the others because Raleigh Junior often needed such a reminder.

Now Raleigh Junior was eating flawlessly. But he was a sight to behold, otherwise. His face and neck looked like red-hot small-mesh chicken wire had been wrapped suddenly around to sear and to mark, so many and so uniform were the scratches on him, scabbed over neatly already. Though the scratches were deep, there was nothing wide enough to require more than the merthiolate that his father had painted them with the night before.

"Beck should not have put Smitty in jail," said Raleigh Junior.

"All right, son. All right. And this is a special friend, Jim and Joe. Sweep the floor out and put all the beer cans and trash in a sack and don't dump it up there; bring it here. I want the new cabin spotless by mid-afternoon."

"Yes, sir," Jim muttered, attacking the sausage.

"Fine, sir." Joe was the big eater though he never got fat.

"I want a special job on the cabin."

"Yes, sir," Jim said again.

Later that day when the party of three men had rolled out with two bucks draped on their car, Jim, Joe and Raleigh Junior went to the new cabin, which was the farthest to the east under the hill, a half-mile from the ranch house, and they began to clean it. They had walked past four other cabins, only one of which was occupied by hunters, now, and they set about the cleaning. Raleigh Junior took the broom. As always, he would do most of the tedious work, and the others knew it. They had learned to love him for it: not with respect—the respect had been gone thirty minutes after they had met him—but with a kind of awe that had fit in well with the love in absence of respect, and with a tenderness which along with the love engendered a deeper sort of respect which neither of them could have explained . . . .

When Raleigh Junior had the worn and stubby broom in his hand, had propped the doors open at either end, and was brushing at the concrete floor with skill, he said: "Beck should not have put Smitty in jail."

"Okay, June," Jim said. "Be sure and get in the corners."

The two watched him work for awhile. Later they would gather up the empty things that had been thrown about.

The new cabin was, like the others, built inside and out of native stone set in concrete, over a concrete floor and with four-by-six beams below a plywood ceiling and a shingle roof over that. It was one large room with a bathroom set in one corner. But there were four single beds, drapes at the three windows, shades, throw rugs which Raleigh Junior now had on a chair, and pieces of new oak furniture with an expensive rough finish. There was even a brass lamp in the cabin, adding touch enough to make it a cottage. It was comfortable.

But now they had not bothered to light the gas heater or to build a fire in the corner fireplace; they all wore their jackets and could see their breaths before them in the still air of the cabin.

Raleigh Junior swept and the others watched and listened to the wisping noises of the broom. Far away somewhere there was a shot that popped and then rolled across the valleys and hills, a swelling, marching sound.

"Thirty-ought-six," Jim said.

Joe sang, with no tune at all, lines he had picked up from Raleigh Jones: "Somewhere there's music . . . how faint the tune. Somewhere there's heaven . . . how high the moon . . . ." He got a crushed paper sack, then, at the bar-kitchen, crackled it out and open, and began to gather cans, paper plates, and trash, and to put them inside.

Outside the cabin the air from the north was beginning to move a little once again, having fulfilled the usual rule that clear-day dawning shall be calm. Beefy-boughed juniper cedars caught the signal and began to move again with small shiftings, sighing. In between the cedars and out in the open places the spindly skeletons of mesquite trees altogether bare of leaves stood in crooked silence and moved not at all. The ground that ran flat beneath them was covered with sparse buffalo and curly mesquite grass that had been burned by the cold and lay down flat now like a dead lawn. There were few rocks here in the parklike setting of the camp, and many nights and days of frost, melting, frost, melting, frozen rain and a little snow, then melting again, had given the ground a peculiar puffy look of softness under the trees. It was frozen and hard now with the cold. But it looked soft. Raleigh gained the front door with his pile of dirt, small sticks, bits of paper, and leaves.

"Don't sweep it out, June. Let's put it in the sack," Joe said.

"All right."

He stood looking out into the warming sunlight, squinting a little.

"I wonder where Rover is," Raleigh Junior said, without a question. "He is mad somewhere and I can always tell when he is mad because he turns his ears around like when you hear behind you. And he goes off into the bushes for two days."

He had turned and was looking back inside the cabin at the others.

"He turns his ears around and will be gone two days. Then he will forget and come back."

Joe came with the sack and squatted down with it at the pile in the doorway.

"Beck put Smitty in jail and Rover turned his ears around," said Raleigh Junior.

He thought about it a little and heard the others laugh so he tried a laugh also. It came out pure and unfettered after he had tried for a time.

Four

It had been dark under the winter starlight for many hours before Mason arrived.

Earlier, after sundown, Raleigh Jones had gone out with his supper comfortable beneath his belt and had stood for a while on the tight gravel near his back door and had looked to the west down toward the gate, wondering if the Masons were on their way. The norther was still blowing steadily; he had seen four ducks low down and yet far away, too, above the cliff and the river beyond his gate, not flying in formation as migrating ducks do but hurrying like frantic darts, giving no thought to position. They had been a nervous etching against the pure sky, and somehow perfect; had they been twenty feet lower over the water he would not have seen them against the cliff that was already black with night. When he went back inside and reread Mason's last letter, he decided to sit up for awhile and wait.

Smitty had come in earlier, grinning, but with quietness; Raleigh Jones had sent him back to town with the flashlight, and later he had driven in again.

"Always remember to apologize early and then forget it," Raleigh Jones had told his son, watching him. There had been no fine.

"Or else don't apologize," he had said. "But then you won't forget it."

Now it was nearing midnight and the three young men were asleep in their bunkhouse which was merely the south wing of the great ranchhouse, and the others were asleep, too—Raleigh Junior in his bedroom next to the living room—and Raleigh Jones was reading and waiting. He could go to bed at three and get up at five with no regrets.

Mason had left in midafternoon. He had loaded the car in a hurry for Martha's benefit, not wishing to prolong the getting away, then he had kissed her and had held her close, feeling a small surge of love and kindness, feeling also foolish with the clinging of her to him. And he had promised a quick and a safe return.

Then he had been at Frieda's place by half-past three and they were on the road by four o'clock.

"Sit down low until we get out of town," he had told her. He had grinned a little. "Does that sound bad?"

She had laughed gaily at him, almost with reverence, strangely.

"Terrible." She had smiled, and he had seen that her eyes were wide apart, her teeth white.

There had been little talk during the almost four hundred miles and he had been grateful to her for that, finding himself a little surprised and wondering, what she must be thinking . . . .

Once he had asked: "How do you like the lark so far?"

"Wonderful," she had said, smiling. "Wickedly wonderful."

He had seen that she appeared relieved, relaxed, and not at all worried. He had begun to try to remember exactly what he had said when he had proposed the trip.

"Mason," she had murmured, later, without the smile, "you may get credit for saving my life . . . ."

But he had not known how to pursue that, except with a knowing smile, weakly.

And they had not held hands even once during the trip, though he had noticed early that she kept her left hand free and resting within his easy reach. This had excited him some . . . .

Once they had stopped to eat in a small town cafe and he had listened to girlish talk for thirty minutes, finding himself savoring and appreciating it, remembering later nothing of what was said and yet everything, somehow: every moment, smile, gesture. And now it was past midnight and for the last nine miles he had been deliciously alert, tired and yet perched in eagerness with the driving, watching every small rock go by, every clump of grass. For the past fifty miles they had dimly seen occasional deer—all does—near the highway.

"We're almost there," he said.

"I'm ready," she murmured. It was not a seductive murmur but he felt his skin tighten all over, as if he were swelling. Without doubt he was excited.

When he turned the car down off the road and crunched to a stop at Raleigh Jones' green gate which the headlights made clear and neat against the darkness, as he opened his door and almost had one foot out, he heard Frieda's door slam and then he saw her already opening the gate. He watched her, then, fumbling a little, then watched some more as he drove past and waited. She was wearing slacks that were dark and sedate enough, he decided. He decided that he did not mind being represented by those slacks, in case Raleigh Jones were awake to greet them.

Which he was.

The stars were brilliant but austere above them as they got out at the ranchhouse, cold and withdrawn in the black sky, as if the rebuff of winter had muted them somehow, allowing them free speech but robbing away the sound . . . .

"Get out! Get out and come in!"

But they were already out, sampling the cold.

"No. No . . . ." Mason was reaching for the square hand, remembering the horny sureness of it before he experienced it again.

"How are you?" Raleigh's voice was deep, friendly. He was grinning.

"Great. Raleigh Jones, this is Freida . . . ."

They nodded and spoke, each appreciating the other. And Mason saw that he was safe.

"Well! Won't you come in? You're tired after your trip. Mrs. Mason? Mason? Come in and we'll visit a spell. It's been a long time."

"Raleigh, no. Raleigh . . . it's too late. Just point us at the cabin. You'll want to go to bed, yourself."

Later Mason said: "Good to see you again! We'll come down tomorrow and have coffee. Or you come up!"

"I have a fire going for you in the new cabin. The far cabin. Remember?"

"That's for me," Mason exulted.

"It's warm, or should be. And if you want to hunt in the morning, take the southeast corner. Some more hunters are here and I checked with them for you and they will be going north in the morning. So the southeast corner will be free . . . you have four hundred acres free in the morning."

"Everything," Mason murmured. "You think of everything."

When they had shaken hands again and as Jones was nodding as a genial host should nod, Mason and Freida got into the car.

"Welcome, Mrs. Mason," murmured Raleigh Jones, the headlights illuminating his hearty man-smile.

"Thank you Raleigh. It's a pleasure, believe me."

Mason decided that she had raised her voice a bit away from its usual huskiness for his own benefit.

In the car again and realizing that he had not even cut off the engine, Mason found her hand and squeezed it. They watched Raleigh Jones go back into his house before Mason twisted his wheel.

The way was up a ragged hill which made Mason's Buick rock and shudder, then winding along a flat, with bare embattled mesquite reaching to scrape the car with thorns; and when finally the dirt tracks went near the first cabin in darkness Mason found that his heart was thudding. He slowed and looked at the cabin hard, then went on trying to remember where the others were, seeing finally the one car at the third cabin and braking past it, peering, trying to see if it bore an Illinois license. He could not tell. Tomorrow . . . .

Beyond the small clearing he found the new cabin, pulled up, and stopped.

Frieda hopped out and he followed behind, seeing that she was already inside. The door clattered a little, coming closed.

"Oh!" she said, making a squeal out of huskiness that was somehow becoming.

The floor lamp was on, heavy red coals were still in the crumbling shape of their antecedent log in the fireplace, and the warmth was soothing, welcome, luxuriant.
Mason sat on the nearest bed. He was tired.

"Like it?"

"Oh, Mason! It's not a deer cabin! It's a cottage, a honey . . . moon . . . ."

"No," he said. He smirked, preluding a yawn.

He watched her.

"Pick a bed, Frieda!"

She pointed to the one nearest the bathroom; demurely she pointed, making a cute jab with her finger at it, as if she were a silly debutante giving a tentative poke at a bug, holding prim lips as she looked at the bed.

"Or maybe you'd like one of the other cabins?" he teased. "Cold, cold cabin . . . . ?" It was good to tease now, he decided, and establish supremacy.

"Not on your life!"

Mason rubbed his face, blinking, feeling tired and yet excited; not sleepy at all.

"I'll unload the car," he said.

One of them had put in a new bottle of Old Forester; for the life of him he could not remember whether it belonged with his things or with hers . . . and after he had set it on the table and had gone back for bedding and groceries which he could remember packing himself, after he was completely through with the unloading, he stopped his drive and saw with surprise that Frieda was in pink pajamas—flannel for the cold—and a matching robe; and he saw further that the seal was broken on the bottle and there was a tall drink waiting for him in a copper tumbler, without ice, on the table.

He took it, sat on his bed nearest the door, seeing that his bed was made, already, and perfectly; sighed and removed his shoes which were tight and throbbing with the day.

"Oh, boy," Mason sighed.

"Oh, boy," she said. She took a sip and then smiled at him from her own bed.

"Verily the lust for comfort murders the passion of the soul, and then walks grinning in the funeral," she quoted.

"What?"

"Forget it." She laughed in a murmur at him, teasing. "Gibran."

"I will. Bet on it I will."

Mason lay back and took a sip watching her. The drink was powerful.

"And so endeth the day and so beginneth the night, Mason."

"And?"

"And!"

They lay there for a long time, sipping in silence, watching each other without boldness. After awhile Mason got up, went outside to where wood should be near the door, and returned with a heavy but short mesquite log which he placed with care on the shambling coals.

Then he returned to his bed and his drink.

"Comfortable, Freida?"

"Perfectly."

"Not nervous?"

For an answer she pulled her knees up under her chin, wrapped them with the robe, and half turned away from him, staring into the fire.

"No," she murmured after a long while. "We don't have any old maids anymore, Mason."

He watched the outline of her face with the firelight on it and saw that it was sad and motionless, staring into the fire. From the side he could see the angle of her cheekbone and the dainty hollow of cheek below it being dabbed at in flickers by the fickle light. Something there was in the light and the hour and the way she was dressed that stripped away the sham of beauty and left a purer woman, somehow, as if she had rubbed all her makeup off, as if hour and need and situation had melted the guise of femininity and had uncovered a richer, rarer and far more beautiful female who could wear the pale and bony face with sadness, with a fullness that was honest and pure. Here was woman, who gave or withheld great favors, who was always good and kind in the firelight because the guise which went with things that she could not help was gone.

"I want you to know that I didn't bring you here to . . . "

"Mason," she cut him off. "You owe me no excuses. I came.

And I'll offer no confessional."

He cleared his throat.

"But I wanted you to know."

"A man begins to lose his ability to make love. Good love. It bothers him. He tries to hide it from his wife and he comes home drunk so he'll have an excuse—or maybe drinking will pep him up, for a time—and then he gets into affairs to prove his powers to himself again. And because of the new excitement he can prove it to himself, for awhile . . . ."

"No."

She looked at him, smiling, and he saw bitterness there in the smile.

"No," he said again. "That's not it." He was looking at the side of her face again, seeing how bony it was, yet how full with the firelight on it, and promising.

"Well, if that's not it then I had better stop talking. If I show I doubt you, then it will be all the same and you'll feel you have to prove something to me. Then you won't have freedom of will anymore, will you, Mason?"

"You think . . . ."

"Please don't tell me I think like a man! Please don't! Tell me I'm beautiful! Tell me I'm sexy! But please don't tell me I think like a man!"

She was looking into the fire and he could see the strong feeling. Mason chuckled.

"You're sexy, Frieda. God, you're sexy. Now don't you feel like having to prove something!"

"Touché!"

"My father made good love when he was seventy-five, Frieda," he said.

"And like father, like son . . . ."

"Like father, like son. Now if you say 'prove it', I will."

That left the thing in proper balance: a challenge. And he knew that he had brought a lady, after all.

She turned and studied him, then.

"Why me, Mason?"

"I don't know. You ask why anybody and I'll have to answer you fairly. I came here to meet a man. A man who may try to give me trouble. With you here he will not try. Hiding behind your skirts, you might say."

He could see no change in her face, and after several minutes she spoke again.

"Why me?"

"Why did you come?"

That sent her back to the fire with her gaze.

"We come to each other's aid, is that it?"

"I can speak only for myself."

"Yes . . . yes, that's it."

"Want to tell me about it?"

"You haven't told me anything, yet. Really explained it, I mean, about why anyone should want to cause you trouble."

"No," Mason murmured. His drink was gone. He got up, reached for her copper tumbler and poured more bourbon into both, filling the tumblers to the top with water from a wide-mouth jar.

"I don't know that he will," he said, sitting again on his cot, hearing it squall with his weight.

"Will you tell me who he is?"

"No, ma'am."

"Will I be able to guess?"

"I doubt it."

"Then I don't have to tell you anything, do I?"

Mason laughed. With something like relief he watched a smile cross her face.

"By God, Frieda," he blurted. "You're much woman. I have never been unfaithful to my wife, but this time and place are going to be a strain . . . I can see that!"

"Whose fault is that?" She was teasing again, and he found that he liked it better that way.

"Don't you let me know I'm disappointing you!" Mason proclaimed.

"All right. I'll leave you with freedom of will. If I had wanted the other I could be somewhere else right now . . . ."

"And don't let me know you'd rather be somewhere else!"

"No. Far away. This is far away. This is better. And if I wake up and someone is in bed with me that will be all right, too."

"Someone. Anyone?" he teased. "I could leave the door open."

"Don't you dare. Rats might come in." She shuddered.

"Rats! Are you afraid of rats?"

"I," she looked at him squarely, "am afraid of rats. Now. Here. And two years ago I was not afraid of rats. I came to get away from rats."

"Tell me about it."

But she shifted around to face him, boldly and at once, moving as if she were throwing off a weight or a covering; and when her face left the firelight reflection it had lost its peace.

"Remind me to tell you about the rats. Not now. And let's talk about something else besides the sex bit. We sound like kids! We're trying to talk ourselves into something and out of something at the same time and we don't know which is which and it sounds ridiculous!"

"It was bound to come up," he said.

Later he added: "The rats, Frieda. Tell me . . . ."

"Did you bring a gun? I don't see it. Will you hunt in the morning?"

Mason waved at a dark corner behind him.

"In the case," he murmured. "I haven't decided."

He saw that she was nervous.

"Tell me about the rats, Frieda. Tell me now."

Several minutes went by. Abruptly she lifted her copper tumbler and drank it down so that he could see her throat working with the swallowing.

"I came to get away . . . ."

"Just once. Just briefly, so I'll know. I told you why I brought you . . . now you tell me why you came!"

She had turned away from him once more and when she began to speak she was addressing the fire. He could see the struggle in the edge of her face.

"I ran the experiment," she said, speaking quietly. "Rats in four interconnected pens each six feet square . . . and let them multiply without taking any out. Healthy rats with plenty of food and water . . . for months."

She went on quickly now as if she were reading a page in her mind.

"Two of the pens became controlled by boss male rats that kept harems of females and chased other male rats out. The harem females made nests . . . good nests . . . bore healthy young and raised them successfully. But in the other two pens, where no single males took charge, social stress went wild. Some of the males gave the females no rest . . . others turned homosexual or hid in corners. The females stopped making proper nests . . . and their young . . . born on the bare floor . . . died and were eaten . . . all of them . . . ."

She finished and stared without motion into the fire.

"Rats," Mason murmured, trying to be helpful. "Just rats, Frieda. No telling what rats will do!"

"Not just rats, Mason! Overcrowded people will do the same someday!"

Her voice broke and a sob came out; then she gathered her knees close and pressed them to her mouth.

He stood, feeling foolish. Then he put his dry tumbler on the table and went to her, putting his hands on things in order to get there. He put his arms around the bundle of her, squeezing, trying to kiss her ear, looking into the fire. She was unyielding.

"I'm glad you came, Baby," he whispered, feeling emotion himself. "I brought you because you are sexy. And beautiful."

He took note of her one small laugh that seemed to break the flow of emotion; he patted her awkwardly and left again to pour himself another drink. By the time he was lounging again on his bed she was under her cover, lying on her side motionless and facing the fire away from him.

He watched and thought he could see her move a little now and then as if with little sobs; but then he decided that maybe it was the small flickering of the light or perhaps a shifting of his eyes from the bourbon.

Just before three o'clock Mason got up and groped about in a big cardboard box until he found his flashlight. Then he found his coat and put it on, slowly because he had to plan the moves and watch himself carry them out, being unsteady; then he walked to the door and opened it with care. Standing in the open door, then, he looked back at Frieda for a long time until satisfied that she was asleep, closed the door without making any noise, then turned away from the cabin. He flipped the flashlight switch and walked away into the cold, blowing night, watching the oval of pale light on the ground before him.

Mason thought: a man's not drunk unless there's someone watching him and measuring his moves.

Though frigid cold, the night air seemed soft, somehow, and Mason decided that maybe it was because of the silent sound made by the wind in the cedars. It was not the high ahhh-ing sound that pines make in a steady wind; it was more a hint of quiet tossing, as if the moving air made no noise at all in the beefy boughs that were built like an owl's wing for silence, but rather a small whispering that the boughs themselves gave to the wind: a complaint, sleepy and murmuring in the night.

But it was cold. He turned his collar up and went on, looking at the hard ground that itself resembled a real softness made of turf and low, tangled grass. He was out in a small prairie near the edge of the trees. Several times he lifted the light far ahead to help in mapping his course.

He had only two or three hundred yards to go. He went the distance cautiously, slowly, seeing nothing except dirt, grass, trees, and a few small rocks, feeling the cold that was moving around and past and almost through him, stopping several times to shiver in a nervous convulsion and trying to remember how the camp was laid out.

Then his flashlight caught a gleam of chrome and returned it to him. He turned the light off and went on slowly in total darkness. He was approaching the cabin due west of his own, and he remembered that it faced under two great cedar trees; now he knew from having driven by earlier that people were inside asleep and a car was parked in front. From time to time he shone the light briefly as he approached; and as he got near the car he turned the light on and left it on, smothering it against his side and using it as he needed it. It would not do to run headlong into the car and make a noise.

When he had his hand on the cold metal of the rear deck he unshrouded the light again and poked it full at the rear license plate, inches away. Then immediately he clicked off his light.

It was not an Illinois plate. It was a Kansas plate. Mason wheeled and began to stride rapidly back without light. He stretched his legs out with the walking, feeling relieved, walking jerkily because of the cold and the relief and often missing the ground—hitting it too soon or ending with a foot in the air after a step because of the bourbon. When he was a hundred yards away and could see the glowing chinks of his own cabin ahead, he turned the flashlight on again.

Mason sighed. The courier was not here yet. Perhaps he would arrive tomorrow . . . no, today. Or maybe tomorrow. Or maybe three or four days from now. No matter. Mason was ready. And he knew within himself that the courier would come, because he, Mason, represented a source of traitorous funds that the big man might want to tap again, and again, and again.

Back in his cabin, Mason saw that the mesquite log had fallen apart in dissipated, glowing redness—mottling to blackness, that Frieda had not moved.

He stood by his bed and took off his clothes down to his shorts. Then he went to the door and urinated outside, watching back now and then to see if Frieda would hear. It was still warm in the cabin. He went to her bed, then, and stood looking down at her, standing there in his shorts. The desire checked out nicely. He thought of warm arms around his neck, of the breasts with full life in them, of the quick, searching tongue. Then he thought unaccountably of a morning many years ago when he had awakened crying like a baby after having dreamt that his wife, Martha, was leaving him.

Mason turned off the lamp and went to his bed, where he sat down carefully. He sat there a long while, looking at the dying fire, looking at Frieda, trying to think that he was making a mistake . . . . At length he lay down and pulled the three beige blankets up close.

"Hell with it," Mason said. "There's plenty of time."

Then he remembered that he was a traitor, and free from moral scruples. "Hell with it," he said again. "And with the hunt in the morning. And hell with the rats."

The fire was falling apart in the fireplace. Outside the wind moved past steadily in the darkness.

The rich sputtering sound of frying bacon awakened him and he lay there without moving for a time inhaling deep breaths and letting the heavy aroma of it clear his head. The coffee smell was heavy, too, and then Mason remembered to be surprised at how good the admixed smell was in his nostrils; and he raised his head from the pillow and shook it a little to see if he would have a hangover from the drinking, then lowered his head again with something like proud satisfaction. He yawned and turned over suddenly, making the cot squall in protest as he moved.

"Good morning, Love!" Frieda was fully dressed in slacks and woolen pullover sweater. She was smiling from the kitchen-bar near the fireplace.

"You built a fire," he croaked.

"Certainly. It's wintertime." She stood with her left hand on her hip, lifting with a great fork and turning the sputtering bacon—a whole pearly sheaf of it—and not looking at him. She was cooking on an electric portable range on the bar.

"That's supposed to be my job. The fire, I mean."

"Well, I mean . . . when her man is a sleepyhead and sleeps all day what is a poor girl to do? I mean, really!"

She brought him a heavy cup of black coffee, waiting until he had sat and then placing it in his two hands, then leaned and kissed him, laughing a little at his efforts to move his bad mouth away.

"Oh, boy!" Mason said.

"Oh, boy!" she mocked, sounding happy.

After he had sipped away half of his coffee, palming the thick crock cup and watching her prepare breakfast, Mason thought of something to say.

"Frieda, your experiment . . . what have you done with it?"

She was silent and he could tell from the back of her that it had been the wrong thing to say amid the happy things of breakfast-making.

At length she answered, without turning.

"I'm through. I checked the rats over to a friend and told him to use them as he sees fit. But most of them are no good. I told my boss that I was going away for awhile."

"Awhile?"

"Awhile. Someday I'll go back and try to write it up. Maybe. How do you like your eggs, and how many?"

"Scramble eight or ten!"

"There's a message for you in the rats, Mason!"

"Tell me."

"Not now. I can't talk about it. Eight or ten!" she turned on him, trying not to laugh.

"For both of us, of course."

"Eight or ten it is! Clean out the kitchen!"

The preparation of breakfast, if it is done right, makes every house a mansion for a little while, and it is because the friendly aroma is the thing. Now with the healthy fire going and the heater going too, on the opposite wall, with the rich smells tempting and cajoling and making everything right, somehow, taking away the very necessity, for a time, for any future whatsoever, the hunting cabin was indeed a perfect place. Mason got dressed without shaving, returned to his bed to sit, and watched Frieda get things ready. He rubbed his face eagerly.

The cabin was clean, tight, and solid. Outside the wind was low, a mere whisper now and then at the door. And the two windows were frosty on the inside with condensate, and streaked clear in crooked lines where drops had run down. The cabin was a rare moment in perfection, with nothing lacking.

After they had eaten, enough, it seemed, for the entire day, and after they had sat luxuriating in the quiet comfort with the last of the coffee before them, Mason and Frieda left the kitchen mess, put on coats, and went outside to look around. It was after nine-thirty.

They stood and talked about small things in the bright, slanted sunlight away from the cabin, enjoying the brilliant cold; then they walked a short distance away through the scrubby brush and looked under and past and through the heavy green of the cedars that were somehow like nubby mounds of alfalfa on posts, and finally they halted near one of the other cabins. It was empty.

Mason stooped and stared under the trees.

"Here comes Raleigh Jones," he said. "He'll kid me about not hunting this morning. He's got two people with him. Let's go back and put on more coffee."

Walking back, then, far ahead of the approaching three, Mason thought of Frieda.

"He has pecan trees. Maybe later you'd like to go and pick up some pecans off the ground. And the wild turkeys come there, too. Maybe you'd like to hunt them, if not the deer?"

"I'd like that," she murmured.

Raleigh Jones, Raleigh Junior, and Smitty came up to the cabin after Frieda and Mason had been inside again for a few minutes.

"Hello the cabin!"

"Come in," Mason said.

They entered and stood. The two young ones looked sheepish with the coming inside, and Mason and Frieda saw the scratches on Raleigh Junior and looked at them.

"Mr. and Mrs. Mason, my son Raleigh Junior, and Smitty," Raleigh Jones said.

"Sit down," Frieda told them. "We'll have coffee in a minute."

"Junior and Smitty won't stay. They have a project to see about."

"You haven't seen a coon, have you?" Raleigh Junior asked.

"Named Rover?"

Mason stared.

"No," he said.

"He ran away. He ran away and has not come back. And he turned his ears around like when you hear behind you because Beck put Smitty in the jail."

"June," Raleigh said, brusquely, "you and Smitty go on and see about it . . . ."

The two young men made apologetic movements for a short while near the door, then went out again and were gone. The ranch owner sat down after they were gone, on one of the unmade beds.

"Well," he said grinning, "how was the hunt this morning?"

"Frieda," began Mason, "you've got to realize things about this guy. He's a Spartan. He thinks if you get to camp at four in the morning you're supposed to be up and at 'em at five-thirty. And one time I saw a hunter that had felt the call of nature before it was light one morning, and had shucked his pants and had sat on a cactus and he came to camp with stickers in his butt and do you think Raleigh Jones would pick them out for him? Hell, no!"

Raleigh Jones laughed, long and loud. His laughter was a virile magnificent sound that overwhelmed the small cabin for several moments. Frieda blinked and watched him slap the table with his horny palm.

"You find out who your friends are, don't you?" he thundered.

"You find out you don't have any friends," Mason grinned.

"I don't remember you or anyone else picking the stickers out for him, either. I remember him squatting out in the bushes that day over an old busted mirror with a pair of tweezers in his hand!"

Mason pursed his lips.

"He asked you first," he said.

Raleigh Jones' laughter rang big in the cabin.

"I furnish the land and the deer," he said. "Picking out stickers is not in the bargain and feeding the deer and tying them to a post to be shot is not in the bargain and taking healthy hunters to their blinds in a jeep and going to get them is not in the bargain!"

"But you will go pick up a dead deer!"

"Sure. In the jeep. What desk-bound executive can pack a deer in on his shoulder, and live to tell it?"

"They're soft," Mason grinned, prodding him.

But Jones, who had apparently delivered long and loud on the subject before, felt himself being baited, looked at Frieda, and laughed some more.

"Do you expect more hunters in the next day or so?" Mason asked.

He tried to smile along with the asking, so as not to give away his interest.

"Sure. We have several coming." But Raleigh Jones was wound up. He began to talk.

Yes, he had seen them, he said. The hunters. He had seen hundreds of them in the twenty-five years that he had been here and had leased for hunting. Hunters who were oh, so few in number and the vastly more numerous who called themselves hunters because they carried guns and were lucky enough to kill something . . . .

He had seen a party of five who came to hunt once except for one of their number who came to drink, and drink he did, for four days; and on the morning of the fourth day when the others, deerless as yet and frustrated with the sterility of effort which had chanced to be their lot, were in the hills and hunting hard, the drunken member had staggered from his bed to relieve himself at the cabin door at eight o'clock in the morning, had seen a deer and had been able to reach his rifle from where he had stood, and had shot once . . . at a random image picked from six or seven interweaving in his eyes, and had hit a twelve-point, two-hundred pound buck dead center in the heart not fifty steps from the cabin. And it was worthy of laughter. Still, years later. Because he had gone directly back to bed without having gone to see . . . .

And he had seen fools who had insisted on hunting with M-1 carbines and military ammunition which meant steel-jacketed bullets which were no good because they made a smooth, neat hole that bored through and did not tear, and it was atrocious because when a deer turns to run after such a shot and such a hole, his skin slides over the neat hole and he does not bleed outside and cannot be tracked. One such hunter had shot at a deer eight times and it had been figured later that at least six of the bullets had hit . . . and they had never found the deer . . . .

And he had seen a deer shot and apparently dead and one of the hunters had carried the deer to a barbed-wire fence and had thrown him over and after crossing the fence himself had reached for his deer and had seen only bare ground because the deer had run away at full speed. Which was dangerous, he told them. They can kick you and run the sharp hoof all the way through you like an ice-pick.

And there had been hunters and still more hunters—and they were getting more numerous—who wanted to hunt from warm cabins where there were cards and whiskey and peep-holes in the walls to shoot through and flood lights outside to show the deer feeding in the dark at corn that had been placed there every three days for two months . . . but he would have none of that sort of thing.

"It's amazing, Frieda," Mason interjected. "People come here expecting that sort of thing, and trips to a legitimate brush blind in the jeep, and after they meet Raleigh Jones they are ashamed, and they hunt like a man is supposed to hunt."

"Where is the glory?" Raleigh Jones demanded, making red and white knuckles on the table and looking at Frieda.

"Where is the payout? The hunt is the thing. Not the kill. The kill must follow the hunt, to be any good. People have to be reminded!"

And he had seen deer shot all to pieces and get away, and that was bad. He himself had once shot both forelegs away and one of the hind hoofs and had had the deer run three miles away from him. They are athletes, he told them. You have to wreck them to get them.

"Why do you hunt then, Raleigh?" Frieda intoned.

He looked at her carefully.

"All the predatory enemies of the deer are gone," he said, peering. "If they were not harvested, almost as a crop, they would overpopulate and that would be bad."

Frieda shuddered.

"If you only knew," she murmured, turning her face away.

"What?"

"I agree," she said, then.

"Of course, all the predatory enemies are not really gone. We have an occasional cougar here, that feeds on the deer. Once every three or four years somebody sees signs of a cougar. But the wolves and coyotes are gone. When I came here almost thirty years ago one of the big spreads had twenty-five thousand dollars worth of hunting dogs. Pack hounds. Think of that! They did the wolves in, but good! And this is sheep and goat country now, and everything that is good for sheep and goats is good for the deer. Some cattle too, of course."

Frieda was impressed. Her mouth was daintily ajar as she listened to Raleigh Jones. Mason saw it and smiled to himself.

"When do you expect someone else in, Raleigh?" Mason asked.

"Oh, any time. There are several more coming. The season only lasts a couple more weeks, you know."

"I know."

Mason did not feel like probing further. He was afraid he might give something away.

After they had talked for an hour and the coffee was gone again they heard a shout, then another. They were glad shouts, with exuberance.

The three of them put on coats and went outside. They saw mild activity at the other cabin which had hunters.

"Let's go see," Raleigh Jones said.

Two hunters were there, and Joe, and Raleigh Jones' jeep. The hunters were of different ages but the olive drab fatigues they wore were the same and the beard stubble which they both wore made their faces look alike, except that the older face had gray patches in the stubble and the younger face had three smears of blood on it— drying, now—on both cheeks and on the forehead.

Raleigh Jones introduced them and he used the same surname twice, and immediately. Mason had forgotten the names. It was a failing which he had never been able to correct: he was always too interested in the faces.

"I thought you both looked alike!" Mason told the grinning pair. "Father and son?"

The younger one nodded happily. He had just killed his first deer and his father had patted the blood on his face with the directions that he should wear it all day.

"I feel like an Indian," the young man laughed. He was a little giddy.

"You look like one," said Raleigh Jones. "You see, Mason, this is refreshing. This is the way to hunt. You see, these boys have class. Most people who hunt nowadays don't know the niceties of the game. . . ."

"Niceties!" Frieda said.

They all laughed at her.

Then they inspected the deer, which had just been unloaded from the jeep and was lying on the ground: flat because he had already been gutted and his flanks were together—the eight points of the antlers neat and well formed, perfectly symmetrical, brown as nut meats and cobbled along the main branches and smoothing out to a waxy white at the tips, sharp yet finely rounded; eyes open and all pupil: clear turquoise; having depth which ceased somewhere far back not as if a retina or something else were the back wall but gradually, as the sun-probed deeps of a cold tranquil stream beneath shady pecan trees: holding the pooled, wide-pupiled fright still as if the ghost had flown leaving the fright and the terror in the deeps to cool there, having no further need of it and so forgetting, fleeting with a pride which the exact and unforgiving seconds had, ticking, precisely freed of panic as a wintering northern pond its southbound duck . . . .

Every Man Also—73

"Look how their tongue always hangs out," the young man said. He laughed a little. "Only it's not much of a tongue."

"They eat vegetation," said Raleigh Jones. "That's the reason the tongue is narrow and thick."

It had been a good shot, a heart shot. And now the legs were stiff, long, and sharp: the forelegs together as one; the hind legs together as one. They would not bend at all.

Frieda squatted and smoothed the tight hair on the buck's side, carefully avoiding blood smears which tangled the hair.

"He's hard," she said.

Later, she murmured, in surprise: "Why, he smells like a spice cabinet!"

Mason watched her with interest, noting that she was not afraid of the dead animal, not squeamish about putting her hands on it. He thought: the gal has spunk. And fire. The rats must have really got to her. That's all.

The young man began to describe the kill, and everyone listened to his garbled, exulting words, especially the father and Raleigh Jones, who was interested for his own private mental catalog's sake in where the buck had been taken; Mason noticed that Joe, the hired hand, was beginning to fidget and was trying to draw Raleigh Jones' attention aside. At length the two of them—Joe and his employer—retired a few steps away and held earnest conversation.

"He ran exactly five steps!" the father was saying.

"Right!" the son enthused. "And I didn't get the shakes!"

This was a happy moment for them. The deer was not just a deer to them. It was a vital piece of manhood. And they did not understand it; but that made no difference.

At length Joe got on the jeep, started the engine, and drove away, twisting hard at the steering wheel.

Later, after Mason had congratulated the son again and had noted with interest that the father was taking a pride of ownership in his son's deer, he, Frieda, and Raleigh Jones left the happy pair and walked back toward their cabin.

"I'll go back to the house, Mason," said Raleigh Jones. "Got some figuring to do. Joe—that's the boy on the jeep—told me that it happened again last night . . . and that's where I sent Junior and Smitty a while ago, to see about it . . . something happened again last night that I've got to figure out . . . ."

"What?"

"Somebody stole some feed. It's been happening. I've got a shed on the north side of the place, at the north end of the oat field, where I keep feed in sacks . . . and some hay. It's open so I can't lock it. Just a shed. And somebody has been coming in there late in the evenings and stealing sacks of feed. Easy to do. It's on the road, kind of. I sent June and Smitty there to see about it, and Joe drove by and checked them out before he brought the deer in, just now."

"What will you do?"

"I don't know. Maybe post a guard. What would you do?"

"Post a guard," Mason said. "Hide him."

Raleigh Jones nodded thoughtfully. When he had seen them to their cabin again, he cheerfully invited Mason to tear himself away from his wife, though he could understand, he said, his reticence in doing so, and to partake of the less exciting delights of the hunt, this evening.

He parted with: "I know it's difficult. But that's what you came for. You can do the other at home!"

Mason laughed. And when Jones was gone, Mason saw that Frieda's eyes were shining and there was a dusky texture on her throat and cheeks.

"You're blushing," he said, laughing.

"I am not!"

"Ah, ha! Ha! Ha!"

"Shut up, Mason."

But he drew a smile.

And Mason thought that Raleigh Jones had lines in his neck. He had lines in his neck but it was because of the sun that he had lines in his neck because his chest was deep and full like a young man's. And though his chest was deep and full his belly was flat, also like a young man's; in fact he had no belly at all . . . .

Mason thought these things, watching Frieda blush.

"Ah, ha! Ha! Ha!" he said.

"Would my Love like some more coffee?"

"I'll slosh," he told her, remembering. He was still teasing.

In the early afternoon of that day Mason left Frieda at the ranchhouse to look at the furnishings and to get acquainted with Mrs. Waskom, who was at the time the only other woman on the place, and then he drove alone into town for supplies. He bought coffee, bacon, eggs and bread for three days, picking the number of days at random with the realization that it might be too many or not enough—and hating the uncertainty of it—and also some random canned goods, another bottle of Old Forester, and soda water. Then before he left the drive-in grocery he grabbed a sheaf of current magazines for Frieda. He took no thought concerning the names of the magazines. How does one pick magazines for a lady Ph.D. who has a phobia about rats?

When he arrived back at the house of Raleigh Jones he went in and was surprised to find Frieda and Mrs. Waskom wrapped in earnest and long-lived conversation over coffee; and he listened to the run of the talk for a time then considered that there was nothing surprising about two women talking if they got along; and decided to leave.

"Frieda, I'll go after deer this afternoon. I'll come back and get you when I get in."

She nodded.

"Guess what," she began.

"What?"

"Helen Waskom and her husband both have the M.A. in English, and used to be college professors."

He could see that she was impressed.

"Good," Mason said, thinking that maybe he should have shrugged, or frowned.

"They came here to find the quiet life," Frieda said.

"Freedom, Mr. Mason," smiled Helen Waskom. "We've been here a long time."

"There is that, sure enough," he mumbled. Then he stood around for a little while trying to think of things to say to bolster his weak statement, saw that the women were going pell-mell again, gave up and left.

At the cabin he unloaded the groceries and magazines, got his .270 out of its case and worked the action several times, feeling the hard shock and slam of it with satisfaction, loaded it by pushing shells in a tight trapslot, then put on a sweater and then the coat over it and walked out of the cold cabin into the day which was now fairly mild and beginning to edge again toward the cold. The sun had two hours of pale sky left beneath it in the west, and there was no wind. Mason turned toward the hill to the east. The father and son had left with their deer and their pride at noon; for a while at least he would have the whole place to himself. Not that he could cover it all in two hours and be back by dark! But he resolved to see a large portion before coming in.

His way up the hill was open enough but rugged, and he found that he had to watch his feet with care in their placement from rocky ledge to rocky ledge; not so steep was it that he had to use his hands, but steep enough that he had to use extreme care in stepping. Mesquite thorns pulled at him now and then, rocks rolled now and then, unsettling his feet, and he had to stop and rest three times before gaining the top. Then he rested again, standing, blowing, looking out across the valley that was beginning to haze now with the early evening, then went on. Mason carried his rifle in his right hand, pointed straight ahead.

The top of the great hill was flat and wooded: the ground puffy and soft now after the melting in between great slabs of gray rock and clumps of yellow grass; the heavy draperies of juniper cedar obstructed view everywhere, growing all the way down to the ground and no higher than twenty feet, lying across his face and shoulders as he went from open space to open space like friendly towels of stiff and heavy green.

He thought of the deer again, then, and reminded himself to go slowly and carefully, watchfully. Almost on cue he heard a crashing and a blowing as if a man with a head cold were quickly using his handkerchief, and, squaring away with rifle half-raised, he watched two deer bound over and under and through the brush of the dry land jungle and out of sight in a hurry.

Does. Two of them. He had seen the tails high and weaving from side to side like pampas grass plumes. ·

After he had watched them go for five seconds he paused and remembered. Does blow when they see or smell a man and the sound of the blowing is the sound of a quick Bronx cheer. And they wave their tails high and fluffy.

He thought: just like a woman.

Bucks on the other hand—especially when the hunting season is weeks old already—whistle through their nostrils, high and shrill and almost like a bird; and then they go hell-bound through the brush with antlers low and outstretched, twenty-five feet between gathering, leaping footprints, with the white and fluffy underside flag of tail hidden, tucked down and under like a craven dog.

But it is different when they walk, unafraid. Then it is that does move the head back and forth almost like a chicken, and bucks carry the antlers high, making them float, keeping them away from branches and brush that might entangle.

Mason walked for an hour, steadily, bearing to the east and then, at the east fence, to the north. He saw twelve deer, all of them moving away from him with speed; and not a single one had antlers that he could see. And in each case he had only seconds in which to look.

At length he turned back toward the west and came to the lip of another hill where he paused for a time. The great valley lay before him again. The sun was poised on the hill beyond, yellow and pulsating and hazy; shadows lay already in the valley, mounting and thickening there. Away to the south he could see Raleigh Jones' quiet house, and, a little nearer, the four cabins. Directly beneath him now was a field, the road to town on the far side of the field, and, near the road, the shed where Raleigh Jones kept feed that was being stolen from time to time. The shed was not in the open: a point of brush came into the field and partially hid it.

Mason found that he enjoyed the scene. He sat down on a ledge of rock to watch the sun dip out of sight. Already it was colder, and he knew that if he sat there long, after the walking, he would soon be shivering and stiff.

He was three hundred feet above the valley floor and a half-mile from the road, and as he sat now and gazed through the cold yellow light, squinting because he was looking almost directly into the sun, seeing down into the layering haze of shadow that was almost twilight already on the floor of the valley, on the field of young oats whose bright green had turned to velvet now with the loss of color donated already to the approaching night, Mason thought of the road and looked at it. It was along here that his courier would come soon—only hours away now, certainly—with a hundred thousand dollars for Mase Mason; with perhaps the hint of a thought of a bullet for Mase Mason in case the opportunity should arise; with perhaps a woman along for the comfort . . . not sport, with the winter wind outside.

A day had passed now and he had not come. Mason knew that he would come. He told himself again that he himself represented a valuable hireling in the scheme of things; that the operator could not afford not to pay him . . . .

His eyes fell suddenly to the sturdy shed, which was big enough to hold two or three hundred sacks of feed and which had been built closed enough but unlockable by a trusting man. And he, himself, Mason, had suggested posting a guard, hidden: apotheosis of stealth-in-righteousness and the vital measure which seeks and sees and decides shoot the son of a bitch without a moment's loss because he is the thief with hand of red here, now, and no jury in the western world will entertain other than the deed done and well . . . he, Mason, prescribing and by prescribing giving the only answer and giving it truly; from the lips of a thief far greater than any who might stop to pick up a sack of feed from among two hundred and who, tallying probably with an eye toward return, was certainly no rank felon because the need was there anyway and whether he paid it back or not he was no traitor because the need was there and it was right . . . anyone who steals feed from among two hundred fat sacks and carries it on his back and lowers it, strain and lower-back pain and sweat of guilt, onto the rotted floor of an old car trunk, with care lest it go on through to the road, deserves to hold his head up, his eyes level . . . but others write the law, and these eyes are the level ones.

Feed is a holy thing. Feed is public domain . . . almost.

But life is not like that, Mason thought. The Great Thief thought; the Traitor thought.

Suddenly, watching the road which had had no traffic at all on it since he had sat, watching too the sun redden as it touched the hill and begin to drop faster also as it touched the hill, grotesqueing out of shape with a ragged bottom, hurriedly now, Mason felt terrible. Something had dropped, fallen, inside of him. Guilt washed over him in a sickening wave; the first he had felt; and he really felt ill. For a long moment he considered, thinking that he might be sick to his stomach.

It was a strange thing and Mason did not like it. He coughed minutely, almost retching with guilt. He tried not to think of the last game of the Warriors.

Then he saw a movement below him.

Someone came out from below the hill, far under him. He saw smoke waft up and away lazily, and he thought that he could recognize Jim, the wiry one, in the near-twilight of below. He was carrying a rifle.

Jim, if it was Jim, walked directly across the field toward the shed, veering a little to the right and aiming now at the brush fifty yards behind the shed.

"Whist!"

Mason heard the sharp sound secondarily, and knew that Jim had made it: almost a quiet whistle. Then he saw another figure rise out of the brush; materialize almost from nothing in the brush and walk out to meet him. He saw the fat coat collar and recognized Smitty. They met in the edge of the field, squatted as ranch people will do when they meet, and talked while Smitty built a cigarette and lit it, puffing away then the blue vapors that drifted south and disappeared. At length they arose again, and Mason could see that they both had guns and that Jim, the replacement, had also a long, five or six or seven-cell flashlight which he tried now against the ground.

Then Jim was into the brush and had disappeared and Smitty was hurrying hungrily toward Mason, far below. The guard had changed.

Later, Mason got to his feet. He was stiff. It was almost dark and he knew that he would have to work his way down into the valley very soon in order to be able to find his way to his cabin in the dark which was rapidly coming down. He had to stop every hundred yards or so to shiver.

By the time he reached his cabin the night had moved in. He went inside, turned on the lights, spent five minutes building a fire and seeing that the three big logs which he put on would catch, then left his now unloaded gun standing in one corner and walked out of the cabin again, leaving the light on.

Mason got in his car and went to get Frieda. His roommate. The thought caused him to smile wryly behind the wheel.

It was custom in the Jones household to eat at sundown, but

tonight, for some unobserved reason—perhaps it was because Frieda had aroused the talk in Helen Waskom to the extent that she had put it off; seeing that Raleigh Jones approved of Frieda and so the late start was all right—supper was not yet ready when Mason rapped at the wooden back door, was admitted, and came in blowing out his chilled breath and removing his gloves and his coat.

"They're in the living room," Mrs. Waskom said as he went through.

In the living room he found Frieda, Raleigh Jones and Raleigh Jones, Junior, and any thoughts which he had concerning beginning a conversation and having people listen were quickly dispelled. Something was underway.

Frieda looked from the sofa at Mason, wide-eyed. Then she winked. Mason sat down in a rocker.

"Now," Raleigh Jones was saying. He sat in his great chair that had broad, flat, red arms, and he was holding his left palm out before him.

"Here are three pieces," he said. He poked at them with his right forefinger, tumbling them in his palm: three small cellophane-wrapped cubes of caramel candy.

"I want you," he sing-songed, intoning, using the Goldilocks-and-the-three bears inflection which builds interest for the juvenile story-master; and with the great ease of familiarity, "to go to the stack lot and bring me back a handful of alfalfa. This means that you will have to go inside, because straw is outside but the alfalfa is baled and on the inside. You bring me back a handful of alfalfa from a bale and these are yours . . . ."

Raleigh Junior was on his feet, laughing. He laughed with interest, almost gaily, then he stalked through the busy kitchen and slammed the door. He had gone outside into the total overcast blackness without a coat or a light; and the verve of the slamming behind him was a statement of strong pride.

"We've done this," Raleigh turned to Mason, "since he was ten years old. To teach him not to be afraid of the dark. The stack lot is a half-mile away and there are no stars out." Raleigh Jones spoke with pride.

Mason blinked. He rocked minutely, beginning to warm a bit.

"For three candies?"

"Yes, for three candies."

"Why not three . . . ."

"Sir?"

"Nothing," Mason said.

"You started to say something . . . ."

"No. But he forgot his coat."

Every Man Also—80

Later Mason stood as if he were ready to leave, but then he read something heavy in Frieda's glance toward him and saw that Raleigh Jones was also looking at him, questioning, not believing; and he used the standing to take off his sweater which had been beneath the coat, then sat again.

He tried to make conversation. But it did not take. The three of them sat there, mostly in silence, for twenty minutes. From where he was sitting Mason could see Helen Waskom in the kitchen: sitting now on a tall stool with hands in her lap, a meal ready which she had not announced; which she would not announce until . . . .

The door burst open and in he charged, wild-eyed and blowing, clutching a handful of green straw which he held out in triumph before him; stalking then through the kitchen, feet pounding, face radiant with overwhelming success, directly to his father.

The exchange was made: three candies for a handful of hay.

Mason saw that everyone was looking at him. He licked his lips.

"Well done," he said.

"How's that, Coach?" Raleigh Jones demanded.

"Well . . . well done!" he managed, again.

Raleigh Junior's eyes were alive with happiness. A grin that would have done justice to a Queen of the May suffused his face with radiance. And he laughed with real happiness, chortling.

"I ran into the stock lot fence," he said. "It was dark! It was real dark!"

"Well done, son! Well done! By God, there are not many men that can do that without a light! And now let's eat, if Helen has it ready. Masons, you will eat with us tonight!"

"No, Raleigh," Mason murmured. "We'll go on up."

He saw that there was doubt so he pursued it, wanting somehow to get away.

"I have a stew already on," Mason lied.

"Tomorrow night, then."

"All right. Come on Frieda."

At the door Mason turned.

"Will you have anyone in tonight?" he muttered adding hastily: "If you do, I'll be on the north side in the morning, so you can tell them."

"I'm expecting a man from way up north," Raleigh Jones said, leaning on the door and looking out at them.

"But I don't know when he'll get here. If it's tonight, I'll tell him."

Mason sighed, trying to make it sound smooth.

"Good night," he said.

"Good night," Frieda said. Then: "I'll see you tomorrow, Helen!

And Raleigh!"

"Good night. Good hunting," said Raleigh Jones.

They got in the Buick and drove to their cabin in silence.

Mason could feel the guilt still ice-edged around his stomach. "How about a beverage?" he asked.

"Pour!"

"I got soda

"That's fine."

Later, warming both inside and out, he decided to begin the conversation after seeing that she was indeed in a dark mood.

"The three candies."

"Should have been something else! Oh, Mason!"

"That's what I thought," he muttered. "That's exactly what I thought. Was that all that was wrong with it? Tell me. You're a psychologist. I sat there watching the thing and knowing it was all wrong and not being sure. What was wrong with it?"

After a while she said, directing her voice at the fire: "He is retarded. But his father, man that he is, has built into him something else . . . ."

"Is that it? Is that all?"

She did not answer. She seemed very sad, and withdrawn.

"I had the funny feeling," he began again, "as if it would have been all right . . . . Hell fire! It was a good trick! I'd hate to think that I would have to go half a mile twice in the dark, whether I knew the ground by feel or not . . . but the candies were wrong! Three beers, maybe. Or three dollars. But three candies! A child's reward!"

"That's it."

"What's it?"

"The three candies," she murmured, still looking into the fire. "That's where they've failed."

"What has failed?"

Mason saw that her drink was gone already.

"Let's talk about something else, Mason. Let's talk about the new hunter who will maybe get here tonight."

"No. Let's have another drink and then you cook."

"I'm not hungry," she said. "But I'll cook, if you are."

"I'm not, either."

But they had the second drink, and after his was almost gone Mason realized that he still felt bad, and, looking at Frieda, he realized again that a similar mood of depression was hard upon her.

"You talked with Helen . . . ." he began.

"But Helen is not the one. Raleigh Jones is the one. Do you know that his son is a middle-grade moron and he has by his refusal to believe and his overt manhood made the boy into something else?"

"Is that good?"

"Good doesn't count! He has done it, Mason!"

"Has he made his son into a whole man?"

After thinking about this for a while, and after finishing her second drink much too rapidly, she replied.

"He is a whole man as long as Raleigh Jones is present."

"Then . . . he is not."

"Maybe. Perhaps you are right. But the effort! The planning!"

"Except for the candies!" Mason said, realizing that he was getting drunk, thinking not about the boy but about his empty stomach, his guilt, and the coming courier who had a hundred thousand dollars and a deer rifle.

"Yes."

"How old is Raleigh Junior, Frieda?"

"I'll guess. Twenty-five . . . ."

"Sometimes he acts twelve."

"Yes. And I'm sorry."

"You're sorry?"

"Yes. Oh, I'm so sorry!"

"What has that got to do with it?"

"I'm supposed to be sorry. Professional pride."

"Okay, Frieda. Okay, Miss Frieda."

"Don't Miss me."

"Why not? Because you have not missed nearly so much as I think you have?"

"Maybe."

Mason laughed out loud, feeling like laughing for the first time.

"But I have changed my mind about the candies!" Frieda announced with sudden finality. "Why not three candies? Yes, and maybe that's the answer to the whole thing, that Raleigh has taken his son and has made him into something other than he really is and the candies were the right reward all along! Something he likes and understands! Why not?"

"I can't argue with a professional," he said. "Only you said that Raleigh made him into a man so long as Raleigh is present and I wonder if that is good. Is it good to be something you're not?"

"What does that mean?"

"I don't know," he said, looking at his empty glass. "Maybe it's whiskey talk. Maybe it's the hard sauce talking already. The loud mouth. Maybe we'd better eat something."

"I'm not hungry," Frieda said again.

She was sitting on her bed. Now she drew her feet up on the bed, clasped both arms around her raised knees, and looked deep into the fire.

"Man that he is," she mused, lowering her chin to the knees.

Mason got up and began to rummage in the food box for something to eat. He found a half circle of cheddar cheese and cut off a three-sided slab, then drew a handful of crackers from the cracker box. Before he sat down again with his cheese and crackers he had fixed two more drinks.

"You appreciate a real man, don't you?" he asked.

"I do indeed. There was a time when I did not."

"Do I qualify?"

"You qualify. Something tells me that before this night is over I will tell you how much you qualify!"

"But Raleigh Jones . . . ," he began for her.

"Man that he is . . . ."

He could see the dark something pouring from her eyes that were lit, now, by flickering firelight. And she was very serious.

Mason munched the crackers and cheddar cheese, filling his mouth with the round, goaty taste of it.

"Tell me about Raleigh Jones, Frieda."

After a long while of looking at nothing but the fire, Frieda began to speak. She murmured dreamily without moving, almost as if she were speaking to or into the fire itself.

"I put rats in four interconnected pens each six feet square. I gave them plenty of food and water and I let them multiply for almost two years. And I watched them. Two pens had only one ramp each instead of two, and here a male rat in each chased all the other males out and could keep them out by sleeping at the foot of the ramp. In the other two pens this was impossible because they had a ramp at each end. In these, the middle pens, the rats got so used to crowds that they would not eat unless a crowd was eating. They would go to the crowded hopper to feed, though the same feed was in all the hoppers. We called this a behavioral sink. Follow the crowd. Just like people. If the group doesn't do it it's no good. Just like people. This was in the middle pens. And also in the middle pens the rats didn't have time, after a while, for the necessary things, like proper courtship. Just like people. Some of the male rats gave the females no rest. Some of the male rats became homosexual. And some schizophrenic—they walked about in a stupor and hid in corners. And after a while in the middle pens the females lost the ability to make nests and they lost the ability to move their young about so that the nesting boxes, the burrows, were not properly occupied homes at all and the young were born on the floor and died and were eaten.

Ninety-six percent of the young died, in the middle pens. And here some of the male rats became what we called probers, and chased the females into the burrows without proper courtship and it was in the burrows and nesting boxes that they often came across the young who were not in a proper nest and ate them, and the mothers would not protect them.

"But in the end pens where the male rats—only two—one in each pen—had harems and had also territory that was their own because they could keep it, everything was normal. And the two males did not chase the females into the nests but waited outside like gentlemen for the females to come out for the mating. And here everything was normal because the two males were fighters and could have the territory and call it theirs and theirs alone and here their women rats were normal and happy and their children were normal in normal homes and survived . . . ."

"Raleigh Jones has land of his own," Mason said. His cheese was all gone.

"Man that he is . . . ," she agreed.

"You think the rats are like people, Frieda?"

"I know it." She looked at him then. "Did you know," she went on, "that we have proved now, where people are concerned, that not only is the proper sexual development of a son dependent upon his having a proper masculine father to watch and copy, but the proper sexual development of a daughter is also dependent upon her having a dominant, masculine father to watch?"

"Proved?"

"Yes. Proved."

She looked back into the fire.

"Behavioral sink," she murmured. "It is a good term. Follow the crowd. We're all becoming city dwellers, Mason. I can see it in the people. And it will get worse . . . the population crisis will make it worse. Already the women are becoming like men and the men like women."

"But Raleigh Jones has land of his own," he said, trying to keep the childish sound out of his voice.

"He does, indeed."

"A two-fisted son of a bitch!"

"Exactly!"

"But can you relate all this to people? I mean really? Rats aren't people."

"Yes."

"Show me. I'm not sure I believe you."

"Okay," she said. She licked her lips. "You consider the successful male rats, the territorial ones, the ones with power . . . ."

"Okay. I'm considering."

"Note that they only approach a female with respect, if you will they do a dance . . . asking permission. Always. They don't have to think about it . . . ."

"How do you know they don't think about it?"

"I don't, of course . . . but, listen . . . ."

He waited.

"It's the lesser rats that hassle the females. Same with people. The males with power, integrity, always ask. There is something in the hormones here that dictates this: all up and down the animal kingdom there is this law of nature. The male makes the advance, the female sets the pace."

"I've heard of that," Mason said, teasing.

"Note that only the male who doubts himself forces the female."

"Okay."

"Now look at this new thing . . . date rape on college campuses. Only the male who is confused does it—and it's a big thing now because many are confused. And a part of his confusion is that he— neither he nor she—understands 'the male makes the advance, the female sets the pace.' Because our liberated female society has taken that away. Now that she wants to make the advance and set the pace also; instead of saying, 'You pay me, then I pay you,' the female is now saying to the male, 'You pay me, then you pay me.' The equity is gone. His role is gone, for the male. The female wants to have her cake, and eat it, too . . . ."

"And it confuses him," she went on. "He says, 'Hey. She must want it as much as I do, no matter what she says. After all, aren't we just alike in this thing?' The roles are blurred, now."

"Okay," Mason shrugged. "He could still listen, when she says 'No!'"

"You don't hear me! What did Marlene Dietrich say?"

"Who?"

"Marlene Dietrich . . . what is she famous for?"

"Playing whores . . . I don't know. What else?"

"'All real men are gentle' . . . that's what she said. And it's true. She was right. It's the same thing. And what is so bad now is that with our feminist media we are in danger of reaching the point of no return. It is one thing for me to say and for you to say 'All real men are gentle'—and that it is not just the male who rapes but only the crippled male—emotionally—who rapes, but they'll never hear us say it because the media is feminist. In the bad sense. Their driving force now is to sell the idea that testosterone is bad . . . top to bottom." She looked into the fire. "Behavioral sink is upon us," Frieda said.

"So what do we do about it?" Mason asked.

"Ah!" She looked at him. Then she began to grin. The grin grew and grew.

"That's where you come in, Mason! Don't you see?"

Later Mason drew a big breath. Then he shook his head.

"I don't have any ball players that sleep at the bottoms of ramps . . . . All of my kids are just people . . . ."

"Ah, but consider!" She was hot with it, now. "Consider date rape. Athletes are the worst offenders. Now. What happens when you get your boys together and tell them what I just told you? Explain that date rape comes from feminism, and why. That 'the male makes the advance and the female sets the pace' *is* valid because it comes out of the hormones . . . out of the ground . . . that it is a law of nature . . . ."

"And is not rational . . . ."

"And is not rational . . . but nonetheless true!"

Frieda was shouting at him now.

"Then," she pointed, "then see if the date rapes come from your boys. You will have re-defined a role for them they never knew— enhanced manhood!"

Mason stood up. It was too much.

"Aspire to sleep at the bottom of the ramp," he said.

"Aspire," she said, "to sleep at the bottom of the ramp!"

"I don't know," Mason told her.

"I do! Know it, Mason!"

She gave him a long glance that had a storm in it, unspoken.

Frieda grabbed her drink, then, that she had not touched since he had put it down near her, and she gulped it down halfway before looking at him again. And then he saw that she was beginning to feel strong emotion, that her face was warped and out of shape with crying, though no tears had shown as yet.

"Raleigh Jones," she almost shouted. "And you, in a different way. You are holy, Mason! I know it! You are holy because you deal with the making of manhood! You who deal in your job with the setting up of artificial situations in your athletics which present young men with strife to be conquered . . . you are thrice blessed! I'm corny now and I'm sorry for it but listen to me! You are the most important man in the world and others like you and there are not many of them . . . you set up artificial situations of strife and you make the young men fight through them and you build them into what you call two-fisted sons of bitches and I'm telling you now that the world does not recognize it or recognize you, but it will! I have seen it! A vision! When the population crisis is hard upon the human race it will be up to the individual people themselves to solve and they'll never solve it in behavioral sinks! They'll solve it by the men that you have created because they will be there with the aggressive capability which you have given them! Honor, yes; and morals, yes; and learning, manners, and compassion, yes; but all these in a man who is a two-fisted son of a bitch! A man who can take and hold the end pen!"

She was gasping.

Mason's heart was thudding. He did not know what to do, so he did nothing except stare at her with his mouth open. Four times he tried to lick cheese from his lips, but it was already gone.

"Holy," he muttered, soberly. "Me. Holy."

"Yes! Oh, yes!"

He went to her and embraced her. She was crying openly. He began to pet her to assuage the crying, thinking: holy. Me. Holy. And in his own stupor with the bourbon and with the new high flight of feeling he did not realize what he was doing until he saw with a start that he had been kissing her and that they had both been lying on her bed where he had pushed her back, and that now both of them were almost completely undressed in the warm cabin before the fire. And he had done it. Mason came to his senses.

He sat up and looked at her, stretched out, still crying. Both still had their socks on, and that was all.

She was unbelievably beautiful to him, now. For a long time he looked at her, seeing that the crying was slowing and that she was watching him.

He looked at the great, perfect breasts, flat now with the reclining but pearly white and raised softly; large ungravid nipples pink as a young girl's, the warm, fascinating hollow and rise of loin . . . .

"No," she murmured.

"Last night it was yes!" He was eager, now, freed by the guilt which he had felt.

"No. I'm sorry." She covered herself with her hands.

"What's the difference, Frieda . . . ?"

"I don't know."

"Raleigh Jones? Is he the difference?"

"I don't know. Let me up."

He let her up. He turned away while she put on her pink gown and robe, still seated on the bed. And he found with surprise that the chagrin which he felt was light, superficial, manufactured; in the light of what she had told him he found that he could accept the defeat with grace; and, accepting, be a man and smile with the thinking that it was not at all important.

"Holy," he told her. "You called me holy. And because of my job."

"Yes. How would you like an omelet before we go to bed?"

"Okay. Holy. That was what you said, wasn't it . . . ?"

"Yes. Holy. It sounds corny, doesn't it? And thank you!"

"No. No, it doesn't sound corny."

Mason redressed, went out, and returned with more wood for the fire. He sat and watched her begin to cook; wondering at himself, at her.

Of course he could only partially understand what she could only partially tell: Raleigh Jones. Raleigh Jones and the rats. As if "fifty million rats can be wrong" and then "fifty million rats are wrong. Wrong because I have proved them wrong." And Raleigh Jones with his two-fisted capability and his ability to hand-mold a man from a crippled perennial adolescent and his land which was in part only economic advantage but that was all right too because money is muscle. Among other things. All history a stream and all civilization not a part of the stream at all but instead homes and households millennium-free on the banks; and in her fear which the rats had given her the stream of history seeming and becoming by the light of the modern population scare a sludge of struggling tangled bodies lost in the stream's sink: the man on the bank two-fisted because Mason had made him two-fisted and had given him aggressive capability so that he was perfect even now—now before the crisis was at hand: saying get away from the crowd. Scorn the crowd because we have proved them wrong. Needed now because society already was slipping into a pale antecedent crisis before the great crisis: not a father in a million wanting his daughter to become a nestless bitch but fully four hundred thousand of the same million turning away from the fact and giving in to rank luck because when you deal with one female you are dealing with fifty, and the kids organized and the parents not; needed to raise the figurative and the potentially material fist and legislate his harem in the end pen on the bank: not mate only but children, also, going against the broadcast right of the now pale but darkening sink and saying draw the line now! Now! Now, by God! and backing it up with the force of personality which lay among the cultured spheres of his being like a golden egg hard-boiled—boiled perhaps by Mason and his ilk; not having yet the knowledge of correct action in his mind beyond a compulsive hunch and the conviction that he as executor needs no excuse; backing the decision with the hard gold and finding the hunch fully as pure-golden. Because sink-bound rats forsake the quality and the quantity in food for the crowded food and give themselves away with the act—and the act now witnessed, recorded, proved: that not famine, nor plague, nor bomb, not yet any other subtractor stands so ready or so unique in horrible ability as the new-named reaper, mob . . . .

Mason drew a gusty breath.

"How about the Nazis, Frieda? They were tough and two-fisted and they put scars on their faces to show manhood." Mason's tongue was slow so he enunciated very carefully, with the result that he spoke more clearly than usual.

"But they forgot everything else. That's not the point. The manhood is to protect the other values, the worthwhile things."

Later he said, looking at the back of her as she scraped the omelet free from sticking in the skillet: "And I have seen my ball players who have the two-fisted capability as you call it do ridiculous things. Stupid, childish things . . . ."

"Now you're talking about maturity, Mason. That comes with years, usually."

"Yes."

Still later he said: "I know it. I have believed in it for a long time."

"I know you have."

Mason was aroused. He sat taking deep breaths and watching Frieda prepare the meal.

"Now I know why you came," he muttered.

"Now you know."

"Are you glad?"

"I am."

She served two omelets: one huge omelet cut in half, really, and he could see the puffy light snowiness of it and smell the cheese and see the triangular bits of browned bacon sticking in it here and there. She rigged the table with knives, forks, and napkins, then poured cold water from the wide-mouth jar into copper tumblers for them to drink. He pulled up two chairs.

It was good. Later she cleared the table and Mason got his rifle from the corner and began to inspect it under the lamp, making noise.

"This is the second night and I haven't seen anything to shoot at yet."

"You'll hunt in the morning?"

"Sure. I came to hunt," he lied.

She left the connubial kitchen things to go to the bathroom and he, knowing that she would not want him sitting there listening, went outside in the black cold where he relieved himself and stood for a long time staring into the darkness.

He thought: holy. Blessed. And because I am a director of athletics. Hit 'em on the helmet. Hit 'em on the socks. Hell yes. Hell yes. Go Tech jocks. God. God almighty.

He drank deep breaths of the frigid night air: exhilarating

breaths. And something new was born, submerged, in the being of Mase Mason. Submerged and yet vibrant, all-encompassing, vital. He remembered the impromptu speeches which he made long ago in behalf of his athletes. They came back to him now as they had not come back in years: shouting in his fuzzy consciousness, triumphant.

When he went back inside he was still breathing as if he had been running.

Frieda was already through with the kitchen things. She was sitting before the fire again on her bed, knees up and clasped, and the fickle light was making dancing shadows on her face. She was smiling.

"Know what I'd like?"

"What?"

"I wish I had a kitten. Here. Now. A kitten to pet."

"You can pet me."

She laughed. He saw that she was happy again.

"You are not furry enough."

"I'm sweet. And by the way I'm pretty damned furry."

"Sweet you are. But . . . I wish I had a kitten. The fire and the hour demand a kitten. And some ribbons. Shiny, red ribbons."

"I could go down to the ranchhouse and get Raleigh Junior's coon . . . ."

"You're laughing at me!"

"I am not."

"Forget it."

Later she wanted to know: "When will you get up so you can hunt?"

"Five-thirty. And you'll get up, too, to make my coffee."

"Okay."

"Because I'm holy, you know. And blessed."

"That you are!" She laughed again. The cabin was happy once more.

But Mason was still thinking of their conversation earlier, and he was sitting there trying to conceive something which he could feel. At length he had it.

"All this about the two-fisted male, Frieda . . . how about the career female?"

"You've been talking to one of them."

That was all. The hour was late. Very soon they both turned their covers back and went to bed.

But as the fire fell apart little by little in the fireplace Mason put his hands behind his head and watched it: seeing the scintillant logs settle and section themselves in ragged little squares, the spectre of cold appear and begin to play across the glowing squares in black spotted stealth insidiously here and there, the sections darken and fall from the log at the ends, crumbling, the cold death gaining until it was a glow now that shot across and through and losing ground all the while until the settling had shrouded the whole thing with ash and had made a mound with cracks and crannies through which peeked the adamant, embattled, futile red. And with the failure darkness: another name for cold; creeping on vacuous feet that inched through the room until all was cold and dark and it was ridiculous to be awake because his senses had closed shop and had gone every one inside.

But inside was turmoil. Mason could not sleep. He thought of getting up and pouring more bourbon and decided against it and with the decision came also strange and alien pride, so that he nodded his head to himself.

He had heard strange words. Unexpected words. And the words had penetrated him to his core and had begun for him a chain, a flood, a turmoil of memories which garbled and shouted and gleamed, intermixing with the present and with a future which he did not recognize at all . . . .

The wind got up outside. Somewhere something flapped intermittently and then regularly in the wind: a loose tag of canvas somewhere under an eave of the cabin. And then he heard foil crackle on the table and knew that a mouse was getting at the groceries. It would be a deer mouse with big eyes and ears, and not a house mouse like they had in cities.

He thought: a two-fisted mouse, no doubt.

Mason grinned into the dark.

His windup alarm clock hammered its wicked little rhythm into the darkness. And once he heard a sound which could have been the slamming of a car door: but it lulled him, oddly, and he forgot to be interested because he could feel now the presence of Someone coming and near at hand: an old and faithful Friend who began to tuck the ragged edges of him neatly back upon themselves, smoothing, making him a perfect warm bundle that asked nothing because the perfection of warmth and the lack of ragged edges was sufficient unto itself and needed not.

Later in the deeps of the night Mason's activity awakened him and his senses swimming in his head told him that he was warm but that his feet were cold. Cold because they had been on the floor. But he immediately forgot about them.

Five

Jim arched his back and grunted, throwing straight up into the warm sunlight that was bathing them there in the lee of the ranchhouse. He threw high enough so that the can went into the windstream above the roofline and swept as it fell a little to the south. "Now!"

A hand jabbed quickly, the motion a single direct one, the little single-shot .22 spat and the can took off on a wild tangent, singing with no tone, out of shape, suddenly crumpled.

Raleigh Junior had handled the small rifle like a pistol. Now he snicked the bolt back, punched in another shell, and lay back against the house again. He exaggerated the position, going limp all over and resting the gun on the ground. He smiled a rag doll's smile, sitting, waiting.

"Thirteen," said Smitty. He was sitting cross-legged on the ground also, and leaning against the house that was warm with sun. He was eating pecans, cutting them open with a pocket knife, expertly; one end off and then down one side exposing the red middle rib, down the other side exposing the other red middle rib, the other end off, then the whole thing flaking apart and the meat halves perfect and untouched into his mouth and the left hand going for another.

"Thirteen," he said again, looking at Jim. When he spoke he bared his teeth and worked the lips over them a little, like a dog eating grass. The teeth were messy with pecan meal. He could open the pecans so rapidly that he had trouble keeping up with the eating.

"All right! Wait a minute, God damn it! I got to get some more cans!"

"What's the record, Smitty?" Raleigh Junior asked.

"Thirty-seven." He said it vacantly, watching the pecans. He could have sighed and made a show of answering the question again, but he had learned long ago that such carrying on was a waste of effort.

"And it's your record, June, and my record is fifteen and Jim's record is twenty. And Joe's record is six."

Jim threw again. Again the can got into the wind and took off to the south a little as it fell.

Junior was limp. His left hand was palm up on the ground, his legs straight out before him, his right hand limp on the ground and curled around the walnut grip of the little rifle without pressure. He hung his head down as if he were falling asleep and watched the flight of the can with eyes only, smiling up through and past his brows as he sat.

"Now!"

Again the jab and the shot, and the can, almost on the ground this time, took off bounding and clanging and lodged in the bare branches of a mesquite bush some distance away.

"Higher," said Smitty.

"You come do it, then!" Jim yelled at him.

"You do it. I done my bit. Only have him shoot when it's higher. We got no call to shoot out into the brush! Fourteen."

They did it again and this time Jim waited until the new can had hit the ground before he shouted "Now!" and the bullet took the can perfectly after the first hop that was vagrant to the left because the can was not a perfect sphere: so that the shooter either had to be possessed of uncanny quickness in aim or the rankest luck because no one could have predicted which way it would bounce. The can flew away like a crumpled line drive, landing skidding, clanging and throwing gravel.

Smitty glared. He stopped his spray of pecan hull pieces.

"Jim!"

"All right! But why have I got to stand here and throw the Goddamn cans? And yell *Now*? You come do it if you want to see it done!"

Smitty sighed. "You got to holler for him to shoot because if you didn't holler he would shoot them all up high and he would go to six hundred and we'd be here all day!"

"No we wouldn't! There ain't that many cans!"

"All right. Oh, all right. Only when he shoots low it's out into the brush and he'll hit a sheep out there, or something. Fifteen."

Jim bent over backward groaning with his hands on the small of his back, like an old man with lumbago.

"You God-damn ham," Smitty said, laughing. He began to cut pecans again and eat them.

They went to twenty-six, then stopped because Raleigh Jones had come out the door carrying something. He looked to his right at the three, watched Smitty get to his feet, then strode off toward the east carrying his bundle. They watched him. At the wire gate a hundred yards away he stopped as if considering, stood there looking at his small brown bundle and hoisting it a little as if weighing it, then turned back and retraced his steps.

His feet crunched in the tight gravel as he came up to them.

"Jim. Here's some cake. Take it to Mrs. Mason."

"Whoopee!" Jim threw his can far out into the mesquite.

Raleigh Junior shot after it and missed, after it was almost on the ground and already hidden, far away.

"Tell her this is for her . . . and tell her to tell Mason that two guys came in from Dallas last night and that I'll have them hunt the south half until he wants to get with them and change . . . ."

"Yes sir!"

The transfer was made and Jim walked away, bounding some with his skinny stride. Raleigh Jones went back into the ranchhouse. Raleigh Junior got up. He held the little gun pointing down.

"That's all, huh, Smitty? That's all for today because I missed the last one?"

"That's all, June. Do you want some pecans? Sit down here by me and I'll peel you some pecans."

He sat again. Smitty took the little rifle from him, held out his hand for the shells and got them, took them into the house and then returned to sit as before with his back against the house in the warm sunlight, and began to peel pecans as before. Every third pecan he peeled he gave to Raleigh Junior.

The raccoon humped out from under the house wearing his tiny harness; he accepted a pecan half and took it somewhere for inspection and washing.

After a while, eating the pecan halves, Raleigh Junior thought of something to say: "I'm the best with the gun, huh, Smitty?" He described the question too well with his eyebrows, the face pure and eager beneath them.

"That's right."

"Why is it, Smitty?"

"You got the best eye, that's all. You got a talent for it." When Smitty spoke while eating pecans the sound came rich from far down, as from a half-closed cave.

"Talent."

"That's right."

"I remember one time Dad said talent was developed in private."

This caused Smitty to look at him carefully, having to remember again that the memory was good for rote things, for some things.

"Yeah."

"Then why does my talent come when people are around, Smitty? You and Jim and Joe? You're always around when I shoot and then is when it is the talent."

Smitty chewed, watching with eyes narrowed.

"It's because we love you, June. And want to be a part of it. We're proud of it."

"Oh."

"Yeah. And we help you build it because we know talent when we see it. It's still private, you see."

"Oh."

"And that makes it partly ours. See?"

"Oh. Yes, I see."

Later when the sun was high and the south side of the ranchhouse was not the hothouse that it had been when the sun's rays had cornered in and trapped in the house-angle, Joe walked up from the wire gate.

He was tired. He sat on the ground with them with his thirty-thirty upright between his knees and blew out his breath in a grand exhalation. Smitty and Junior looked at the dark good looks of him.

"Well, some more were stolen."

"How many?" Smitty paused in his pecan shelling with the question.

"I don't know. Two or three. Hell, I can't count two hundred sacks and come out right!"

"Don't tell the boss that!"

"I know. But we got to cover the early morning hours if we're gonna catch him. That's when it happens."

"We got to cover every hour?"

"What is it, Joe?" Raleigh Junior asked.

Joe said: "Somebody's been stealin' feed, June."

"Oh."

Later Joe got to his feet, saying: "I better report in." And he went into the house. Smitty decided then that they had eaten enough pecans, and, pausing to peel one last one for Rover, who had appeared again from beneath the house in a begging mood, he went into the back door of the house and through the kitchen into the living area. Raleigh Junior stayed outside with the raccoon.

"Hell fire!" Raleigh Jones was saying.

Then, when they were there except for Jim, who had not returned yet from the hunting camp, Raleigh Jones held a conference. He would have called it a conference, but in reality it was he who did all the conferring.

"Smitty. Joe. I want you to know that I have called the sheriff about this thing. And he has offered his help. I want a guard posted around the clock. Smitty, you will go from noon till eight tonight. No. Jim will go from noon till eight tonight . . . we'll tell him . . . and then you, Smitty, from eight till four in the morning, and Joe again from four in the morning till noon tomorrow. I want it started today at noon! Tell Jim when he comes back! He'll have time to eat and get up there!"

"Yes, sir," Smitty muttered. And Joe nodded.

Raleigh Junior came through, then. Nobody said anything to him.

"Sheriff Hodges said he'd do something about it," said Raleigh Jones.

Smitty thought and then wanted to know: "What can he do unless we can catch the thief or track him? Up to now there's been no sign."

"I don't know but he'd better see about it! That's his department. That's what we pay him for!"

"Yes sir," Joe said, watching the powerful feeling.

By the time Jim had returned and was told of his new guard duty the steady north breeze had sighed itself out, at once, within minutes, as if it had been pulled back and away by a thoughtful hand; then within minutes again it backed around into the east and began to blow softly through the stiff live-oak and mesquite flat, coming now in puffs that were still cool but spongy somehow and soothing, quiet and without the tang of before, lulling. And with the new breeze the sky milked over and then lowered into gray ridges that scudded across from the east, without hurrying.

Jim stood outside the back door before lunch and looked at the sky, at his watch, and kicked at the tight gravel with a shoddy boot, thoughtfully.

Raleigh Jones and his son came out. The rancher had already washed his hands for lunch and was drying them now with a limp, ripped-out flour sack.

"Mrs. Mason said thank you for the cake," Jim said.

"Oh. Good. Did she eat any of it?"

"Yes, sir. I did, too." He snickered.

"Good. It will rain by night. You see, June, it rains when the northers come and it rains when they play out, and this is the best time to hunt deer—in a light rain and after. Because this is the rutting season and the bucks chase the does and they have to run in the rocks, which hurt their feet. But rain makes the ground soft and then they can run a lot and not make their feet hurt. So a lot of deer are running around during rutting season when it rains. And that makes it a good time to hunt. The best." The voice was rich and tender with the explaining. The three of them stood close together and looked at the sky.

Raleigh Junior had listened intently, with obvious wisdom. And his nod when his father had finished was an eager caress: a love pat almost, with its wealth of dedication and filial devotion-to-please.

"And the ruts are in the mud, Dad! Rutting because the ground is mud, then."

Raleigh put his arm around his son's shoulders as he looked at the new clouds and smiled slowly. But the smile did not reach his eyes.

Jim coughed a small cough.

"You know," he began, "maybe he's got something. It will rain sure, and then if anybody comes to steal feed he'll make tracks. That would keep the thief away, don't you think, Mister Jones? Don't you think . . . don't you think we could forget about . . . I mean . . . ."

"Hell, Jim, I didn't teach you to talk like that! Speak up!"

But there was distant warmth in the white-haired man.

"Well, if it rains we won't need a guard at the shed."

"Yes, we will. And we'll have one. Come on in, men. It's time for dinner."

But later Jim still had something on his mind. He had been absolutely silent throughout the meal and now, assembling himself for the trek, he did things too hard with his hands.

He was in his and Joe's and Smitty's big bunk room in the south wing now, getting ready, and after a while Raleigh Junior came in and began to watch him.

"I could ask Joe to swap," Jim muttered. "But he just got back and I could ask Smitty to swap but hell no, he's your dad's favorite and has to be there between eight and four which are the most important hours now."

He paused, then, and found the long, garish flashlight which he realized that he himself would need during the final few hours of his watch, taking it from a dresser top and laying it on his bed before him.

"Where you going, Jim?"

"Aw . . . !" Temper, for a flash of a quelled moment; then a smile, grimmed on his face.

"For a hunt, June. Want to go?"

"Sure."

But he paid no attention. Jim was frail, with a wiriness that reminded of quirts, whips, and leather in general. He had a square chin with a considerable beard which he kept shaved meticulously close all the time: sometimes shaving twice a day; and three scars that ran across with no apparent relation to each other sat awry on the chin like pale chalk streaks on a blue brick. When he smiled he showed considerable gum but the teeth were white and well-formed. He was something of a dude about his hair, which was brown and long at the sides and which he kept combed back laterally so that it came in from each side and met in a vertical line on the back of his head.

One of his rear pockets was ripped loose at a bottom corner; the slick billfold showed a little through the hole in his faded jeans. When the jacket was on and tugged just so into place, unhappily, he found himself staring at Raleigh Junior.

"What did you say?"

"I didn't say anything."

"Yes you did. I said I was about to go out for a hunt and did you want to go . . . ."

"Sure."

After a while Jim murmured: "That's what I thought you said." He adjusted the hat, fanning up the brim on both sides with quick, practiced, vacant movements of both spread palms.

"A frog he would a-wooing go, heigh-ho! says Rowley! And whether his mother would let him or no with a rowley, powley, gammon and spinach, heigh-ho! says Anthony Rowley!"

Junior took it up, then, moving his hands: "So off he set with his opera hat, heigh-ho! says Rowley, and on the way he met with a rat. With a rowley, powley, gammon and spinach, heigh-ho! says Anthony Rowley."

"Now pray, Mr. Rat, won't you come . . . ."

"All right! All right!" Jim said.

He took off his hat and stood spraddle-legged and crimped down a little before a dresser mirror that was filmy with old and dubious history of fly specks and neglect, and combed the hair carefully: doing the whole thing three or four times and then repoising the hat and patting it down with care. Then he grabbed the silver flashlight, reached in a disorderly closet for his slicker, then stood back and looked at Junior.

"Come on," he said. "Let's go."

They went through together and Jim grabbed Junior's coat and slicker, then they paused in the kitchen where the rifles were kept unloaded behind an antique breakfront. Jim reached and got his thirty-thirty. He turned to the table where Raleigh Jones and Smitty were having coffee.

"June wants to go," he said simply. Then he waited.

Raleigh Jones studied. His mouth opened a little. There could be only one answer, and Jim knew it: the knowledge shone straight ahead in his direct gaze.

"All right."

And that was all.

After they were several hundred yards from the house, walking through a newborn mist, with Jim carrying his rifle and Junior carrying the great flashlight, Jim began to sing again.

"A frog he would a-wooing go, heigh-ho! says Rowley . . . ."

"And whether his mother would let him or no . . . ."

"That's enough, June. We got to be quiet, now."

"Okay."

"Atta boy!" Jim was happier now.

Their way was along a sheep trail: concave and rounded soft dust on the bottom speckling now with the tiny quiet rain, never anywhere more than ten inches wide and with lips at the edges straight as if drawn with a ruler: made by the down-headed woolly followers in single file as one section of anything follows another without thought: one sheep's ideation being and consisting wholly in the stub of tail before his downcast eyes and immediately above them; his own stub of a bobbed tail serving similarly as brains enough as if in evolutionary accident for the sheep behind him, and so on—success lying in blind following, nothing failing like success.

The path was too narrow for them. And it was deep enough to turn an ankle in. But they gave the small problem no thought, walking on from experience at the edges.

Spectral mesquite trees stood all around them without leaves here in the flat. There were leaves of other kinds on the ground here and there: mostly live oak leaves like small curled beetle shells, and some elm, packed in rows and small banks at the bases of tree trunks by the north wind and now blown out occasionally by the wetter wind from the east, some scudding across the path before them like a tiny light horse cavalry to hang and pile again, shifting. The misting rain grew heavier. The slickers darkened into black.

"This is the time to hunt," Junior whispered. "It's raining."

"Yeah."

Jim had a date that evening. In a house up ahead, three-quarters of a mile to the north of the feed shed toward which they were walking, crowded close to the road in cobble-stoned peasantness beneath a windmill that stood a few feet beyond Raleigh Jones' north fence, a ranch foreman's daughter already had her tape player warmed and was running through her tapes a tentative first time to see what should be culled out. She was twenty and almost an old maid already in her mother's eyes and she had soft lips and thick ankles and some reason to believe that Jim was almost in love with her. He was. She had a warm smile and a wit and well-formed breasts, also. They were at the early kissing and late hand-holding stage, and he had figured her for a virgin and was happy with it.

"June, when we get there, we will watch the feed pen, see? The shed. Not for deer, though. Somebody has been stealing your dad's feed, and we're going to try to catch him doing it. Got that?"

"Yes."

"And when we see somebody stealing feed we'll see who it is. That's all. Got that?"

"Yes."

"You know everybody around here . . . ."

"Yes."

"And we have a gun. But all the gun is for is protection, in case the thief . . . the stealer . . . has a gun. Then in case he has a gun and is ugly, then we may have to use the gun we have."

"Okay, Jim."

After a while Jim went on.

"We'll sit and watch the shed from a blind. That's all. And after a while I may leave and go somewhere but I'll come back in a little while. You can sit and watch the shed for a little while by yourself, cain't you?"

"Sure, Jim."

"And not go anywhere. Not go out of the blind because I'll be back in a little while. You can do that, cain't you, and wait for me? Even if I come back when it's almost dark?"

"Sure, Jim."

"Good boy. I have somethin' I got to do. Got to!"

Woman. A song in the wind, woman. She lies and it comes out truth; she speaks truth and it comes out a lie. She sometimes does wild and wicked things and when she does it is because she has not free will and cannot help it. Free will is a saddle on man's back and woman sits invisible therein, holding her script which is incomprehensible to man and written long before man could read; written by the hand of Eve and guided by the moon and the tides and other cyclic things unheard of; she reads the more ancient script and finds she had it memorized already from birth. In a world where feeling and passion cannot be trusted and have caused laws as checks, the paradox is that the greatest truths are those that touch the heart beyond knowledge of the mind: the genius of woman is that she knew them first. And tries to tell of them and is wrong. And feels them and is right, and makes a fool of thinking man . . . .

"Good boy!" Jim exulted.

The rain came down upon them: not the heavy splashing summer rain with every fat drop yearning for the earth, but the near mist of

December, drops heavier than mist but coming silently and with stealth, falling down along and through the stark and naked brush and the corpulent cedars like a misunderstood blessing in a dream, feather almost with quiet landing.

They left the sheep path beneath a high bluff, swung stiff legs expertly over a seven-strand barbed-wire fence, and walked out into the field and headed toward the point of brush that came out from the north into the field near the road. The ground was lightly crusted here between fanning sprigs of green oats, and soft beneath the crust with deep plowed ground. The going was slower now.

"Nobody will come," Jim said. "Nobody will come because of the rain. He would leave tracks."

"Okay."

"But we got to sit and watch just the same. That's the way it is when you have a program."

"Okay."

They saw the shed and approached it, passing into the few mesquites that were there, already black near the ground with the rain. Thick cedar posts formed the risers of the shed, and there was some planking horizontally on the west side and the north side; the east and south were open. Fat sacks stood in leaning rows on dry ground beneath a very wide sheet-iron roof that sang now with the driven raindrops. It made a haunting music that was far away though they were right there listening.

"Nobody's been here today . . . ."

"We're here, though."

"Right. Let's go to the blind."

The blind was a forked mesquite trunk, now dark and soft with cold moisture near the ground, and a pile of cedar brush that had been felled somehow by accident or by unknown design so many months ago that all the nubby leaves were gone already. They sat against the big mesquite trunk—each one taking a low branching fork for his back rest, and peered over and through the tangle of gray cedar twigs that were an extended leg's length away. But when the ground is wet you do not extend your legs. You prop knees up in your face and make yourself as compact as possible to avoid the cold moisture.

They did this.

Settled, fifty yards away from the shed and looking west at it through the cedar shambles, Jim consulted his wrist watch. He drew himself together for the waiting.

"I'll stay here an hour with you, June, then I'll leave you for a little while. But I'll be back."

"Okay, Jim."

They sat without talking for a long time. Jim played with twigs with his fingers, now and then rolled a cigarette with tobacco from a small, flat can—taking off his hat and putting it over his knees and rolling beneath it—and smoked, then got out his pocket knife and scraped some of the letters off the back of the tobacco can, making the words say something far different than they had said originally; and all the time the rain came down benignly, steadily and yet without really getting things wet.

Junior never took his eyes off the shed.

Jim looked at him from time to time, marvelling. Once years ago all of them had gone into the city and Junior had seen a policeman sitting on his quiet motorcycle at a curb and talking on his two-way radio. After that he had copied the scene many times in a child's play-acting, staring straight ahead vacantly and yet with the look of eagles on his face, speaking nonsense or garbage or sometimes pertinent words into his cupped hand . . . . And now the same look was on his face: intent making the profile as carefully direct as a polished carving. His hair was wet and beaded with the rain now, and drops ran down his cheeks and his neck, but he took no notice.

Once he said: "Jim, when will the stealer come?"

And Jim said: "He won't be here today, June. We just got to be here in case he does."

The whole valley was shrouded, completely gray, calm. There was not a sound to be heard. Away to their left across the road the cliff beyond the river was almost invisible. It was as if, a couple of hours past midday, the world was taking time out from everything for the cold sojourn of the winter rain. Twice during the hour, and no more, cars went by on the road and they could hear the sleepy singing of the tires on wet asphalt.

At three o'clock Jim got to his feet. He raised and lowered each leg in turn, trying to relax them from the cramped sitting.

"Ain't going to be anybody here, June," he whispered. "But if somebody comes, see who he is."

He paused, and looked far to the north where he could see a windmill head above the trees, cocked and not turning. He had not been positive enough. After all, he was leaving a trust in Junior's hands for a while.

He walked three steps and turned again, feeling sure that no one would come.

"Don't let anybody steal any feed, June." Lightly he said it, jokingly.

"Okay, Jim." The jaw was set, almost comically. And he watched the shed.

Jim took a last look, then said quietly, "I'll be back in a little while. Before dark. Be sure you stay here."

"I will."

Then he was gone, walking quickly with his wiry stride out through the mesquite flat north of the field. He made no sound as he went.

Six

Mason had hunted all day long.

At six-thirty he had loaded his pockets with apples, kissed Frieda, and made a quick, aberrant and almost disinterested check of the cabins, noticing a new, white Oldsmobile with Texas plates, then had taken to the hills, leaving Frieda alone. He wanted to think. And to hunt. He had taken his binoculars with him and they had been bulky and troublesome all morning, hanging from thin leather straps from his neck, banging against his chest and belly and getting in his way.

Early, before sunup and while his hands had been hurting beneath the gloves with the cold, Mason had decided that he would stay no longer than an hour in any one place, that he would keep moving all day. He was aware of the controversy. Some hunters say that the only way to hunt in the brush is from a blind. "When you move you don't see the deer. The deer see you first." Others who seek to cover lack of patience or to exhibit quietness afoot and good shooting skill say that they kill just as many while moving. Usually they do not. But today Mason was one of them by choice. He had felt that he could not be still today.

At sunup he flushed a buck near the east fence, had three seconds in which to get off a shot, and fired during the fourth second, shearing a small branch from a live oak tree axe-clean with his bullet.

Enthused, he went on, feeling only mild chagrin because now he had finally seen a buck after looking only at does. Then later he saw five more does, singly, bounding across dead cedar with the wobbling furry stalk of white tail high behind them, or standing still like sharp and tight wisps of blue smoke, alert, watching him, blowing their outraged and quaint insult at him as they decided to go and moving the head first before the running, back and forth like a chicken.

When the norther had blown itself out and the wind had retreated around to the east Mason had been eight feet off the ground in a gnarled cedar. There he ate three of his apples and watched a hundred-foot clearing, thinking of Frieda and the rats and of Mason and the athletes. When the clouds came he got down again and moved on toward the north and west with only questions in his head and no answers.

The ground was puffy and soft, with clumps of yellow grass and slimy green lichen-like things, the rocks all great concrete-like slabs protruding out of the earth at shallow angles, the trees and brush quiet and clutching.

When the mists had come he had been moving through dense cedar, and as the cold rain began to make itself felt on his face and neck, Mason came to the head of a shallow draw on the hilltop where the cedars were so thick they formed a real brake and nothing grew beneath them. Here where the trees reached into one another and shook hands continually he had to squat low now and then to go beneath them, and he found that here he was immune from the mild cold droplets. Here he also found that on all fours he could see for a long distance in every direction with only the ragged brown boles obstructing his view, as an upright man in a forest of pines might find his viewing moderately obstructed: upright he could have seen nothing but heavy green in his face. The felted ground sloped down to his right.

So he had begun to crawl in his exuberance, like a schoolboy, thinking: here I am hunting deer and not being able to get Frieda and the rats out of my mind and why is that? Like she said, there was a message for me in the rats and I know it was the rats with aggressive capability in the end pens and why in hell can't I get it out of my mind and I know why and it's because I've got to put the rats into the language of people before I can forget about them and be at rest about the thing. Holy. She called me holy. I've got to figure it out.

Crawling, he found that the only bad thing was the thing hanging from his neck. The binoculars swayed and bumped his arms. There was nothing he could do with them. The ground was like a sloping carpet beneath the cedars, prickly in minute feeling through the gloves and yet soft, stoneless.

And then, crawling like a boy with his gun flat against the ground in his right hand and the weight of the swaying binoculars at his neck, he looked up and saw, very near, an animal sneaking away from him: brown like a horse and almost as large, only hindquarters visible because it was going directly away, walking, almost crawling with head down as he had been doing to dodge the horizontal foliage that intermeshed four feet from the ground: a great deer with tail tucked out of sight; not hurrying; moving only, away, as from a swarm of gnats and unafraid.

Mason's heart jumped toward his throat. He sat quickly and fielded his rifle and fouled it briefly with the binoculars. When he was aiming finally it was at nothing.

Immediately he crawled on, rising then to his feet and running, taking the stinging slap of heavy wet cedar in his face as he hurried straight ahead to more open ground.

He came to a clearing and skidded—fell, almost—to one knee according to plan with cedars on both sides of him, and began the interminable agony of raising his rifle.

The buck was standing fifty feet away, watching him, turned broadside.

Mason had heard all his deer hunting days about buck fever. He had killed a dozen deer within the last twenty years and he had always scoffed within himself at the tales of neophytes shaking and not being able to shoot, of experienced hunters standing stock still and jacking all the shells out of their guns and thinking later— swearing—that each jacked-out shell had been a shot; of violent trembling. But it had never happened to him. It happened now. And it was a dream. His rifle would not come up to his eye level. His rifle weighed five hundred pounds and he could not lift it.

The buck was brown-black instead of gray and as tall as a horse at the shoulder and the rack he presented head-on was as thick as a man's two wrists at the base, three feet across and a foot high, square. The muzzle was broad and almost grizzled, with a wide blue band around it as if smeared in a hurry with blue clay. The eyes were calm, unafraid. And readiness was there, and alertness, but overall was great and final calm as if he knew nothing would happen.

Here was a deer who had seen hundreds of hunters, mostly from afar. He was wise and he knew the power of the thunder stick which Mason carried. But he stood unafraid, watching. He who had been shot at and shot stood with calm now as if he knew the script.

Mason began to tremble. He lowered the rifle. And then the buck was gone: dematerialized, vanished. With no motion apparent and nothing left to indicate direction.

Mason sat for a long time on the bran-like dead cedar leaves and drew in his breath.

Then he had it. Somehow he had it: the most important thing in the world is children and the next most important thing and tied in inextricably with the first: the right male with aggressive capability. Not just any male. The right male. The thinking male. And herein the problem and the struggle, herein Mason's worth and necessity.

After a long time he got up and moved on toward the west. He was not following the buck anymore.

With labored breathing he tried to analyze. Something there had been in the buck's baiting him and then standing stock-still for him to run into, almost, that was like the matador's deliberately turning his back on the bull when the latter's head was down and he was doubting . . . and Mason, like the bull, had been transfixed, charmed, learning about himself.

"God," breathed Mason. He began to shake again, remembering. But maybe he was still following the buck. Yes, that was it: no remembrance of the buck having moved before he was gone and no sound either to denote passage; yet the buck had been facing west and surely had he turned before he had left Mason would have remembered that. So he must have gone west into the deeper cedar that sloped gradually down until it ceased abruptly at the cliff's edge overlooking the field.

Carefully Mason went on. He stooped, clutching the binoculars against his chest. He remembered then to look for tracks and cursed himself for not having thought of it sooner but now it was too late. He did not want to go back. On he went, mildly downhill, wondering at himself.

"You fool," he said under his breath. "You poor fool!"

From time to time he stopped now and sat down watching openings in the brake, making himself as compact as possible because of the rain, but he saw nothing except the great heavy wetness of the cedars and the oddly dry, brown felted ground sloping away beneath them.

At length with a sigh he came to the opening at the cliff's edge near where he had been the afternoon before.

He was glad to see open space. He walked with care to the very edge of the precipice, found a well-anchored boulder that was two feet high and flat on top, and sat. The rain came down upon him. But it was small and not very wetting, so he forgot about it.

Mason wondered why it was that when a man most wanted to think, then it was that something tried hardest within him to convince him he was stupid.

He sighed again and raised the binoculars, looking out across the valley at the other great, sheer bluff a mile away and shrouded now with rainy afternoon gloom.

He sat there for a long, long time, without moving, drinking in the wild, qualified freedom of murky space.

Mason was an expert with the binoculars. It went back to his scouting days of coaching. And now, looking at the wet black asphalt of the old county road beyond Raleigh Jones' feed shed far below him, he wondered when his courier would come. And then he wondered some more at himself, for thoughts of the courier seemed less important now. But his wallet was still the same size. He wondered.

He picked out a doe far away across the road in the river bottom, beneath a bare pecan tree. He watched her for half an hour and counted the times within that period that she raised her head from feeding. Only twelve times and of these only five with head turned looking behind her; and he decided that she must have already bred.

There were no individual clouds visible now. All was slate gray. The terrain spread colorless beneath him as in a dream seen in black and white and dirty shades of gray, like an old movie with the projector jammed and its light dim. He could not even see the rain anywhere, nor could he hear it, but he could feel its low lulling on his head and the chill of it behind his shoulders as the wind gusted. The cliff across the valley was wet and dank, not rosy now as it was in morning sunlight nor yellow as by day but gray like everything else, furry almost, and remote: farther away than it really was because of the shrouding. Mason had never seen such calm. And he knew that very shortly now it would be dark. It was already darkening, as though the sun were far away now somewhere in a different world and had left a timetable behind by proxy, and a message not apparent.

His binoculars were 7-50: night glasses. They were wide at the front and gathered much light, so now he kept them to his eyes as he looked, somehow enjoying the dreamy calm, realizing as soon as he tried to look with naked eye that it was indeed getting late early, and dark.

A car approached, creeping, on the road to his right. He put the glasses on it. Watching a moving object that he knew was making a noise and yet hearing nothing, not even after time lapse, had always seemed spooky to Mason, and he had never become used to it.

He saw that the car was a new Chevrolet, white with splashes of thin mud on the sides and a radio aerial like a fly rod on the rear fender.

He watched the car drive slowly into the shallow ditch on the left side of the road, creep some more, and stop near some mesquite trees that came out to the road north of the field.

He watched a man get out and slam the door. Carefully Mason listened for many seconds for the sound of the slamming, but heard nothing. The man must have shut the door more softly than he thought.

The man wore khaki clothes, it seemed, though they, like everything else, were gray now. And a hat with a wide brim: gray or white.

Mason watched the man as he stood by his car for many

moments, then began to move toward him, into the brush, across the fence with practiced ease, and then disappeared from sight in the mesquite tangle, heading, apparently, for the feed shed.

Mason followed with interest, seeing pieces of motion, seeing now and then the whole man as he came and got closer, noting the stealth and the care of him, hearing nothing. He still had a long way to go before reaching the shed.

He could seem him, then, more clearly. He watched the careful footsteps on the soft earth, the turning head as he came. Soon Mason could make out a chrome revolver on the man's right hip, and laced boots, and then he saw that the khaki clothes were a uniform without markings and the flat, wide-brimmed hat a mark of authority by its difference . . . .

Mason lost the man from sight, then, in dense brush, and the next time he appeared he was close enough for Mason to see the expression as the man walked with care up to the feed shed.

Then he was lost behind the building for minutes; and then he came with caution around the left side of the shed—the south side— creeping, almost, yet standing erect, and Mason could now see his face clearly. It was a young face with a broad forehead beneath the hat brim. He was peering into the shed.

A shout sounded, wordless. Mason had seen the startled expression on the man's face before he had heard the shout and he knew that someone else had shouted. But he could see that the man was startled, for he raised his left hand and tried to grin and then moved his lips in shouted answer with the left hand raised and the smile and the right hand making an abortive move toward the right hip and then plainly arrested short of the revolver though threatening almost for a brief second. And then Mason saw the smile broaden and heard another wordless shout from nowhere, and then he saw the man's lips move as he shouted back in answer, in greeting, somehow not loud enough for Mason to hear.

Mason was a pro with the glasses. He had learned long ago to read a quarterback's lips from the top row of any stadium . . . .

"It's me! Beck!" the man's lips said. And the left hand lowered into ease and the right hand jerked up a little from where it had been into ease also and Mason was surprised that he could see the face so well at this distance or that he could see so much because he saw then a small dark round spot appear on the man's forehead above his left eye like a horsefly lighting or, more nearly because he could see so well, like a small round piece of liver blown there as from across a schoolroom by a spitball expert's pea shooter, sticking.

And then there was not time for change in expression as the man went down still smiling, and Mason could tell from the way he turned and fell backward on his right hand and his hip came down and drove the stiff fanned fingers of that hand into the mud that this man would never rise again.

Mason lowered his binoculars.

The shot had sounded. Small because it was away from him. But growing as it returned from the hills beyond the valley, marching along them in majesty, roaring into chaining nothingness throughout all the hills for miles around as each and every one of them had its say: the clamor taking an eternity, it seemed, to run its finally whispering course of dying thunder.

Mason could feel his heart in his wrists, then, and in his neck. He blew out his breath in a long, sectioned sigh, and did not know it. A figure came out of the brush below and walked tentatively up to the fallen man, almost on tiptoe. Mason put the glasses on him and saw that it was Raleigh Junior.

Mason watched him get within fifteen feet of the body, peer carefully, then turn and begin to run toward the ranchhouse.

With exuberance he ran, high and lightly in the mud, like a child exulting over a secret held precious and close. He was swinging both hands, carrying nothing. Mason remembered the pride with which Raleigh Junior had run to his dad with the grasp of hay in his hand, seeking payment of three cubes of caramel candy with high pride, with shining eyes. The running and the demeanor were exactly the same now.

Mason watched him go without slowing until he was a speck in the great field to his left, almost into the edge of approaching darkness.

Mason stood. He thought briefly about going to the fallen man to see if he could help. But the binoculars had already told him that this would be a waste of time . . . .

He took the glasses from his neck, folded the strap, and began to move along the cliff to his left, seeking a path, carrying the binoculars in his left hand and the .270 in his right. He would go to Frieda first.

At his cabin door later after what seemed an eternity of dodging brush and trees, of twisting and doubling back and of running into brush with his face, of interminable and haunting rain at the back of his neck, Mason charged inside upon a warm nighttime scene.

Frieda was in her night things by the fire, reading; he could see the rudiments of an evening meal's beginning all laid out and ready for him at the bar-kitchen. She arose with a smile.

"I was beginning to worry . . . ." Then she saw his face.

"You can go ahead and worry," he said.

"What? What is it?"

"There's been a tragedy."

"What? Tell me. Tell me!"

But he was shedding his wet things and not looking at her.

Later he said: "A man's been killed. Raleigh Junior killed a man at the feed shed." He sighed, not really believing it, pursing his lips with the surprise of it.

He looked at her glow, at her slack mouth fading the glow with its concern.

"You said someone had been stealing feed. The thief? Did they shoot the thief? Tell me, Mason!"

"No. No, I don't think so. An officer. The sheriff, maybe, or one of his men."

"Did you see it?"

"I saw it." He sighed and sat down near her in his shorts, watching her face measure the news with care.

· "But Raleigh Junior! Surely not! Surely he wouldn't be on guard! Raleigh Jones would never do that! Let the boy stand guard by himself!"

"I don't know . . . Frieda, I don't know . . . God! I don't! But that's what happened!"

They studied the thing for a long time, watching each other with concern.

"I'll have to go down," Mason muttered. "I'll have to go see. I may be needed."

"I'll go, too. Do you want to eat first? It's ready, almost."

Mason drew a gusty breath and looked about him at the tight, warm cabin that was now less than cheerful.

"No," he said.

Later he said it again in finality: "No. Get on your jeans. We'll go down now. To the house."

"I'm glad. I'm glad that you don't want to leave me here."

"No, of course not." He was redressing, gathering again the rifle and glasses.

They rode down the rocky road to the ranchhouse with the spectre sitting between them in Mason's car and keeping them silent; they were almost there before he remembered to turn on the windshield wipers.

At the door of the ranchhouse in the complete darkness, seeing the wide line of light beneath the door and square pools of the same light on rocky wet ground under the kitchen windows, Mason hammered with his fist. There was no answer.

He opened the door and went in, Frieda behind him.

There was no one in the brilliantly lit kitchen, and no dirty supper dishes, either; he could hear a rocking chair going in the living room.

They went through.

Helen Waskom was there, and her husband. And Smitty and Joe were there with them: all seated—none got up as they came in—and all with the deep eyes of concern in their faces, all mysterious with the not-knowing.

"Where's Jones?" Mason wanted to know.

Smitty was rocking.

"He left out of here a while ago," he said calmly, almost belligerently.

"And Junior?"

"He went with him."

"Where did they go?"

"They didn't say. The only thing they did say . . . the only thing Mr. Jones said . . . was that none of us was to leave the house. And I been trying to talk Mrs. Helen into fixing me some grub . . . ."

"Mrs. Helen," Mason said, "get up and fix him some grub!"

She got up from an ancient leather sofa and smoothed her skirt with pudgy hands as her husband stared.

"I just say," she sighed. She went into the kitchen.

Mason went closer to Smitty.

"What's up?" he tested.

"Damn if I know. I know the boss is on a tear. But I learned a long time ago that when the boss is on a tear you wait to be invited. And I ain't invited, this time!"

"You don't know anything?"

"Hell, no. What do you know?"

"Nothing," Mason lied.

After a long time of staring and of having his stare returned by wide, innocent eyes from all over the room, Mason pushed Frieda ahead of him into the kitchen where Helen Waskom was banging and slopping a supper together that would resemble a breakfast when it came to being, because of the speed.

"Will you eat?" Helen wanted to know, bulging almost with ill-will that had been forced and put upon.

"Frieda will," Mason told her.

"You?"

"No."

Mason drew Frieda to the door. He paused to think, seeing that she was awaiting his decision with wide eyes; and this caused him to grin. He pecked a kiss on her cheek, then put up his hand for some whispering into her ear.

"Call the sheriff. Hodges is his name. Call him in town as soon as I leave. Tell him that his man—Beck, I think his name is—has been killed. Tell him to come to Raleigh Jones' feed shed immediately! Got it?"

She nodded, eyes big upon him.

"Good girl! Call his office. Then call his home if he's not at the office. Hell, call his home first! It's too late for an office call!"

"Okay. Anything else?"

"No. Only tell him to get here in a hurry. You won't have to elaborate. Tell him Beck is dead. He'll come. They'll have a book of numbers by the phone."

"All right."

"And don't worry about the people here hearing you. They'll all listen, but it's all over now anyway, and won't make any difference."

"All right."

"I love you. For what you are."

Mason kissed her full on the lips, quickly, then was gone out the kitchen door again before Mrs. Waskom had had time to look.

He got in his Buick and was racing the engine before he knew it, then cooled it to a more sedate pace and pulled away, circling, heading for the wire gate to the field. He would have several gates to open, and it would take time. No matter.

The Buick crept along the flat-rutted road toward the main gate and the highway, then turned off to the right on flat ground that crunched beneath the tires. Then the headlights were lowering through the spectral wire gate that began the eighty-acre field at its south end; showing the misting rain that was swimming through the cold wire.

Mason got out.

On impulse, then, he cut off the lights, killed the engine, and felt for his binoculars on the seat. The field would be wet, soft; there was a road, somewhere along its edge inside the fence, but Mason did not know where, and he did not relish the thought of taking a heavy car in, getting lost, getting stuck . . . or at best having headlights scream announcement of his coming.

He raised the binoculars and began to glass the impenetrable darkness a half mile away, thinking half-mile in his mind and seeing only blackness that could have been three feet or fifty miles for all the light he saw—then lowered them and began again, going to about the shed first and then working toward the right up under the bluff, seeing absolutely nothing, striving only to keep the glasses from straying too high into sky which was now one with the cold and wetting earth.

A light. A light? He could not be sure: a match maybe, sizzled out or waved away at once, or a flashlight flicking briefly and then hidden by plan.

Mason considered. Then he made up his mind. He reached into the back door, slid the .270 off the rear seat, snapped three shells into its side in the dark, racked the bolt once and checked the safety with a blind forefinger, then felt for the wire fence, groping.

He had brought no light. He would have to go out through the middle of the field trusting his sense of direction only and the fact that he could walk in a straight line and the possibility that he could soon see a light somewhere near the shed.

What if they had not gone to the shed? What if they had gone somewhere else and only a lightless dead man awaited him in the mud near the shed? Or nothing at all near the shed, a half-mile away? Mason sighed and trudged, finding that the main thing was keeping his balance, holding the binoculars then out in his left hand and the rifle in his right and raising the lighter binoculars with a stiff left arm higher so he would be balanced and so he would walk straight and not make an arc to the right. He thought: like a sliced golf ball. Me. Like a golf ball sliced into the bluff. I wish I could drive one a half-mile.

Then the thought occurred to him that he had better get the idea out of his head about curving to the right because subconsciously he might do it; or, reacting, he might subconsciously curve to the left: reason there for doing both or either or neither and he could not tell what he would do. But whatever he did, it would be with luck. Which way he went would be luck and he would not know, but he had to keep going, thinking straight ahead, asking for a light . . . .

The cold constant rain came down on him without notice, without feeling, and he imagined that it was dissolving away the land in the blackness. Mason trudged. He knew that every step slid backward a little in the mud but he could not tell how much. He was awash, and helpless: driving with purpose and with the power of sight in one hand and the power of might in the other, both useless and ridiculous now because he could not see and he could not hear and he could not feel. Awash in a black and raining night with the land dissolving away beneath his feet, but with purpose. He kept going, looking straight ahead as nearly as he could, and grinning at the futility. Something in Mason's history caused him now to grin at the futility and to keep going; and his grin might have been merely a shadowed reflection of a thought and numbed feel of contracted facial muscles imagined also, because of the cold dark.

But Mason went.

A light, briefly? Maybe not . . . .

And then again . . . ?

Then he saw it: not flickering exactly but as if a lantern had been shown briefly from behind a great rock far away and then withdrawn, teasing almost. But sure! He had seen it, this time! And it had been directly before him, perhaps four hundred yards away.

He went forward with new interest, swinging the binoculars and the rifle, leaping almost with each step in the silent mud, peering through brows that were beyond dewing into dripping and seeing nothing but remembering. He grinned some more, playing with the tightness in his cheeks.

He saw it again and again and again, and then later in constant intermittent gleams seemingly from the same spot as from an anchored buoy far out in a black chopping sea or a distant streetlight behind tossing trees; then it seemed that it was the light moving and the intervening things—trees, brush, arid tangle now slackened and softened in darkness and cold—still.

It was like a child's code with a lantern, with no glow apparent, a tiny point of light still that shuttered or that moved and he could not tell which.

Something took him at the right knee, hard, like a dog bite, and something a knife's edge of time later at his chest, caving. Then he heard the dull and wet metallic squall of barbed wire pulled under tight staples and knew that he had run into the fence at the field's edge, that the shed was off to his left now and that the light was up under the great cliff.

Mason backed away from the tight wires. The one at his knee tugged and then let go at once sharply like the last stiff turn of the key at a coffee can and he knew that the barb had gone into his leg. He would have to be careful, now. He would have to be sure that he made no noise now.

Carefully he mounted the fence, standing on one side and then standing stifflegged on the other, letting the depressed top wire come up with stealth, with silence. Then he turned and found the light again, still only an intermittent, blinking point, and went on. He was careful of sticks on the ground.

Gradually the light grew in Mason's sight and became more constant. He avoided trees and brush by contact, working his interminable way up the faint slope that was rocky and uneven now, and grassy; seeing the light grow until it matured into a constancy with a thin aura of glow around it that did not blink and disappear. He thought he heard a voice, briefly.

Five times he knelt to crawl between low-hooding cedars.

Finally a scene began to appear in pieces. He stopped from time to time to build it. He thought: Frieda has long ago called. Long ago.

And Hodges has been on his way minutes already now and it's only nine miles . . . .

There was a Coleman lantern on the ground. Above it was a gray boulder with a great unwieldy warped head seemingly unbalanced eight feet from the ground, and beneath the boulder Mason could see Raleigh Jones' virile white plastered head bobbing, weaving, working. He could hear nothing. He went on.

He eased around to his right, using stealth. Then he saw Raleigh Junior, sitting. Then he saw the boy called Jim leaning against a thin mesquite trunk, sitting. And he could still see Raleigh Jones' head in full flight of hard and feverish activity beneath the impending boulder, close up under it, working.

Mason got as close as he dared. He peered through the top of a bush which he did not know, which had leaves like holly but sharper. There he considered, and decided that he should arrive. He lowered his binoculars to the ground and left them, took the .270 in both hands in the stalking regimen, flipped the safety off, and walked out into the tight clearing beneath the great invisible bluff.

He saw that Raleigh Jones was knee-deep in the ground and digging, and that he was using a short spade almost like a toy with great strength and speed at the very base of the boulder and under it and that Raleigh Jones' shirt was dark brown all over with a vast sweat. Raleigh Junior was to the left and Jim was to the right and in between on the ground was a brown, rolled cocoon that was man-sized and unmoving in an old army blanket and he knew who that was.

Jim saw him first. He made eyes like a wild cow, licked his lips, and Mason could see the three scars on his chin that were white as streaks of putty. Jim tried to move and could not. Mason saw that he was tied to the tree, sitting against it.

Raleigh Junior saw him. He got to his feet, smiling. He began to walk toward Mason.

"Mr. Mason . . . ."

Raleigh Jones started, dropped his spade, turned, then sighed volubly and relaxed his frantic, instantaneous climbing efforts as he saw Mason tall and still in the light and as he saw the .270 pointing at his own chest. Slowly he got out of the hole.

"Mr. Mason! It was Beck and I got him! With one shot! He was the stealer and I got him and Dad said it was the best shot he ever saw! We'll have to be sure and tell Smitty! It was Beck!"

He was there smiling before Mason now, with pride, smiling a pure exultation that went as face value for the lump-in-the-throat glory of a boy of ten who had just soloed with a gun for the first time and had a butchered, scrawny, mangy squirrel to show . . . . His hands gamboled before him.

But Mason was watching Raleigh Jones. He saw the sweat glistening, saw almost the steam, saw the eyes wide yet shrouded as though by a deathbed fever known for what it was, recognized, hailed.

Raleigh Jones grunted. He sighed, and sat down on the edge of his pit, watching Mason.

"And I helped wrap him, Mr. Mason! I helped Dad wrap him and helped Dad carry him here . . . ." Raleigh Junior laughed gaily, breathing hard.

"No," Mason said. He was still looking at Raleigh Jones.

Then he said: "The Coleman is low. Pump it up, Junior."

Later he took the rifle off Raleigh Jones after seeing that he was beginning to tremble, and went and sat down beside him with his own feet in the pit, looking at him.

"I saw it happen," Mason said.

"June," Raleigh said without looking, "untie Jim."

"Yes, sir."

Raleigh Jones grabbed his knees and drew them together and then put his chin on them, trying to stop the shaking, sitting on the lip of wet ground which he had carved.

"I'm sorry," Mason said.

"Oh," Raleigh whispered into his knee, staring into his pit. "Oh. Oh. Oh, God. He was coming to check the shed. And Jim . . . oh, God."

"I'm sorry."

"Tell me about your hunt. Did you see anything?"

"One big buck, up on top here."

"I know him. Did you get a shot?"

"Yes. No."

Raleigh Jones nodded. He looked as if he were chewing his knee. Abruptly he said: "Now Jim, you stay here."

Jim made no answer. Mason turned and saw that he was licking his lips and massaging his wrists, hard.

"You can't do it, you know," Mason muttered. "Rules, and all that. Sounds funny . . . ."

"Yes."

"I mean me saying it. Me saying you have to obey rules . . . ."

"Why you?"

"I mean no unfair advantage. And me saying it. That's the funny part. Me saying that everybody has to have an even chance. Or something."

Raleigh Jones sighed. He was beginning to hedge the shaking a little.

"Not funny," he murmured, looking without sight ahead of him into the wounded earth.

Raleigh Junior came up to them, getting ready to speak.

"Dad said it was the best shot he ever saw!" he said again.

"You see, Mason," Raleigh Jones explained, pointing, "the center of gravity of this boulder is high. Undermine it with a pit, then go around on the other side and dig just a little bit, and you can push it over, face down, on the pit on this side. Go above it a little, cause a small slide to come down, and cover all signs of digging . . . ."

"I saw it, Raleigh. I saw it happen. From the cliff. From where I left the big buck."

The blackness hooded them tighter, it seemed, pressing in upon the lantern, the gnarled and dripping black spectres of brush delineating the scene on all sides quietly, without life. The small, volumeless rain continued to come down on shoddy and imperfect and sympathetic ground.

"It'll be all right," Mason whispered to Raleigh Jones. "I'll see that you have help. It'll be all right. We have to do it this way. Believe me. I know."

He touched the wet shoulder and was surprised to find it hard and round as a river rock and almost scalding to his touch.

The white head stared ahead, resting on the knees.

After a while Raleigh Jones murmured: "Listen to the Coleman. You can hear it sizzle in the rain. I never knew that."

"So you can," Mason said.

They sat there a long time in the cold, dim hemisphere of light with the rain coming down, the drops aiming straight down as though to gain the center of the earth, and entering it, too, for all they could tell, for all the sign that was left after they touched; a select few frying instead and dancing, shrinking in little white balls around the edge of the Coleman lid for a short while then falling off or sticking and vaporizing like pygmy genii into oblivion . . . the only nervous one there Jim, and he with the fright of his young life having made ghosts of the scars in his chin, that were returning to normal color now and seeming no more to be marble splinters with shadows around them. Jim was pacing, hands in pockets, carefully avoiding looking at the corpse.

They waited. Without talking about it at all and without Mason telling the others that they were waiting, they waited. Everyone seemed to know it. At least everyone waited. Raleigh Junior walked a little as Jim was doing, now and then looking at the trophy on the ground, sighing as if he were waiting for the bragging and the talk and wondering why they did not come, his hands playing small, nameless games together in front of him. He was puzzled. His face had on it the look of a man awaiting his chance to speak; but he said nothing.

Raleigh Jones stretched his heels out to full length in the hard virgin mud that he had created, and seemed to relax. He dropped his chin on his chest and Mason could see the deep etchings, crossing, in his neck.

"You're right," Raleigh Jones murmured. "Rules. The game. If you can't afford to lose, don't play . . . ."

"What?"

"Thank you. Thank you." He seemed to yawn, but that was not exactly what it was. "You saved me, Coach. Me? Raleigh Junior? Who can say?"

Raleigh Junior came over and sat with them, then, and he was still smiling. Mason was glad that he had sat because he had been watching him now and then, fearful that the boy would go over and admire the wrapped man and perhaps stroke him in glory and Mason had been afraid of that because of the feelings it would have elicited in himself.

He reached and gripped the boy's shoulder in rough friendship, seeing the purity of the smile and finding it almost frightening.

"The rain is heavier, now," Raleigh Jones said.

"I believe it is," Mason said.

Mason heard it then. Like a small short sound a cat might make at night under a house: the taut outcry of wire. He wondered if the others had heard it.

He heard nothing more, but waited for what seemed to be five minutes and was probably much shorter, then turned, hearing nothing, and surprised to see that he was the last of the four to turn, to look.

Mason had never seen Sheriff Hodges. Something in the name had suggested that the man should be overweight. He was. And there was another man with him who was not overweight. Standing there quietly in the rain with the glare coming up from the ground and making their white faces grotesque and puffy beneath their broad brims, they looked like a comedy team; and Mason had the strange feeling that the slender one was about to reach for a microphone.

Raleigh Junior got up and stumbled toward the two men, beginning to talk, beginning to tell them. When he got to them he had his left hand out in order to explain and to show, eagerly, smiling, and Hodges took the left hand and with a quick motion had the handcuffs on it, then stooped quickly from the hips and came up with the right hand and then had the cuffs on that hand, too. But he had been almost gentle. He had known the Jones family twenty years.

Raleigh Junior held the hands out and looked down at them. A long time he looked at them, while the smile passed into complete lack of expression on his face. He turned and looked up at his father, at everyone, at each face in turn. And then he began to cry. He sat down on the ground and looked at the handcuffs, crying. He cried openly, like a little boy, making an honest sobbing, and the rain fell on his head in the glare of the lantern and ran with the tears in little rivers down his face.

Later that night, after Hodges and Raleigh Junior and Beck had gone into town in Hodges' car, and the other deputy had taken Raleigh Jones, Jim, and Mason back to the ranchhouse in Beck's car—barely having remembered in time to unroll Beck from the blanket to get the keys—Raleigh Jones sent every one of his wide-eyed hired hands to their rooms with a quiet, firm-voiced declaration and an order.

"My son killed a man tonight," he said. "And is in custody. Go to bed. Go to bed and pray if you can . . . . But go to bed. Get out of here."

When they were gone and Frieda was building Helen's coffee pot in the kitchen, slowly because she was unfamiliar with it and was having to try to read the markings, Raleigh Jones stood near her and said to Mason: "Jim will be gone in the morning."

Mason nodded. He saw that Raleigh Jones was as weak as a rabbit and still trembling, and he could smell the rank sweat on him, dried now and stinking.

"You'll fire him."

"No. He'll be gone. And it's just as well. He won't want to look at me again and I'll have a hard time treating him right now and he knows it. It's just as well. And maybe it's my fault."

They turned out the lights in the rest of the house and sat in the kitchen listening to the great electric coffee pot thump and gargle, and Mason saw that Raleigh Jones was dead tired. He sat at the table and held his forehead in his hands.

After a while Raleigh Jones said: "You know, everyone is afraid of dying. I used to be. But now I know the secret. And it is to be tired and exhausted when the end comes. That makes it welcome. It's simple."

"Don't talk that way," Frieda told him.

"It's true."

"All right, but don't talk that way." She did not look at him.

"Yes ma'am," said Raleigh Jones. He tried to wink in fun at Mason.

Later, when they were thoughtfully sipping at the scalding turbid coffee, Raleigh Jones told them something else.

"I'll shower in a little while and then I'll go to my son," he said.

"You need to go to bed," Frieda murmured. She was holding her cup in both hands and staring at him with wide eyes. Mason had told her of the pit, and of the work which had gone into it in a frantically short time.

"Yes ma'am, but no ma'am."

"Call me Frieda. Oh, call me Frieda, Raleigh!"

There were light glances at her, then, almost amused; and Raleigh's look had wonder in it.

She was breathing so hard that both men could hear her, and Mason winked at Raleigh Jones.

After she had poured them all a second cup and Raleigh Jones had gaped and stretched and had shown signs of gathering energy, he got up and went to the back door. He opened it and stood, waiting, and after a very few seconds the raccoon came into the room, shuffling, high-backed. Raleigh sat again and made clicking noises with his tongue and the raccoon came to him and he picked it up.

"How would you like to go to town, Rover?" Raleigh whispered, smoothing fur. "And make a young man happy? How would you like that, huh?"

Rover nosed about. He was dry so he did not have to shake water loose, and he was glad to be getting warm, happy with the whole prospect.

Mason saw that Frieda was crying, then, with her face averted. He sighed.

It was warm in the kitchen, brightly-lit and basic with the comfortable necessities of feeling: proximity to food, heat, friends; a seeming life-lifting lighted island in the black, trackless void of tragic night . . . they all looked at the raccoon and watched his patient nosings. With filled eyes Frieda looked over her wrist, her hand to her mouth in some sort of quelling effort.

Rover grew warm. He was happy and showed it with ceaseless small activity.

"We'll go," Raleigh Jones told the raccoon. "In a little while we'll go."

"Do they. . . ," Frieda began, uncertainly, "do they allow animals in the—I mean, where Junior is? Do they allow animals there?"

There was no answer, beyond a slow look and a growing grin. The grin spread until it attained happiness from its somber beginnings, with feeling and power. It was the first time he had smiled since the tragedy and it was a statement of policy and a doubtless prediction given with pride, with careless and sure abandon.

"They do," Mason muttered. "If they didn't before they do

now."

After they had all had a third cup and after Frieda was finished with hers—the last one to do so—Raleigh Jones stood, as if they had been having a conference and he, as owner and proprietor and executive boss instead of host merely, had called the conference and so held the situation within his power to call an end to the conference, and he signalled the end by stretching and by announcing his bath with a sigh.

Mason got up and Raleigh Jones reached to shake his hand. He held it.

"Except for you, Mason, we'd all be outlaws, tonight. Now none of us is an outlaw. Not even my son."

"Okay," Mason muttered. "We'd better be going."

Mason went out the door and walked the few hundred sightless yards to his Buick, drove it back, went back inside for Frieda and his rifle, then the two of them drove up to the camp. It was ten-thirty. Mason could hear strong emotion in Frieda's breathing as she sat beside him on the way up. He looked at her and saw that she was thinking severe woman-things.

When he had built a fire and seen that it was catching with real magnitude, he fixed them both a drink, using the bourbon, and sat watching Frieda prepare his meal. It was cold in the cabin.

"Easy," he said. "A sandwich will do. You've already eaten."

"Okay. A hot egg sandwich. With bacon and cheese . . . ."

"Fine."

"Mason, I want to go!"

"What?"

"I want to go! Into town."

"Tonight?"

"Yes! Tonight!"

Suddenly he was hungry. He watched the preparation with hollow interest.

"Make two of them," he said. "And make yourself one. Three."

"Will you take me into town?"

"Okay. If the sandwiches are good enough, and warrant it."

She tried to laugh. She was breathing hard, and Mason, watching her, thought oddly that she was like a mare that he had seen once that was ready for the stallion . . . that she had purpose and would accept no wrong advice and no failure . . . and no substitute. She did not touch her drink.

Mason saw how it was, thinking of the rats, of the successful male rats in the end pens, thinking of them as shadows on the wall of his own whole life's experience: the gift of male to female not protection only but freedom from the rains of stimulus, females being affected by stimulus because they were other-directed, and reacted. Females reacting because that was what their inner beings required: reacting. He remembered his own love-making and how his partner always had to be prepared, reacting physically. Males acting and females reacting and the whole secret of the successful male rats in the end pens that they absolved their females from the rain of stimulus that was to be had in the crowd, that they made them immune by isolating them and allowing them some freedom from the rain of stimulus pressure, to pick their own . . . and this the secret and the answer. Human females in the U.S.A. in trouble now because they have too many stimuli which require reactions: television shouting, radio shouting, headlines screaming, magazines persuading, everything suggesting competition, and fast transportation by car and faster communication by telephone robbing away self; the problem the same as that facing the middle-pen rats: too much intimate communication involving too many people—causing the synthetic rain. And like the inept middle-pen males, the human males standing dumbly by, watching the too-personal war being lost and not even recognizing it as strife. Others having end-pen isolation like Raleigh Jones with his unasking outlook and his individuality and his freedom of land possessed . . . and now Frieda craving it and not understanding it though she was a lady Ph.D. because she was a reacting female first. And Raleigh Jones being grief now and holding out an invisible hand to her fear: allowing her the other half of the mystery which was the female's craving to be allowed to sacrifice for love and thus be worthy, without which a female will crave and seek the rains of stimuli and the middle pens . . . and failure.

Mason sighed, wondering if it were all true.

"God," he said.

"What?"

"Nothing. Blasphemous nothing. Hurry up with my sandwiches. Two of them! Then I'll take you into town!"

"It's a deal," she told him, frying with dedication.

They ate hurriedly without realizing it, and then there was a time when Frieda went into the bathroom to freshen herself without actually taking a bath, and then shortly they were on the road to town. It was near midnight. Mason listened, and could still hear her breathing. He began to prepare his speech to Raleigh Jones, knowing that Frieda would say nothing. She was his ward, now, and nothing more. It was a strange situation.

It was strange that he thought he knew what to say, that he thought he knew what was in her head without actually asking or yet trying to figure it out: as if he had followed somehow because the strength in her had been that plain, that vital.

She looked out the window as they went, from time to time watching the road ahead briefly and it was then that he saw by the diffuse reflection of the great headlight fan ahead of them that she had put on lipstick and was almost eagerly beautiful. She was still breathing as if it were hard to do, and he saw when she looked at him once that her eyes were black with strong feeling, her pupils expanded until each blue iris was a thin line around the periphery.

"What will you do in town?" Mason asked her.

She looked at him.

"They might . . . they might need me . . . ."

He saw that she did not know how to talk of it.

"I believe it."

Later she murmured: "Does Raleigh . . . have you ever told him who I am? What I am?"

"What you are?"

She regarded him then with fright almost, and he smiled quickly, making it a joke.

"Does he know that I am a psychologist?"

"Every woman is a psychologist."

"Oh, Mason, say things for me! Please! Don't do this! I—I can't say the things . . . ."

He saw that she was about to cry again.

"Easy. Easy, Frieda. Everything will be all right. I know. I understand."

They sped along, the Buick floating through the curves along the hilltops, pushing the lighted cones ahead, passing with speed through great cuts that had been blasted in the hills, sheer sliced-out rock towering above them now and then on both sides, the heater going unnoticed and unappreciated in the car because of the feeling.

"I wonder how he is dressed?" Mason mused. "Most of the ranchers and farmers who get into town once a year for a special occasion . . . they wear a twenty-year-old blue serge suit that is double-breasted and with a tie that is six inches wide and red and white, flowery . . . ."

"Don't! Mason, don't!"

"What difference does it make? A man is dead, tonight! A man is dead tonight by horrible mistake!"

"Yes.

Later he said: "Yes, that's so. Leave it to me, Frieda. You have a surprise in store. Leave it to old Mason. Old Mason has been around, too, and knows the score."

"Old Mason had better slow down." She laughed with that, the way a child laughs on Christmas Eve, through a cramping throat, with hurting force.

They came out on a long slope and headed down, winding slowly. The town set ahead of them, far down, dotted with lights that were mostly white points, now, with the late hour. Most of the neon had been turned off.

Mason saw that Frieda was sitting on the edge of her seat, putting a hand on the dash.

The Buick sailed through the bridge, coasting, tires making the regular, slow, concrete-section double thump and the steel structure going by overhead like a gaunt and spectral web that the lights never quite reached; then Mason braked the car to a crawl beyond the bridge.

"Do you know where it is?" she insisted.

"Well, no . . . ."

They were on the main street, then.

"We could ask."

He saw an Exxon service station on the right and pulled up on the outside apron. Three men were there beneath the lights, looking purple because of the pure light whiteness and the blue uniforms of two of them.

An attendant came over and Mason rolled down his window as the man came around, stooped, and peered.

"Need any help, sir!" It was not a question.

"Where's the jail?"

The man was old, with bad teeth. He stooped some more and looked at Frieda, at her eyes.

"You mean the hospital. Har, har, har! When it happened to me I went off and forgot the main thing! Forgot the wife! Had to circle the block and go back and pick her up!" He sputtered saliva, slinging a rag with good fellowship, standing and looking over the car at his cronies and getting ready to tell them the good joke.

Then he stooped again, looking at Frieda.

"But that was long time ago," he said. "The jail's over there. Only one light on, downstairs."

He had pointed across the car. Mason began rolling up the window.

"Anything I can do?" the attendant shouted.

"No. Thanks."

Mason pulled off the apron and made a complete turn in the street, going north then for two blocks on gravel.

"Do I look pregnant, Mason?"

"Only from the neck up. Maybe expectant is better."

The car slid in the gravel a little, though he was going at a walk, and then he got out, went around, and opened Frieda's door. When she got out they stood for a moment looking at the stained and cracked glass, the ponderous old masonry that had to be guessed at now in the cold darkness. They walked the few steps and Mason turned the old knob and pushed the door in.

The outer room was like that in an ancient courthouse, with old oaken benches that curved, a single obscene hanging light bulb, and the distant, documented, and almost guessed-at smell of tobacco, urine and sweat—centuries old in flat presentation and quiet insistence.

Raleigh Jones got up from a bench, holding a soft and tattered magazine. He was smiling a little. No one else was there.

"Hello," he murmured, coming to them, showing surprise.

"Is he . . . ," Frieda said. Mason looked at her and was reminded of a matron in an old church, after the service, fawning at the minister.

"He's asleep. He went to sleep as soon as I brought Rover. He went to sleep happy . . . and Rover, too. Happy."

They stood close together beneath the bare bulb, looking at each other. Mason put his arm around Frieda's waist, clasping the hand that had sought his on the other side, seeing that Raleigh was trying to smile.

"Smile, Raleigh Jones," Mason said. "Smile. I have brought you the manna."

"What?"

"We'll get to it in a minute. Is the boy all right?"

"He's fine. Asleep. The coon, like I said. And Hodges told me he was leaving me here in charge. How do you like that? How do you like that for a friend? And he said he had something in his eye, but I think I know better. Only I noticed that he took my boy's key with him."

"Well . . . well, that's all right."

"I guess so." Raleigh's whisper was coarse and easy.

Mason could feel Frieda playing with his fingers unknowing. He saw that her attention was lost in Raleigh Jones' face.

He was dressed as he always was, with clean khaki pants that showed new creases, leather jacket and a silk scarf for the occasion: white and fluffy at his neck, tucked neatly. He was casual and basic, not really dressed, yet somehow debonair. The luxuriant white hair was coarse and neat, the brown eyes sober, direct. He might have been a horse owner at the practice track.

Mason drew a loud, gusty sigh. He got ready.

"The lady wanted to come," he began, feeling wounded. He wished, now, that she were somewhere else, so he could talk.

Raleigh nodded, looking at Frieda. He licked his lips, and Mason wanted very much then to feel his pulse, to be allowed to count it.

"The lady," Raleigh said.

"Not Mrs. Mason," Mason began. "Frieda Colbein, Ph.D."

Raleigh Jones stared. His eyes narrowed a little, and Mason planted his feet and got ready.

"You have a man coming from Chicago, Raleigh. Right?"

There was a silence.

"Answer me," Mason said.

"Yes. Sure. N. L. Nielson, from Chicago. He'll maybe be here tonight. Sometime between . . . tonight, he said. He said to save him a cabin, and he sent a hundred dollar bill. Nobody ever did that before. Nobody ever came that far before."

"Have you met him?"

"No. This is his first time. He called me two weeks ago on the phone."

"Well," Mason said, breathing hard. "Your N. L. Nielson is coming to see me. On a . . . on a deal we made. And I had reason to fear him. I won't explain, and I'm not sure that you'll understand, but anyway that's the way it is. And because I feared him I thought I should have someone along. So I brought Frieda, an old friend. Frieda is a Ph.D. in psychology at Tech, at my school. And I have not touched her."

Raleigh Jones stared, his eyes not narrow any more. He stood motionless.

"I could have brought my wife but was afraid she would find out something . . . so I brought Frieda, who is no maiden and who came to get away from something, but the important thing is that I have not touched her. Do you believe that? And I have tried! Now do you believe it?"

Raleigh Jones stared. He had rolled his magazine and was feeling it.

"Why are you telling me this?"

"Frieda is a psychologist. She . . . she knows things about Raleigh Junior. She can testify in court for you, as an authority. When they read her credentials the jury will have to listen to her."

Raleigh Jones licked his lips. Frieda stood there with her own lips parted. When Mason did not continue they both looked at him.

"She wants to help. That's all."

The bare bulb seemed hot to Mason. The ancient acrid smell captured his consciousness and insulted him, now, and he wanted to get away.

"You know," he began, groping, "your boy . . . well, he could use a person who is an authority on . . . ."

"Say it, Mason. God damn it, say it! I hate namby-pamby talk!

My boy is retarded! It's no secret! I've faced it since he was one year old!"

"All right, then."

Later Mason said again: "She wants to help. Will you let her?"

"I'd let her have my house, if she wanted it!"

Mason stared at Frieda, trying to grin. He saw that she was beyond speech, trying to rub the skin off the fingers of his hand that she was holding.

"All right, then . . . ."

After a while Mason went outside by himself to escape the discomfort, feeling jittery. He listened and could hear them talking inside: Frieda's voice low and sedate, capable, comfortable. Mason sighed again into the cold night air. He realized that he was dragged-out tired.

The wind puffed on him from the north, refreshing with mild cold since he had just come from stale air. Stars looked down, tiny, countless, remote: oh, so remote! The night was absolutely silent except for the voices now and then inside, droning. But then he heard laughter: Frieda's first, then Raleigh's. Mason felt tired some more. He tried to look at his Buick in the dark and could barely see it. He felt lonesome now, almost deserted.

The town had no sound at all. Not a car, not a dog; nothing. From where he was standing he could see a single street light on the courthouse corner, with a high moving pecan tree nearby. And that was all. Soon he began to get cold.

Mason walked out by his car and urinated on the gravel. Then he turned around and went back inside. The two of them were sitting on a bench beneath the frightful bulb.

"Well," Mason said.

They looked at him.

"I'm going to camp, and to bed," he said.

"I'll stay, Mason," Frieda intoned.

"I'll bring her when I come," said Raleigh Jones.

Mason made a contrived sign of blessing, then, and left.

On the way to the car he thought: and I didn't say it. I didn't tell him at all what is really in her mind but that's not my department. That's not my department at all and it was good the way you said it, Mason, to leave the other part out. You did a noble job. A noble job! And the noblest part was to leave the main part out. That's her department. That's their department.

When he had his car door open and it was lighted inside and he was putting his right foot in and getting ready to follow it, he saw that Frieda was there with him. He withdrew the right foot and found himself, standing again, in an embrace, with something wet along his cheek.

"Thank you," she said.

"Okay!"

Then he got back in the Buick and shut the door. He saw that she was already back inside the building.

Mason inserted his key after fumbling a little, gloried in the big sound of the engine that was his very own, backed out onto the sleeping gravel street, and moved toward the south and the highway.

Traveling then, gaining speed on the bridge for his run at the great hill, he thought: Atta way to go, cutter. Atta' way, lover. Boy, you really wow 'em, Mason. You wow 'em and hold 'em, you do.

It was after one o'clock when he approached the ranchhouse, and he saw that the kitchen lights were on. The thought struck him that the whole house had been dark when he and Frieda passed by more than an hour ago. On impulse he stopped his car and got out, approached the back door, found it unlocked, and went in.

Smitty and Joe were sitting at the table, their eyes wide and apprehensive on him as he entered. He saw that they were drinking coffee, both wearing only shorts in the warm kitchen. Mason went to the cupboard, got a cup, poured, then sat with them, looking at them, seeing that they had both been to bed because their hair was disheveled. Both were smoking cigarettes that they had rolled; he saw a flat can of tobacco and a book of cigarette papers, half empty, in a neat stack by Joe's coffee cup.

"Well," Mason grinned.

"Well," Smitty said. He looked, with his great nose, like a sleepy, crafty pig with eyes too wide now for real sleepiness or real pigness.

"You boys can't sleep now. Is that it?"

"We been asleep," Joe said.

"Did you see it?" Smitty demanded, sounding gravelly. "Mrs. Mason said you saw it happen."

"Frieda," Mason told him, watching to see that it took.

"Frieda. Frieda said you saw it happen."

"That's right."

They waited for something more, watching him.

"It was Beck, of course. You know that. And the bullet took him neat above the left eye . . . ."

"God o'mighty," Smitty breathed, looking bothered.

"But how is it you boys are up? Can't sleep?"

Joe said: "A hunter came. He beat on the door."

"A hunter? Who?"

Joe drained his cup, then took a last drag on his dying cigarette, cupping his hand around it, holding the flat stub with all five fingertips.

"Guy named Nielson," Smitty said.

"Nielson."

"That's right. From Chicago."

"You sure . . . I mean . . . Illinois plates on his car, and all that?"

"Hell," Smitty said, "I didn't see the plates. I doubt it, though. He said he had flown in. To somewhere. Probably a rented car." Smitty was regarding Mason with surprise: mild surprise, after the strong surprises of the day.

Mason thought: of course. He would fly down. You're stupid, Mason, to look for Illinois plates. A man like that wouldn't drive that far.

There was a silent time, during which they sipped and studied each other.

Joe asked: "How far was the shot . . . ?"

"Fifty yards . . . That's a guess. A perfect shot . . . ."

"Yeah," breathed Smitty. "Perfect. It would be."

"Was he alone? Was Nielson alone?"

"No," Smitty told Mason. "A woman . . . a gal was in the car. Fingernails like Fu Manchu and a fancy white hairdo. You notice these things because you don't see stuff like that much in deer camp. When a guy brings a woman you can always tell when it's not his wife."

"Which cabin?" Mason was trying not to smirk, with fatigue as a successful ally.

"North cabin. Next to yours."

"Oh," Mason said. He nodded thoughtfully.

It was almost suffocating warm in the bright kitchen, stale with lateness of hour and flatness of smoked-out cigarettes. The young men and Mason looked at each other with eyes that smarted.

"Beck," Mason remembered, speaking the name without willing it, as though his mouth were hooked now to his subconscious, "Beck. He had a family?"

Smitty and Joe consulted with studying glances.

"A wife," Joe muttered. "Kids, too, I guess. I don't know."

"A son, maybe," Smitty said. "That's right. A young son . . . ."

Mason sipped, watching them.

"Okay," he said.

Later, when his coffee was gone, Mason decided that he had the thing well enough phrased to give it to them, the main part of it, leaving out the parts that were not his affair, and he slid back his chair and plunged his hands into his pockets, making fists.

"I would like one or both of you to help me now. Do something. Move Ms. Frieda into Raleigh Junior's room. Now. Tonight."

He saw that they were floundering and unable to read the thing, so he continued.

"I came here to meet someone. I brought Frieda with me for help. She is not Mrs. Mason. Her name is Frieda Colbein and she is a doctor of psychology, a Ph.D., a friend of mine. And we have spent several days and nights now in the same cabin but I want to tell you and have you understand that I did not bring her here for the usual reason and that's why you were fooled, and thought she was my wife. I have a good wife but could not bring her under the circumstances . . . ."

He saw that they were overwhelmed, listening with gaping mouths.

"Frieda is a psychologist and can be the number-one witness for Raleigh Junior because he is retarded . . . a moron, something . . . you know. And tomorrow I will probably leave. Maybe. But she will stay. She's in town now with Raleigh and Raleigh Junior. And I don't want you to tell anyone I told you these things . . . let your boss or Frieda tell you if they want to . . . and you play dumb, and all that, but it is important to me for you to know that I have not touched her. Not here, not anywhere. She came for another reason; I brought her for another reason. And I even tried, which you will believe, but had no luck. I'm telling you this so you can show her respect, which you will have to do. You see, the important thing is not that nobody ever—the important thing is that I did not. This is the whole thing, to you, because you know me. And I swear to you before God that I did not, that I have not . . . ."

Mason was looking at two stupefied young men. Smitty licked his lips and nodded. Joe stared, mouth open.

"You see how it is," Mason said, feeling large and tarnished.

He watched them both build cigarettes, Joe first and then handing the makings to Smitty, and he realized that it was because they were embarrassed at his words and at the surprising magnitude of the thing and did not want to look at him. But he saw also that they believed him.

"Frieda . . . Doctor Colbein . . . will stay. She'll have a part in the hearing. The biggest part. I'll probably have a part, too, because I saw it happen. But I've got things to do so I'll probably leave sometime tomorrow or the next day and let them call me back if they want me to testify."

Smitty had it, then. He nodded, making new smoke.

"Jim is gone," he said.

"His things?"

"He took a few, in a bag, and hit the road. I told him I'd keep the rest for him."

"They may want him, too," Mason muttered. "For the hearing. Or trial."

"I'll know where he's at," Smitty said.

"He won't be far," Joe said. "He's got a girl here."

Mason nodded. He stretched and drew a great, needed breath.

Later Mason said again: "I'd like to move Frieda into Raleigh Junior's room. Now. Tonight."

"Let's go," Smitty told him.

"Me for the sack," Joe said. "If one will do."

"One will do," Mason said.

"I'll get up early," Joe explained, "and go to the feed shed. And count the sacks again, and look for the thief. Business as usual."

"As usual," Mason agreed, seeing that Smitty was grinning wanly at Joe.

They scraped chairs and got up. Mason put the cups in the sink and ran water in them while the young men disappeared into their part of the house. Soon Smitty was back, dressed in his faded and worn jeans, vagabond boots, and fretted leather jacket that had been torn here and there by brush.

"Let's go," he said. He was wide awake.

They moved her in, expertly, shivering, both looking at the north cabin but not talking about it as they passed going and then coming with her things, seeing the bright blue Chevrolet that was most assuredly a rented car because it had local plates; carrying her clothes and her suitcases without putting the whole thing together, in bits and pieces, piling and stacking things on Raleigh Junior's bed, on the dresser, hanging neat things in the closet.

"You tell her, when she comes through," Mason told Smitty.

"You tell her, or Joe, if he is up and you are not. You tell her that she belongs here. She will know it, really, already."

"Okay," Smitty said.

"And she will stay here. With you as chaperone."

Smitty laughed. The sound burst from him eagerly, rupturing the spell of the whole evening, making things comfortable and liveable again.

"Hoo, boy!" he said. "Fancy that! She won't want that!"

Mason laughed with him. They had just finished unloading Frieda's things.

"You're right," he said. "She won't."

When he was back in his cabin, Mason stirred the coals briefly into rejuvenated warmth, put two new logs in upon them, set his clock for a very early hour that was before sunup and not far away at all, now, and got into the bed after undressing to his shorts. He lay there watching the baby fire, hands under his head, thinking. Two or three times he checked his alarm clock, making certain that he had really set it. And at length he slept.

The licking flames made small shadows that moved on him as he slept.

An alarm clock is monster enough under any circumstances. Set to go off within four hours of the end of such a day as Mason had had, an alarm clock sings a strident discord that just has to be a lie: and some important measure of a man lies in whether he, the sleeper, can believe, under such conditions, and can rise after closing the switch and silencing the outrage instead of lying back and making untruths in his mind.

Mason remembered the day behind and then the day ahead and sat up on his protesting springs. For awhile he was coming back from somewhere else, breathing hard, then noted that the two logs which he had put on the fire were disassembled shambles now, still red, and that the cabin held a small chill that was not at all vicious yet, merely waiting, hovering, impatient.

He got up, went to the bathroom in red-toned darkness, then returned to his bed to put on his shoes before building the coffee pot. He thought of Frieda and Raleigh Jones, seeing their images in his mind against the stark backdrop of yesterday, trying to search out whether they had come to the cabin while he had been asleep and had found her things gone, having to concede that if they had come he had been unaware . . . .

With coffee perking then, he dressed, spent a few grudging moments wiping clotted mud from his shoes, went out for more wood which he threw heavily in upon the coals, then sat again waiting for the coffee, yawning fiercely.

Mason was washed out. He felt dead. He clasped his tired hands and looked at them.

Little flames shot up tentatively around the new, cold logs after awhile, bursting high with fingered stealth once, twice, many times in absolute silence, then sputtering and purring underneath as the real fire came with the heat and the burning. And the chill began to recede in the cabin, losing ground, making insidious retreat from the fire to the corners, sinking, cowering away, its truth having become untruth before the new supply-line of the enemy; dragging back darkness with it into diminishing corners as failure of any kind breeds more and calls attention to it.

Mason poured coffee when it was done. He stood before the fire and looked down into it with the leaping red and yellow lights on his face, drinking the turbid and scalding fluid, thinking. At this time he felt, oddly, that if a man were smart enough he could think things through and solve all the problems of the world. The fire made him think this way, and the sufficient and replenishable coffee. He knew that it was not true.

At length, working on his second cup without having eaten yet because he was not hungry, Mason thought of his binoculars, which he would need in a very few hours. He moved about the cabin, holding his hot cup high in his left hand, putting the right hand upon aberrant shadows here and there, turning things over, feeling, rummaging, having finally to concede that he had misplaced the binoculars. Then he remembered. He had lowered them to the ground behind a bush the night before as he was getting ready to appear and impose upon Raleigh Jones' digging, and he had forgotten them. The binoculars were still there behind the bush, beneath the great cliff that overlooked the field and the feed shed. Mason listened. It had long since stopped raining. At least the binoculars were not getting wet any more.

He went to the door, opened it, and looked out toward the western sky. Stars were there: unnamed and trackless with the lateness or the earliness; he would have sun in a couple of hours—sun in an open sky.

He thought: that's good.

With his third cup in his hand he got his .270, laid it upon his bed, and rubbed the eyepiece and the objective of his six power scope lightly with his handkerchief. It would serve. It would be needed, and would be sufficient.

Then he went back to his fire and stood with his back to it, sipping coffee and waiting. He had not considered turning on any lights in the cabin.

In summertime, morning bursts in the hill country like a flower opening—after the mockingbirds have had their conclave, shouting quarter-mile notes at each other in the first hint of light—then coming on and opening, with noise and rosy glow. In dead of winter it is not that way in the hill country. In dead of winter the morning creeps in, a hungry spectral cat, and nothing is heard. Nothing at all.

Mason propped the door open so he could see it begin. He found three stale and cardboard-like sweet rolls and he ate them with the last of the coffee, standing close to the fire so the chill of the open door could not reach him, and he had to look at his clock from time to time in order to see the daylight coming down. Once he went out and saw the light in the east above the cedar-furred hill behind his cabin, calm, sedate, cold; pure as a muffled treble note from a tower bell—and as remote in aloof and self-sufficient planning. He went back in and stood before the fire, hailing its warmth, waiting out the grand plan at his open door, sipping with growing impatience.

When finally he could make out the few trees and bushes beyond the doorway and it was cold again in the cabin so that he had begun to turn alternately front and back to the fire, Mason closed the door, turned on a lamp, and began to get himself ready. He found that he was trembling, that his extra shirt and then his coat were moving oddly as he put them on. He found a floppy old felt fishing hat that he had brought but had not yet worn and put it on his head, pulling it down tight and binding above his ears, testing the brim several times to see that it was low enough but would not fall down in his face. At length he turned up his coat collar against the back brim of his hat, and pulled on his gloves. Then after standing motionless for a long time, thinking, he grabbed his .270, turned off the lamp, and eased out the door.

It was cold, of course, as it always is on winter mornings beneath a clear sky.

Mason stood outside the door and waited until all his senses had made their slow change, then he began to walk. He walked a single step at a time, north and west, almost as if he were playing a game in which stealth and lack of speed were rules. There was no hurry. A new man would certainly not arise early and hunt in a strange place after having arrived in the dead of night, with no direction, no familiarity with the lay of the land, no knowledge of where the other hunters would be . . . .

The cold crept in at his toes and into the fingers of his gloves, cutting and stinging. He could sense and almost see his breath hanging out before his face, a misty shroud, ghosting away; and the cold snuggled in against his face, wrapping, like something wet.

Mason went on. From time to time he stopped, stooping, peering, trying to remember the north cabin from the first day he and Frieda had walked that way after breakfast, trying now to set the memory right and perfect in juxtaposition with the fused and vagrant shapes of trees and brush which he could see now, having to feel his way almost, remembering his feet on the now hard ground to see that he made no noise.

He was shaking. He had to stop and work with it now and then. Soon he could see the cabin, asleep behind great cedars. It was bulk still and nothing more. Mason thought, from almost a hundred yards away, that the morning sun which would climb over the hill in an hour's time would probe exactly and without interference full at the cabin door. He saw that the Chevrolet was to the left of the door; from where he was now he would have a clear view of the doorway.

Mason halted, shivering, and tried to look about near where he was for cover. Almost immediately he found it: two cedar trunks. He saw when he stepped to his right that he could sit against one and have the other in front of him so close that he could touch it. He crept in, crackling small branches on the ground, and sat. He saw with pleasure that he was in luck. The cedar at his knees was a foot thick and branched less than three feet from the ground, making a perfect and solid support for his .270.

Mason settled and tried to relax. He poked the rifle into the forward tree, sliding it through, seeing with satisfaction that it aimed itself unobstructed at the cabin door. He could not have done better with advance planning.

Soon he found that when he was relaxed the shivering stopped, but that it came again from time to time and when it came it was a wild thing that gripped him almost like an unfriendly orgasm, wracking him completely. But he could get ready for it; and as he sat he found that the episodes got further and further apart as he worked at relaxing. He could see small brush details near him now. He could see how the tiny puffs of wind shook everything small all the way to the ground—not waving, but shuddering stiffly because they were skeletons.

He thought: skeletons with futures. Futures tied to the sun.

The sun. He would welcome the sun. Never had the sun seemed so deliberate, so independent, to Mase Mason. He rediscovered faith, sitting there, practicing making himself as compact as possible so he could not be seen except as part of the two cedar trunks.

His butt began to ache. Very soon it became unbearable, and, feeling with his left hand, he found that he had been sitting on a dead branch with two small, sharp, broken limb stubs that were stabbing him. He swept it away, then tried to settle again and found that comfort which he had had before was now playing a coy game of hide and seek with him. He spent fifteen minutes shifting, then gave up and embraced the small misery of seat-ache.

He could see, now. He could see details of the cabin, of the car, of the velvet ground that stretched away frigidly beneath the brush and trees and intermittent tangle.

Then real light came, without fingers yet, but he could see the yellow bar sweeping across the top edge of the cliff beyond the road, beyond the river on another man's property, far away to his left. He watched the bar broaden downward. In impulse he put the scope on it, pointing the .270 at the distant cliff, for several minutes enthralled that he could actually see the light move down over cut edges and crannies in the sheer ochre stone. He could see the motion of it.

But then he remembered and covered the door again, waiting out the minutes that impatience was turning into tangled complexities of time.

He began to listen for an alarm clock, knowing that there would be none. Not on the first morning.

But N. L. Nielson, no matter what his name really was, would not be a man to sleep far into sunlit hours on a first morning when he had so much to learn, so much to appraise.

After interminable ugly time the sun was in the cedar tops above Mason's head. He looked up and tried to watch it come down. He was relaxed now, not shaking anymore. But poised. Ready.

Then the sun was on the cabin's peak, cold splashless liquid, sinking; then on the front and down the top half of the door; then Mason could see the wide fingers forming through the trees and lying out on the brown ground in streaks. It seemed colder to him.

A noise in the cabin? Why fret about it? Noise would come, and the rest of it . . . .

Then there was a noise and Mason caught it: bedsprings shifting, unloading, shifting again; and then he could hear nothing else because he was too far away.

Mason sighed out his breath. He gathered himself as one with the rifle and laid his eye to the scope and saw the cross-hairs neat and etched against the brilliant yellow-white of the faded wooden door and making it square; the exact mating of hairs lining because he had to be doing something, now, with a nail head two-thirds of the way up the door and exactly in the center . . . .

He waited some more. Mason decided that he had always hated waiting. He had never known it before. He became conscious of his breathing, of trying to see how little he could make each breath cause motion of the cross-hairs.

Then when the door opened it opened at once, quickly, without increments and not fully open wide either but open just enough for a man to slip out, so that he was still aiming at the door and seeing the bright shape standing in the sun to the left. But it was a simple matter to shift the rifle, without seeming to move. The crosshairs swung over and stopped, exactly an inch above the bridge roots of the nose.

The face was still. Looking. The eyes were squinting, struggling with the bright insult, the mouth feigning squint also because of the need in the fierce light; gray was in the hair on the sides, intermixed with black and showing shaggy now with the tousled effect from the pillow and the color of the squinting eyes was something which was beyond Mason's range. Perhaps they were blue, after all, which would be likely if the name were really Nielson.

Mason saw the placid expression then and saw that the man was relieving himself on the ground, that he wore pajamas that were green and white. The eyes moved in the still face that was ugly with the hour.

The neck was thick. The man had power: and hollow cheeks going with the thick neck to incite respect for the power. Mason kept the crosshairs glued to the forehead while he looked. He looked sharply, not finding what he was looking for in the face the first time, the second time, the third time, nor for an interminable period of time when all of his surges of effort fused together and made failure almost a part of his effort; and then he had it. He saw it.

Mason thought: Nielson. Maybe your name is really Nielson and we'll play like it is and we'll also play, Mr. Nielson, like you are dead in your prime with a neat hole carved halfway between your eyes. Pow.

But he had not shot. He had stroked the trigger, but the thumb of that same right hand had been sticking all the while into the open breech for continuing and positive proof to himself that nothing could go wrong.

Nielson looked about for awhile, then got cold and went back inside, pulling the door in tight behind him. Had the eyes been brown, after all?

Mason got up. He began to move away, at first slowly then moving faster and then gliding, almost running, skulking through the thin early light like a playful schoolboy, moving on legs that were stiffer than the schoolboy's but with a spirit no older.

When he got back to his cabin he fixed it rapidly for comfort: starting more coffee, adding wood to the fire, removing hat and gloves and coat, turning on two lamps and moving to the table, clearing a space on the table. Mason was moving as if he were in a hurry. And when he finally sat down at the table, it was with several sheets of writing paper and several envelopes from the bottom of his suitcase, and his pen.

He readied a sheet before him, stripped and stacked the pen, then waited, thinking.

"Nielson," he said. "Raleigh Jones is going to prove to Frieda Colbein that people don't have to be rats. And N. L. Nielson is going to prove the same thing to Mase Mason."

At length, with the fire beginning to pop and purr and the percolator thumping behind him, with the gloom of the cabin cut sharply by the lamp's cone of light flattening on the table top, and by brighter, less constant light at the windows, Mason wrote. He wrote with care, with relish.

"Mr. N. L. Nielson of Chicago:" he began.

Mason wrote two full pages, read it back through five times when he had finished, then looked at his watch and noted the time below his signature. Then he addressed an envelope "N.L. Nielson," slipped the folded letter inside and sealed the envelope.

After going to the percolator, Mason sat with new, black coffee, spread a clean sheet of paper before him, and wrote again.

Dear Frieda:

Well, Kid, I could write twenty pages in gratitude to you and at the end you would not understand. Nor do I, really. So I'll not try.

Do a good job for Big Raleigh. He needs you. If he ever lets on that he is looking for a best man, hint to him that I'm him. Or maybe Raleigh, Jr. will fill the bill. At any rate I am leaving. I will probably be back to testify; but I'll let the authorities call me back. As for now, I have business elsewhere.

He wrote for thirty minutes, filling two pages. When he was through, Mason did not know how to end the letter. For a long time he stared at the bottom of the page, read it through, stared some more, then gave up.

"In eternal gratitude, Mason" was what he put down.

He enveloped the letter, sealed and addressed it simply: "Frieda."

Mason played with the two envelopes for a time while he drank the coffee and thought. At length he got up, looked around him at the shambles of living, and sighed. Then he began to pack his bags. Later he began to put his things in his Buick, not being very neat about it.

When he had finished packing, had turned out the lamp, had seen that the fire would dissolve itself harmlessly into death without popping anything anywhere, he put on his coat and went outside with the two letters in his hand. He had calculated the next move carefully but did not like to think about it because it made him seem silly.

Silly.

Mason stopped. He stood there in the cold for a long moment holding the two letters, thinking. Somewhere, someone or something was trying to tell him something. The eyes . . . they had been brown! Not blue! Who ever heard of a man named Nielson with brown eyes?

Mason went back inside the cabin. He took off his coat and sat down again in front of the dying fire.

At length it came to him, in bits and pieces. The eye color was no matter, probably. Neither was anything else N. L. Nielson had inside his head. It was what he had inside a shallow briefcase that was important, and Mase Mason was not doing that part justice.

He thought: too much could go wrong. It won't work, this way.

All night long he had been thinking about it, and until now it had seemed like the perfect next move. Abruptly he tore open the letter he was holding that was addressed to N. L. Nielson, and he read part of it again.

I took a close look at you this morning through my scope when you went outside to piss. You have a scar that begins at your right eyelid and runs up through that eyebrow and makes a little hair tuft where it comes out . . . .

Then he went on to tell Nielson to look up Frieda and give her the money, saying further, "Do what I tell you because I can recognize you and you have never seen me and no picture has been made of me in fifteen years and if you don't do as I tell you then you will spend the rest of your life thinking every stranger is maybe the desperate Mase Mason and a man who will sell out his football team will do anything."

It had seemed like such a good idea. He was so eager now to get back home. He had some things now to tell Charlie. And Martha. But no. He could not take the chance, he decided. He would have to put his very own hands on the money, tainted or not. Traitorous or not.

Mason threw both letters into the fireplace. Then he scrambled the hot coals on them. When they were burning well he put his coat back on, went outside again and got in the Buick. This time he gave no thought to Nielson, but drove to the ranchhouse.

When he got there Helen Waskom let him into the kitchen. She was the only person there, and her smile to him was weak and warped.

"Coffee, Mr. Mason? Or how about breakfast?"

Mason shook his head. He smiled a little.

She brushed back her hair. He saw that she was comfortably overweight.

"What will happen now?" Helen asked him.

"Nothing. Everything will turn out right. In due time."

"Did . . . did you see it happen, like they say?"

"Yes. Is anyone else up? How about Smitty?"

"Smitty. Joe. My husband. They're all up. Warren has gone to the sheep, and Joe somewhere. Smitty is around close, though, I think. They all got up and ate, just like they always do."

"That's it. That's it, Helen. And you cooked, just like . . . ."

"Sure."

"That's the way. There is no other way."

She did not say anything.

"You know Frieda is a doctor of psychology? She told you?"

"Yes. She told me much more . . . ."

"You know that she will stay? To see about the boy?"

"I guessed it. I guessed it when Smitty told me she was here. Here in June's room."

"Raleigh is not up?"

"No. They got in after four o'clock."

Mason nodded. After a while he patted her soft shoulder once more, then went outside to his car, still feeling a little foolish.

Smitty walked up. He had on his coat with the fat wool collar, and he was grinning as if it were an exercise hard to accomplish in cold, alien air because he had not had much practice.

Mason got out his black checkbook from his shirt pocket and wrote a check, using the rear deck of the Buick for a writing table, with Smitty coming near and looking to see what he was doing.

"You don't have to do that."

"How do you know? You're not Raleigh Jones."

"Hell, when Raleigh Jones is asleep I am Raleigh Jones."

Mason laughed. He had written the check to cover his and Frieda's stay up until the time when she had been moved into the ranch house, adding only himself for an extra night's lodging.

"A day at a time," Mason said, "from this point on."

He clasped his pen, folded the checkbook away and handed the newly-inked blue paper to Smitty. Smitty shook his head, not understanding.

"Hell," Smitty muttered, taking it, folding it, putting it into his billfold.

"Hell," Mason aped.

Smitty put his hands out on the Buick's rear deck that was warming now with the sun and Mason looked at the hands and saw that they could never be clean. Grit had worked into the lines and the tracings of the horny palms, making them like treads almost, and the work of grasping things had made them curled so it was doubtful that he could straighten them out flat without pushing against something. The backs were red and scarred from infinite encounters with thorns and wire and barbs on the wire, and the big veins knotted and gnarled into brown-purple branchings that were like an old man's but harder. The nails were thick and torn, and packed.

Mason put his own hands out on the rear deck and stole a glance for comparison and saw that his hands looked twenty years younger.

"And you didn't get your deer this time, huh?"

"No. But I saw one. I saw one I want."

"The big buck, I bet . . . in the green cedar above the field!"

"Right. How did you know?"

"Raleigh . . . Mister Jones used to hunt that one. He's got one track that's warpfooted, kind of, so you can recognize him. I forget whether it's a front foot or hind foot. But Mr. Jones says that he used to hunt him on a horse, years ago, because sometimes a man on a horse can go right up to a deer. But not the big buck. He told me that once he had the buck out in the open and he was horseback and the buck got a tree between them and ran off, and no matter where he went the big buck had figured him out and kept the tree between 'em."

Mason waited. Then: "I got a broadside at him. A few yards away."

"And missed?"

"And didn't shoot."

"Why not?"

"I don't know. Looking at him, my gun got heavy." It was a confessional that Mason had never thought he would make.

But Smitty only grinned. "Tied up, huh?"

"I guess . . . ."

"Buck fever! And you a grown man!" He was mildly teasing.

"And then some. I was a grown man a long time ago."

Smitty shook his head, making sounds of play-shame. Then he laughed.

"But I'll get him. I'll come back and I'll get him. Next year, maybe."

"Hope," Smitty said, "springs eternal. Even when it's the big buck."

"Even. In the human breast."

Smitty was smiling at him now, as a man might smile at an impetuous three year old, to whom proper instruction is yet impossible concerning such matters.

"No. Sorry, no." Smitty grinned some more.

"Yes."

"I guess you can try."

"That's right," Mason told him. "I can try. That's all a poor man can do. That's all a dog can do. Or a stud rat."

Mason looked at the grinning face and saw that it did not go with the hands at all, that it was a clown's face, almost, or the face of Santa Claus when he was a young man just now fashioning his career: the bulbous nose ungodly unbeautiful, the scraggle of pale unkempt two-day beard here and there too thin to be called anything but ugly, the vagrant pimples near the chin and to either side, the small, emotionless eyes . . . .

Then Mason saw that the jaw was moving out of tune a little, that Smitty had imperfect control over his lower lip. The fact hit Mason hard, painfully, surprising him.

He thought: he's grieving. God damn me for making the small talk when he's standing here grieving. A face built for comedy and that's what I took it for and he's standing here grieving . . . .

Mason felt a surge of emotion then that knotted his throat and made it hurt, somewhere deep, above his breastbone. Suddenly he wanted to take Smitty in his arms and comfort him, but something strong prevented it. Mason looked away, his own eyes filling.

He thought: it's an imperfect world.

"It's my fault, Mr. Mason," Smitty said, his voice rasping. "It's all my fault because I got into trouble with Beck and June was there and saw it and because . . . because he loved me he put me right when I was wrong . . . ."

Mason looked and with strange relief saw that the unemotional pig's eyes were still dry.

"Not June's fault . . . my fault!" Smitty said. "And I taught him to shoot!"

"No," Mason said. He grabbed the shoulder, slapping hard.

"Jim's fault," Mason went on. "Raleigh's fault, Raleigh Junior's fault. Beck's fault. Your fault. My fault."

"Your fault! How?"

"I don't know but I'm sure of it. We could figure it out if we tried. Everybody's fault."

Mason could see that Smitty's own father's love for Raleigh Junior was causing the rebellious lips, that his recognition of the tragedy and his grieving included not only June but Beck also, and that the hardest part for him was the inability to understand how such a thing could happen: embarrassment that such a thing could happen in his—and everybody's—cherished world.

"It's an imperfect world, Smitty."

"What?"

"Or maybe you can't say that. Maybe you should say the world is a standard, a constant, a non-variable. And that it is we who are imperfect. All of us!"

"What?"

"Never mind," Mason said. He looked at his watch. It was eight-twenty. No doubt Nielson would be out and walking around by now. Perhaps he would be looking for Mason.

"Tell me more about the hunter who came in last night . . . Nielson . . . was that his name?"

"What can I tell ya?" Smitty said. "A guy. Four legs an' a snout

. . . like ever'body else . . . ."

"With a woman . . . ."

"Yeah. Now that's somethin' else! No bimbo, exactly."

"Fu Manchu nails," Mason prompted.

"Yeah. An' platinum hair . . . done up nice . . . ."

Mason looked at his watch again. He should be there, at the deer camp. Now.

And Frieda should be there with him.

"What time did you say they came in from town last night?"

"Who?"

"Raleigh and Frieda."

"Don't know. It was after four."

Mason walked back and forth. He should be moving, he thought. He looked at his watch again.

"I'm going inside," Mason told Smitty. Then he walked away from him. "Have to take an accounting."

In the living room then, Mase Mason sat down by himself, in the gloom. He had never been good at waiting, he thought, again. Now in his mind he was talking to Charlie. But this was not a memory. This was something to come.

Charlie, we have to make all athletics more available. For a start we will have a lightweight football team for the students who can't make the varsity. For everybody. We'll put a weight limit on it and we'll scrape up games for them and award letters, even if we have to play them against high school teams at first. They will be in addition to the teams we already have . . . .

That was good. Charlie would probably not like it. To hell with him. He, Mason, would do it anyway, and would name a coach who was not producing anymore to the job of lightweight coach. No. Not that. Anybody who had the nerve and the dedication to put on the pads deserved the best. Mase would give the job to a good man. Maybe he would coach the team himself . . . . Yeah! Sure! He would coach the team . . . .

In his mind's ear now Charlie was speaking. He was shaking his head. "Won't work, Mase. The economics of the thing will eat us up . . . hell, you're the A.D . . . where you gonna come up with the funds? What're you gonna charge at the gate, for a Mickey Mouse college football team? Who'll come? And not only that, we don't even have the funds to outfit 'em . . . what're we gonna use for uniforms? Hell, we don't have the money to get such a program off the ground!"

And in his mind's eye Mason reached in his satchel and came out with thirty big ones. Still neatly wrapped. Three stacks each of one hundred hundred-dollar bills . . . a snug paper band around each stack.

"This for you, son of a bitch. Now what do you say? How's this for uniform funds?"

In his mind's eye Mase saw Charlie's eyes pop out. And he loved it.

Mason got to his feet again, then walked back and forth in the still, almost dark living room of Raleigh Jones' ranchhouse. Abruptly he went to the windows, one at a time, and cranked miniblinds. Light flooded the room—the pale light of morning from outside.

He looked at his watch again. Then he sat down once more.

Mason's mind continued to race. Of course he would leave some of the money with Frieda with instructions that it be used to defray expenses incurred in Raleigh Junior's defense; with the remainder going to Beck's widow . . . .

It was strange. All along in his episode of the traitorous act leading to the funded courier, Mason had not wanted to think about the money. His motivation had been hatred and revenge, not personal financial gain, and that had made the hundred thousand dollars a hurdle for him, an enigma . . . something dirty . . . Now that there were good things he could do with the payoff, he was eager. The money was not dirty anymore.

Now Mason looked at his watch again. Dammit woman, he thought, are you going to sleep all day? Then the thought occurred to him that maybe he should go on up to the cabin by himself the first time, leaving Frieda sleeping. No, he thought. Not that . . . that's the reason I brought her in the first place . . . also it is more appropriate than ever, now, because he brought his woman . . . .

Mason got up. He went down the dark hall to Raleigh Junior's room, where Frieda was now asleep. It was nine o'clock.

At the door he emptied his lungs for quietness, then twisted the knob and entered, pushing the dry, thin door almost closed behind him, listening to the small, vagrant squeaking.

Frieda was there, asleep in a double bed that had come from another century. He moved near.

Her hair was out on the pillow, a blue quilt pulled up close and tight; and, leaning as one does to see a sleeping baby for the first time, Mason saw that her mouth was slack and half-smiling against the pillow, that her breathing was easy and untroubled and soundless. He watched for a long while, considering kissing her. But it would have been too much.

It was softly dark in the bedroom, and cold. Lights and shadows played on the single window that had a yellow tasseled shade pulled all the way down before it, and there was no sound there except that of his own careful breathing.

Mason eased on the edge of the bed, sitting. He had made the bed move not at all, but when he looked down at her face again the eyes were open and a smile was beginning. Then the arms were up and warm around his neck and Mason was treated to that fullest and most unexpected of pleasures for a man: the sudden voluptuousness that flooding happiness can bring to a woman. But before he could get lost in it—and Mason was falling fast—she turned her morning mouth away from his and pushed him back into a sitting position so she could look at him.

She looked at him for a long time, with eyes almost too large and lustrous.

"Thank you," she said, breathing the words.

Mason cleared his throat.

"I need you," he said. Then, as she began to look away, he laughed some.

"No," he said. "Not that way . . . I mean I need you up. The guy is here . . . the man I came to see. Can you get up so we can go to their cabin?"

"Their . . . cabin?" She looked back at Mason.

"Their. He has a woman with him."

"What kind of woman?" Frieda arched her brows. "What role?" she teased.

"I don't know . . . according to Smitty, more like foxy mama than bimbo. Fu Manchu nails, he said." Mason smirked a little. "What can I tell ya?" he said. "You know the difference between foxy mama and bimbo?"

Frieda nodded. She was looking at the shade, at the sun color coming through it.

"Give me thirty minutes," she told him.

Mason left the room, went back outside, and got in his car. Thirty minutes would give him time to go back to his cabin and re-establish his presence there. He thought: for Nielson's benefit. Then Frieda and I can walk over. And I'll take an empty briefcase to leave with him. That ought to make communication easy.

At the camp there was no sign of the newcomers. Their rented Chevrolet was as before, and Mason parked again at his own cabin, then spent fifteen minutes moving back in . . . ostensibly. For Nielson's benefit, he thought. Also for Fu Manchu, he thought. Then he went back to the ranchhouse, taking with him the empty black briefcase he had brought along for the purpose.

When he arrived back at the ranchhouse, Raleigh Jones was still asleep, no doubt still exhausted from the strange and violent effort of the long night before; Rover was getting in Helen's way in the kitchen; and Warren Waskom was sitting at the kitchen table drinking coffee. Frieda was still in her bedroom and the door was closed.

"Mornin'," Warren said to Mason.

"Mornin'," Mason said. He sat. In a minute he got up again and began to move about the kitchen.

"Jittery," Warren noted, "like that damn coon there . . . ."

"Guess so," Mason looked at him. Then he sat down again.

"Hellacious goin's on here . . . ," Warren said, ". . . I mean last night . . . ."

Mason nodded. He looked at Waskom in silence.

At length a door opened somewhere and soon Frieda walked into the room. She walked up to the table and stopped, looking at them, posing a little.

"Jesus," Warren muttered, gaping at her.

Mason stared. Then he drew a gusty breath.

She was absolutely beautiful. A new tan, tailored western outfit, complete with dainty soft and feminine boots and an orange scarf, emphasized a figure that until now she had never flaunted. Her face was creamy, the blush just right fading cheek into temple, a lock of hair just so, framing a soft and feminine brow, eye shadow perfect and leaning a bit to evening . . . and mystery . . . the lips full and pouty red. Her hair was casual and soft, falling to correct tailored length.

Frieda smiled, then showed teeth. Mason had had no idea they were so white . . . or that they were all so delicately rounded across the bottoms . . . .

"Well, my man," she said to him, "got that briefcase?"

"Got it," Mason said. He was still staring at her.

"Then shall we?"

Mason stared some more. "Where'd you get it, Frieda?"

She laughed at him, the sound bubbling out, merry and rolling, happy.

Mason got up from the table. The Waskoms watched them walk out the door. Rover was rolling a piece of biscuit between never-still forepaws, measuring it, kneading it. He gave no notice to anything else.

Behind the wheel of the Buick, driving the five hundred yards back to camp, Mason did not look at Frieda. He cleared his throat. "You see," he muttered, "I didn't tell you what I'm doing with this guy . . . exactly."

She waited.

"He's supposed to have some money for me."

"I figured that out, Mason," she said quietly. He gave her time to follow with a question, but she did not. Mason glanced quick gratitude at her. She was not looking at him.

Then quickly he said: "You see, things have changed, in the last thirty years, in college athletics . . . the economics have changed. We compete with the pros, now. Now we have other factors: TV dollars. Small crowds instead of big crowds. Steroids." Drug problems, Mason was thinking. "More changes than I told you before."

"AIDS," she suggested.

"Maybe . . . ." Mason drew a big breath. "The point is, money is short. I have a plan now to form a lightweight varsity . . . a student team, if you will . . . for the kids who played in high school but who can't make the big team."

"We've been over this, Mase."

"Okay. Point is, Nielson has the money I need for the program. To get it off the ground. He owes me . . . came here to pay me. And I never saw him before, and that is the reason you are here to be a witness, just in case."

"In case of what?"

"Beck . . . June . . . deer camp, the mob . . . that sort of thing."

Frieda looked at him.

After a time Mason said: "I want some of the money to go to June's defense. I will give it to you. What you have left over, you can give to Beck's widow. Your decision."

Both stared straight ahead at the dirt road which was nothing but tire tracks going through the brush. Up ahead they could now see the clearing with big trees where the cabins were. There were three cabins in a row and the middle one had a new Chevrolet in front and Mason drove his Buick there now.

Seven

The eyes were not blue. Mason had been right about that. But the eyes were not brown, either. They were yellow: a pale shade of hazel that was close enough to pure yellow to demand a second look, always, whenever anyone met N. L. Nielson.

Now Nielson was sitting in front of his fire, drinking Scotch. He was completely relaxed. He always drank Scotch when he had nothing else to do, and now all he had to do was wait. He waited without enthusiasm; the Scotch took care of the enthusiasm part, making his day palatable. He was waiting for someone named Mason. He knew Mason would come. If Mason did not show up, within, say, three days, well . . . .

Now Nielson smiled into the fire. He had it made.

He looked over toward the window, where a honey blonde about thirty was reading a paperback romance she had bought at the airport.

She appeared relaxed, also.

Nielson sighed. So far so good. Earlier they had gone outside together and had walked about some, but had found nothing in this Godforsaken brushpile to interest them, so had gone back to the fire. Now as she read, the woman toyed with a wisp of yellow hair above her left ear, rolling it adroitly with the fingertips of her left hand. The nails were not Fu Manchu nails at all, but were arched perfectly across the tops like firetruck-red beetles. They danced in the hair, rolling it into a thin rope, then dancing back and unrolling it. Her morning makeup was perfect: of evening quality.

"Cozy, Baby?"

"Uh-huh!" She emphasized the final syllable, not looking up.

Nielson sighed again. He settled in his chair. It might be a long wait. The longer the better, really, for him . . . .

Her name was Doris Elizabeth Morton, and they had been together eight months. During that period of time Nielson had not found a single thing about her he did not like. Now, looking at her, everything clicked again: the pure, serene face of the airhead blonde, the delicate choreography of red beetles rolling and unrolling and rolling again, the emphasis on the last syllable of her thoughtless answer to him just now showing once again quick and unplanned enthusiasm for all his projects—each and every one, as they came. Eight months with no glitches is a long time . . . harbinging years to come, perhaps. And last night, after he had built the fire and the cabin was snug; after he had poured them both a Chivas to celebrate arrival; after he had begun to think about how to assuage her fear of the strange place, the woods, the rough austerity, if fear there should be . . . when they had begun to measure the real livability of the place and he had in foreplay middle-finger-touched her magic place with a tentative stroke as light as that of the red beetles in her hair, now . . . Bartholin's had run out on the floor.

Hey, man! Talk about enthusiasm for a project! Talk about getting with the program!

Now Nielson drew a big breath. Looking at her, he wondered if there were room for him now in her chair by the window.

Then he chuckled.

"What?" she smiled the question, looking away from her book. The red beetles stopped the hair-dance.

"Nothin', Baby . . . just lookin' at you . . . ."

"Just lookin' at you, Kid . . . ?"

"Kid," he remembered, smiling back. "Here's lookin' at you, Kid." Nielson raised his glass.

She returned to the book.

Nielson had not told her about Mason. And for a reason. He knew only two things relating to this assignment: he knew the man's name was Mason, and he knew what Mason had done.

More than twenty years before, Nielson had played high school football, in Milwaukee. He had been good at it; he had loved it. Now he still loved it. He followed the Chicago Bears: just two weeks ago he and Dorie had gone to see the Bears play the Giants.

Nielson knew he could have no respect for Mason . . . after what Mason had done . . . hell, to sell out your buddies was the lowest thing a man could do. And Nielson knew exactly that his thinking this way about the man Mason represented a very great danger for him, for Nielson. He knew he would have to be very careful. In giving him the assignment, Abe, Nielson's boss, would condone no failure . . . in his mind's eye now Nielson saw himself trying to explain his failure to consummate the transfer . . . while his fingers were being broken, one by one. On the other hand Abe and the man above him, whoever he was—most certainly considered Mason a one-shot deal. If Mason were to disappear . . . never to be heard from again . . . .

That is the thing about dealing with traitors. You have to be careful. They are going down . . . and can take you with them if things go wrong. If things get sticky.

Nielson looked at Dorie again. He knew where there was a new white Fleetwood with gold trim instead of chrome. Gold that would match her hair. He longed to tell her about it. He ached to tell her about it. But he had not, did not, and would not . . . at least until Mason was behind him.

At this point she did not even know the name Mason.

Also at this point N. L. Nielson would admit, if asked, to being in love with Dorie Morton. He would jump at it. He would even admit that their relationship had matured. He would jump at that, too. But N. L. Nielson had never heard of S. Freud, nor of his observation that in any mature relationship between male and female, the female mothers the male . . . at least a little bit . . . .

Always.

A car door slammed outside.

Dorie lowered her paperback and the fingernails stopped their red bug-dance above her ear. She looked at Nielson, who drained his glass and got to his feet. He sauntered to the door, listening, relaxed. Mason knocked. He was holding the empty briefcase in his left hand, and Frieda was there with him.

The door opened. Nielson stood there looking at them for some moments before moving aside so they could enter. It was obvious to Mason he was looking at Frieda. Something inside Mason clenched a frozen fist, then exploded, exulting . . . .

"Mason." Mase stuck out his hand.

"Nielson." The voice was raspy. Predictably raspy, perhaps. The handshake was solid, to the surprise of neither man.

The men were not smiling. The women were.

"Frieda," Frieda sang out with a big smile, extending her left hand toward Nielson, upside-down-dainty from the shoulder, then she stepped to Dorie and leaned down—the effusive female—still smiling big. Dorie had not got up. The women hugged . . . an act of Frieda's doing entirely . . . and they might have been sisters, from the look of it. Dorie smiled big, now, without reserve. She put her book down.

Mason noticed the eyes, then.

Nielson caught the hitch in Mason's stare, and smiled, a little.

"Eely volk eely chelovek," Nielson said. He picked up his glass.

"What?"

"Nothin.' How's the deer?" Nielson kept looking at Frieda, walking now to the back of the cabin to fill his glass.

Mason still had not greeted Dorie. He went over now, thinking Fu Manchu, looking at the nails, motivated by nothing so much as the necessity to remove as much awkwardness from the scenario as possible.

Dorie could have been greeting guests on the Riviera. She put up a perfect red-and-white smile and a right hand high in the air with just the right amount of arch in the wrist.

"Mason," Mason told her. Oddly, he thought of kissing the hand she presented, but did not . . . .

"Dorie."

"Dorie," he repeated.

"Mason," Nielson said from the back of the cabin, "how about a Scotch?"

"I . . . ah . . . ." Mason looked at his watch. He was still holding the empty briefcase in that hand. Of course it was way too early for Scotch. For anything.

"Sure. Why not? Why the hell not?" Mason said. He thought: fuck the rules. This is a different game, now.

"How's the deer?" Nielson wanted to know, again. He grabbed a glass. "And how do you like your Chivas?"

"Scarce . . . and on the rocks, in that order," Mason said. He laughed big, looking at Frieda.

She rolled her eyes to the ceiling. Mason saw that she was relaxed. Having fun, even.

"And you," Frieda said to Dorie, sitting down in the other chair so as not to be looking down at her any more, "do you hunt?"

"Only men!" Nielson said. He said it too loud. Then he laughed. His laughter had a lot of chest in it. Dorie threw her book at him. It fluttered and missed by a wide margin but he ducked anyway, and everybody laughed.

Then Nielson handed Mason his drink, and at the same time and with the same motion Mason gave him the empty briefcase. He locked eyes with Nielson at the same time, not smiling. There could be no doubt . . . .

Nielson took the briefcase and put it on the floor against the wall. He grinned.

"Dorie spells deer with an *A*," he proclaimed. "They have two legs. Not four." He laughed big again.

Dorie was looking at Frieda and shaking her head in disgust. It was all in the script.

Frieda said, "That's all right. She knows the difference . . . ."

"Damn right," Dorie said, acting. She looked at Frieda, and crinkled the corners of her eyes, only. "Do you hunt, Frieda?"

"Not me." Frieda knew to say "not I"; she knew also not to say "not I." Now she shook her head fast, violently.

"Bambi," she told Dorie. "Bambi's mom . . . all of that."

Dorie nodded.

"I'll bet you could if you wanted to!"

"Right." Frieda made an issue of the nod in agreement.

"Right!" Mason chimed in, at just the right moment. "Two-legged or four, what the hell!"

Frieda looked about her for something to throw. The host and hostess caught it, and both laughed.

During the next few moments the four calmed down some and, the meeting off to a perfect flight, said nothing. Soon the men were sipping their drinks and the women had their heads together as if comparing notes, or planning something. It was cozy in the cabin. Outside the north wind picked up a bit. Nielson put two more logs on the fire. Comfortable minutes went by.

"You a hunter?" Mason asked.

"Yes and no. I came prepared."

"I'll bet. I got to go back. Hopefully today . . . I'll tell you where there is a big one, if you are interested."

Nielson looked at him, his glass halfway to his mouth. The yellow eyes had in them the slow look of the mob, with the color adding something. Mason did not know what.

"Tell me."

"Up on the bluff overlooking the field. There's a two-acre-wide strip there of cedar that's never been cut. Big trees. It's like a cathedral park. There's a big buck in there . . . I saw him yesterday," Mason said, sipping. "World class rack . . . ."

Nielson lowered the eyes. He nodded. Obviously he was not interested.

"Maybe I'll get up there," Nielson said quietly.

Mason lowered his drink and looked at it. He knew Nielson would not fill the briefcase now, with everybody watching. He also knew the day was getting on, and there were things to do.

"What's to do, here?" Dorie wanted to know. Her voice was carefully petulant . . . the timeless feminine prerogative.

"Oh, there are things . . . ," Frieda said, making it big, nodding big.

"Really?" The voice was completely naive. Everybody read it. Dorie did not know why she was here. Nor did she care.

"Sure. If he goes out . . . leave it to me. I'll take you to town."

"That'd be great!" Dorie grinned, big, not knowing what town was like. At this, then, Mason saw the chink. He watched, and saw Nielson appear to fidget, some. Nielson wiped the moisture from his glass.

"We'll go," Mason said. He took the bull by the horns: "When you are through with the briefcase, put it in our cabin. I leave it unlocked."

Nielson stared.

"There to the east," Mason said. He pointed, watching the eyes.

Nielson nodded, still staring slow with his yellow eyes.

Then within two minutes Mason had finished his Scotch and gave a nod to Frieda. She got up.

"See you," Mason said. "Good luck with the big buck. If you go up."

Nielson nodded.

The guests left the cabin.

Then later Mason and Frieda looked at each other in the Buick, going back to the ranchhouse. Both nodded. They did not speak on the way back.

When they got there, Raleigh Jones was up. He had not dressed as yet, and his hair was tousled. Mason and Frieda came in and Mase sat at the kitchen table with him, where he was having breakfast, with Helen Waskom doing her thing.

"How's Junior?" Mason asked.

Raleigh looked at him. He raised his coffee. Mason saw that his hair needed combing, that he was not the same without it.

Raleigh shook his head.

"Needs his coon," Mason suggested. Then he was sorry for having said it, when Raleigh looked at him. That was the thing about morons. You never knew what to say. Frieda had walked on through to her room, and was gone from the kitchen, now.

Then Mason thought of something.

"How's Senior?" Mason asked.

Raleigh looked at him.

"You know how it is," he said. "You always leave somethin' undone. Unfinished. At least I do. Why is that?"

"I don't know," Mason said. "What're you talkin' about?"

Raleigh shook his head.

"Lots of things," he said.

Mason waited.

"Thinkin' about that hole I dug last night. I can't get it out of my mind . . . ."

Mason looked at him. There was a question but he did not know how to ask it. Then Mason thought about his own empty briefcase at camp, about how he was waiting for it to get full. Hurry, briefcase. Come home, little briefcase.

"I know," Mason said.

"I mean . . ." Raleigh looked at him. "Last night when I dug it,

Every Man Also—155

it was for a purpose. Now it's lyin' there. Open to the sky. Naked. A mistake. I can't get it out of my head."

"Maybe we ought to go fill it in. It's a gash. A wound, in your mind."

"Mase, it's not we. It's me. I."

"Why?"

Raleigh's and Mase's gazes locked. The rancher appeared ragged out, exhausted. Now he straightened his back, sitting taller, and sighed.

"Yeah. Why?"

"I mean," Mason said, "You can look for reasons on and on. When you find 'em maybe they're true and maybe not and you'll never know the difference. But a better way is if you have something you need to do, go do it. And if your buddy wants to help you, let him. What else is there?"

Raleigh tried to grin.

"You'd do that for me?"

"You got two shovels?"

Within five minutes the two men were in Raleigh's pickup, headed for the base of the bluff. The landscape and brush were warming in the morning sun. There was no wind, now, and everything was perfectly still.

"I mean, mistake is one thing . . . ." Raleigh was driving, thinking, trying to get it just right. "A mistake is maybe a mistake when you do it and maybe it becomes one later. What am I tryin' to say? But whether it was one from the very first or not . . . when it becomes one, you don't need to be lookin' at it all the time . . . Mase, is that what I'm tryin' to say?" Jones stared at Mason in something like mild anguish.

"Sounds like Frieda ought to be with us, now," Mason said. "Maybe that's what you're tryin' to say."

Raleigh laughed. Mason had the thought that the laughter was at the mention of her name.

"All I know is, that open hole lookin' at the sky is buggin' me! Bad! Why is that?"

"Maybe because it's a grave. Graves need to be closed."

"Maybe. But it's no grave, now. It is a mistake, is all . . . ."

"Where is Frieda, anyway?"

"She went into town. Took Rover to Junior," Raleigh said. "She took the car. My car. We had that agreement last night . . . this mornin', when we got in."

Mason nodded.

When they arrived at the hole Raleigh stopped the truck and they got out. There were two shovels in the bed of the pickup and Raleigh got them. He gave one to Mason. He gave Mason also a pair of fabric work gloves, the kind that you buy at the grocery store for a dollar and a half. The gloves he gave Mason had not been used.

Without talk the two men began filling the hole, from the pile of loose dirt six feet away. The dirt was black and dry. The work went fast. When, after thirty minutes of work without stopping, they were only halfway finished, Mason took a break. He stopped shovelling, and tested his back.

"Damn," Mason said. "How'd you get so much done, in such a short time?"

But Raleigh Jones did not hear him. He worked on. He made a small explosive noise with his mouth at every shovelful, and did not look at Mason. He pursed his lips, after every shovelful.

Buzzards were wheeling overhead, now and then. Mason had learned to tell the difference between turkey vultures, which had naked heads, and black vultures, whose wings stuck forward when they flew, and whose wingbeats were faster when they scudded away.

The winter morning was ripening into noon. Sun lay out on the land in absence of wind, and it was getting almost hot. The hole filled slowly. Periodically Raleigh put down his shovel and stamped back and forth, packing the earth. He had not said one word to Mason since they had arrived and had begun the work, and now Mason could hear a small edge to his breathing, at each shovelful, a small gasp for air, almost.

"Raleigh."

"What?"

"Let's rest."

"No. Got to get it done."

The hole was almost full, now. Mason was amazed that one man had done this much work, by himself, in digging the hole in the time he knew it had taken him. He could not believe it. It was order-of-magnitude unreal; order of magnitude ridiculous assessment . . . .

"Raleigh."

"What?"

"What do we do if the sheriff charges you with trying to hide the body?"

Raleigh thought, then he said, "He won't do that. I know him. I'll take my chances. It never happened. We were just digging a hole. A man can dig a hole on his own land anytime he wants to."

"Let's rest."

"No."

Raleigh kept on. He dropped his shovel and tramped back and forth. They were almost finished.

Soon they were done, and the way they knew it was so was that the pile of loose dirt was gone. Raleigh stomped back and forth for the last time. Then he knelt, in the new dirt, with the shovel handle sticking up, and began to cry. He cried for a long time, not making any noise. He turned his face away, and his shoulders shook. After a while Mason came near and the crying stopped. Raleigh had still made no noise.

"You okay?" Mason said.

"Okay."

"Let's go back."

Driving back, following tire track dirt roads through the brush, Raleigh Jones opened his mouth several times to thank Mason for suggesting they come, then coming with him. But each time he began to say something, the words were wrong and, afraid he would make a mess of it, he said nothing.

Mason had thoughts only of his briefcase. He was also considering how to phrase something.

Finally: "Thanks, Mase."

"Okay. It's okay. How about drivin' by camp, on the way back?"

When they got to his cabin, Mason got out and went in. There was no briefcase. Also, Nielson's car was gone from the front of his cabin. Mason ran the fifty steps to Nielson's cabin. He peered in through the front window, at the edge. The first thing he looked for checked out: the couple were still here. But the briefcase was exactly where Nielson had put it. It had not been touched. Half-heartedly he tried the door. It was locked.

Mason went back to the pickup, where Raleigh was waiting with the motor running. He got in.

"Everything okay?"

"I . . . ah . . . yeah. Yeah. Everything's okay."

Later Raleigh said: "You sure, now?"

"Yeah," Mason said. "I'm sure." But the wheels were turning in his head.

When Frieda came back from town both Raleigh and Mase were waiting for her. They were sitting at the kitchen table talking, though not many words were passing back and forth. The table was old and round and could seat eight people. It had faded red oilcloth on it; near Raleigh's place the oilcloth edge had fibers showing, where Raleigh had, over the years, scraped the top layer of plastic off with a fingernail. Now he had cancelled lunch, which Helen referred to as dinner, and she was taking a break somewhere.

Frieda came in and sat with them. Nobody said anything.

Later Frieda said: "June is fine."

Raleigh nodded.

"Upbeat," she said. She smiled.

Raleigh covered her hand with one of his own, and squeezed. She squeezed back. Nobody said upbeat because of the coon.

"And the briefcase?" Frieda wanted to know. "What kind of shape is it in?" She looked at Mason.

"Empty. As yet." Then Mason told her about coming by and looking in both cabins, and that Nielson and Dorie were gone, but their things still there.

"They're back," she told him.

"What? How do you know?"

"They turned in the gate right behind me. Coming from the other direction. Apparently just out riding around. Maybe lunch."

Mason got to his feet. The other two looked at him.

"Where you goin'?" Raleigh asked.

"Confrontation time . . . ," Mason said. He was grim. He got out his car keys and looked at them. "I can't wait all day. Might be all week."

"No," Frieda said. "Wait. I have a better idea. Sit down."

Slowly he sat again. He stared at her.

"Better idea," she repeated. Then she got up and went to the refrigerator, opening it. She bent at the waist and peered inside, as if shopping, her hands demurely on her knees.

"Lunchtime," she told the men airily. "I have the munchies. A bit peckish, as our British friends would say." She looked up and smiled brightly.

Frieda found cottage cheese in a carton and put some in a bowl, got a fork and returned to the table.

"You had an idea," Mason reminded. He looked at the new beauty of her, since the makeup job in the morning.

Eating the cottage cheese, Frieda dug in her purse and produced Raleigh's car keys. She put them on the table in front of him.

"Now give me yours," she said to Mason, wriggling fingers at him.

Mase produced them, looking a question at Raleigh, who shrugged big, making a show of it, face and all.

Frieda laughed again. She was having fun.

"You're not gonna do it!" Mason told her. "No. I won't stay hitched for that!"

"No, no," she said. "This is something else . . . ."

It was almost as if she knew something they did not know, now, with the new face. Not quite that she was a new person but an older one exonerated, resurrected, refurbished into a legacy of fun and new horizons . . . party time . . . carnival . . . Mardi Gras. She was a little girl squinting eyes and hunching shoulders and giggling now into a cupped hand, with a friend; the friend doing the same, both jumping up and down.

Mason stared. She did know something.

"What're you gonna do?" he asked.

"You don't have to know. But there is a flea market this afternoon on the courthouse lawn. And I found a craft shop . . . Happy Hands. It's loaded!"

She picked up his keys.

"See ya," she said. "You stay away. You, Mase, stay away from camp! Stay here for the afternoon. I'll have a try at your briefcase."

Mason stared. Jones stared. Frieda got out a lipstick tube and a white compact and thickened her lipstick. Then she got up, waved to them, and walked out the door. In a moment they heard the Buick start.

The two men sat at the table. They were tired from the spadework earlier.

Ten minutes later they heard the Buick again, from the other direction. Standing so they could see out the window above the sink, they saw Mase's car sail by on its way to the front gate, dust boiling up behind.

In the car two foxy females were nodding heads and laughing. Both were talking at the same time.

It was not long before Raleigh Jones went back to town. Smitty came to the big house twice within thirty minutes looking for tools. Warren and Helen were not in evidence, so Mase Mason was left to his devices. He turned on the TV several times, then wandered about.

Finding the morning newspaper in the den, he read it through, then wandered about again. Outside in a cloudless sky the sun had by midafternoon warmed the now windless countryside, so at three o'clock it was cooler in the house than outside. But Mase did not know this.

He knew only that he was getting sleepy and, with Frieda's big fourposter nearby, tightly and refreshingly made, he kicked off his shoes, pulled the shade down, and climbed up on the bed.

Lying on his back, Mason closed his eyes. Almost immediately he was dozing, and within a few minutes he was in a deep sleep. Soon he began to dream.

In his dream it was game day at the big Tech Stadium and from the pressbox Mase put his binoculars on the south end zone ramp and saw Benjie, the receiver coach, lead his team onto the field. They were obviously the Warriors, from their Red and Gray uniforms, but they were midgets. They swarmed behind Benjie, who was running hard to stay in front. Like rats behind the Pied Piper, or chicks behind a mother hen, they billowed . . . fell back . . . scudded here and there. It was very fine. The fans began to throw pillows onto the field.

Right in the middle of the midget Warriors was Moose Drobisch, running with them. He was in uniform, also, of course, and was the only one of the real Warriors coming on the field. The pillows the fans were throwing now were of the flat canvas variety you sit on. Mase had tried them in an effort to boost ticket sales, some years back, but it had not caught on. Now in his dream the pillows were back.

Inside the flurry of pillows now was one Coke bottle, which looped far out and true and hit Moose Drobisch on the head and dropped him.

Mason loved Drobisch. He remembered when he was so green and awkward it had hurt Mason to watch him try to play. In high school he had been gullible, also. A buddy confided in him that the way to be both relaxed and sharp on the field was to masturbate before the game. So Moose had tried it. Before one night game he had gone into a commode stall in the dressing room and had "whipped up a home-batch," as he put it later. That night in the game he broke three ribs . . . .

Then all at once Moose Drobisch was a hell of a player. Overnight. Mase had never understood this. Now in Mase's dream Drobisch was out cold, and lying on the field.

In his dream now Mase remembered the year before when the Warriors had gone to Fayetteville to play the University of Arkansas. The night before for some reason they had stayed in a hotel in Ft. Smith and the morning of the game he remembered his wake-up call had said, "Good morning. It is six o'clock and sixteen degrees." Later, after breakfast, the team had walked around downtown to get a little exercise before getting on the plane and they had gone into a men's clothing store.

He remembered the people were unfriendly because they were the Warriors.

He remembered also the proprietor, who was friendlier, came up to Drobisch and stood up close to him, looking up and saying: "God a'mighty. It's too big for a man and too small for a mule. What is it?"

Now gazing from the press box he was looking precisely at the man on the top row who threw the Coke bottle. He watched him throw it. It looped far out, then got bigger and bigger and then bounced off Drobisch's head and because he did not have his helmet on yet it knocked him out. There he was, in the middle of the field, flat. Occupying acres, it seemed. Bleeding.

Let that be a lesson to you, men. Put that helmet on. What's it for? I mean . . . early! Put it on!

Then for a time Benjie and the Midgets, who sounded like a rock group, even in Mason's dream, tried to play their game around Drobisch there on the field. The other team was a lightweight team also. The whole thing was like a game between two Japanese college teams. Except for Drobisch.

He was out for a long time and finally it was decided that the game was not fair to either side because of the prostrate giant on the field so they called time while they brought in a big stretcher and a firetruck and took Drobisch off the field. They took him to the doctor. And they sent Mason along in the firetruck as emissary. Then Benjie and the Midgets returned to their game.

When they got to the hospital the doctors all drew straws to see who would care for Drobisch, then Mason walked up to the one with the short straw, and saw he had yellow eyes . . . .

It was six-thirty in the evening when Frieda tiptoed into the room and returned the favor of Mason's visit many hours earlier: she eased onto the bed, sitting. He opened his eyes.

Mason was lying on his back with his hands folded on his chest. Now he looked at her, and did not move.

She made a little crumpled pile of his car keys on his chest.

"How'd it go?" Mase mumbled, his voice crusty. Then he cleared his throat and said it again.

She nodded. Then she leaned down and kissed him on the cheek.

"I think," she said, "I got a good scald on it."

"What?"

"Something my grandmother used to say. Had something to do with plucking chickens . . . . It means I succeeded."

"That easy, huh?"

"We'll see, Mase." She got up, then went back to the door. Now it was almost dark in the old bedroom. Frieda turned back to him at the door.

"Helen's almost got supper ready . . . listen to me! Dinner!"

"Supper," Mase told her. "Out here you have to say supper."

"Okay. Anyway, why don't you stay here and eat with us, before you go back up?"

Mason looked at her.

"Okay," he said.

In some moments Mason got up and went into the bathroom,

where he dabbed cold tapwater on his eyes, blotted his face with a towel, and combed his hair. Then he went into the big kitchen. Everybody was there: Raleigh, Frieda, Warren, Helen and Smitty. Smitty had his coat off. Rover was on the floor by the stove, wrist-deep in a bowl of oatmeal.

It was the first time Helen had really cooked since the tragedy. She had the usual pinto beans and cornbread, mustard greens, and there were two shallow bowls on the table with cucumbers, onions and tomatoes—all sliced—covered with vinegar. The only meat was fatback pork in the beans, but there was a lot of it, cut into big cubes with the skin pared off.

Raleigh Jones bowed his head when they were all seated, and said grace. It was the one that goes: "Lord, make us thankful . . . ," and he said it slowly and with feeling. Mason stole a glance and decided Raleigh wanted to say much more, but did not know what to say. Or how.

The food was good and Mason decided the atmosphere at the table was exactly like that of some pregame meals he had sat at with the Warriors, when a Moment of Truth was at hand. When all talk had faded and disappeared and you either did it now or didn't.

Exactly that way. Nobody said anything.

Pregame meals are all alike, Mason reflected. Nobody looks at anybody. Nobody says anything. The food is good but nobody cares. Everybody is thinking about the Moment of Truth at hand, and what luck will be had with it.

But luck has many faces, Mason thought. And who can recognize her, before the die is cast? Or after, either, for that matter? Now it was pitch black outside, in the wide window above the sink. Helen's pintos were tender and good, the fatback in them just right. Still nobody said anything.

Then Smitty was standing, pointing at the window. He was pointing across the table.

"There goes somebody."

Mason stood. From where he was standing now he could not see the car lights.

"Nielson," Mason said.

"Prob'ly."

"Which way is he turning? Toward town or toward the Interstate?"

Ten seconds went by.

"Interstate," Smitty said.

Mason bolted from the table. He hit the back door without being aware of it, then was in the dark and running heavy-footed toward his Buick.

"Oh . . . ," he said. "Oh . . . he better have."

But there was nothing he could do but get the car running and get to his cabin as soon as possible.

Mason was aware that Frieda was yelling something to him from the kitchen door. But he could not hear what she was saying . . . it was like there could be no communication . . . if he hurried and if the briefcase were not there he would have time to catch Nielson on the Interstate and stop him. His .270, he thought. He would have to remember to throw it in the car when he got to the cabin . . . .

But when he got to the cabin and turned on the lights the briefcase was on the table. It was standing up.

And when he opened it there were ten neat stacks of hundreds looking at him. It was all there. All of it. Looking snug and official: one thousand portraits of Ben Franklin.

Mason sat at the table for a long time and looked at the open briefcase. At length he got up and put everything of his that was still in the cabin in the car. The briefcase he closed once more and laid beside him on the front seat.

Back at the house he walked through the kitchen with his briefcase and nodded at everybody.

"It's okay," Mason told them.

Then he sat down at the library table in the living room and waited for Frieda and Raleigh.

Mason thought: quickest game I ever saw. And we won. The Warriors won.

Frieda walked in.

"The Warriors won," he told her.

"I know." She sat down at the table.

"How did you . . . I mean what did you . . . ?"

"Oh, Mason," she sighed. "What can I tell you? A lot of little things, I guess . . . ."

Then she perked up.

"Best to act mysterious," she told him. "It worked, didn't it?"

They laughed. Mase shook his head in wonder.

Raleigh walked in. He was wiping his hands with a towel. He sat with them.

Mason got ready.

"You see, Raleigh . . . . You see, it's the old, old thing about the amateur and the professional. Economics and the Moment of Truth. You can subsidize somethin' just so long, then the time comes when it's got to float by itself or go under . . . ."

Raleigh Jones stared. He was puzzled.

"Simplify," he said.

Mason laughed.

"A long time ago a bunch of us believed in college athletics," he said. "The well-rounded man. You teach teamwork, dedication, staying power, courage . . . pride, maturity. Then the economics changed, like it always does. And some other things changed. Now you have to win, to keep goin' . . . I don't know . . . maybe it was always that way . . . ."

Raleigh waited. He looked as if he wanted to nod.

"The things you have to do to win get harder and harder," Mason went on. "Farther away from the thing you want to accomplish. So the whole thing becomes more and more professional. Maybe specialized is a better word for it. Away from the idea of the well-rounded man . . . . It has become too hard to do. So those who can't do it any more have given up, and they knock the others who still try."

Jones nodded. He was up to speed, now.

"But now and then an iron ass . . . like me . . ."—at this Mason stole a glance at Frieda—"will insist on forcin' the old values on people. So he'll start a lightweight football program, for instance, for the students who are not big enough or good enough for the big team. Because he believes in the teaching value inherent in the sport, so much . . . even though nobody talks about it any more . . . we do, you see."

Raleigh nodded. "Texas A&M."

"Yep. Their Twelfth Man squad. The kickoff squad. Recruited from the student body . . . same idea. They make it work. It's the belief that counts. And the attempt."

Raleigh waited. Frieda waited.

Mason blew out his breath.

"Well," he told them, "I'm in the formative stages with my program. And I need money for uniforms." Mase petted the briefcase. It was still closed. "This is it. That's all there is to it."

Later Mase said: "This money belongs to the Tech Athletic Department. That's where it came from."

Mason stole another glance at Frieda. She crinkled the corners of her eyes.

"It'll have to make its own way, of course," he said. "We'll see. But now we're off and runnin'."

Mase opened the briefcase. The ten rectangular stacks looked at them. Each was ten thousand dollars.

"In any beginning," Mason went on, "you got to cover overhead. We'll do that now. I want to contribute to June's court costs, and I want you or Frieda to give what's left—or take some out along the way—for Beck's widow. Your option."

Mason stacked seven cubes in front of Raleigh Jones.

Raleigh pushed one back.

Mason put it back in front of Raleigh.

Raleigh put it back again.

Mason tore the band and made two equal stacks of the hundreds and put one of these back in front of Raleigh Jones, so the money on the table was now equally divided.

Raleigh pushed his money to a spot in front of Frieda.

She looked at him. Then she looked at Mase. Mase watched, and had the thought her eyes were wet.

Later they all got up. Mason put his share back in the briefcase.

Around ten that night the wind backed around into the north again and began to blow colder. A fine mist started to fall and Mason went outside. It was blackest night and the light from the open kitchen door flooded out into the yard in a wedge. He could see every little droplet in the light, each one wafting like a minuscule snowflake as it floated to the ground. Mason watched for a moment, wondering why they did not hit each other.

Then he went back in the kitchen and put on his coat. Just outside the kitchen window, nailed to the window framing, was a thermometer, fixed so the light from the room went through the window and fell on the vertical scale, making it possible to read outside temperature from inside the room. He went there now and peered. The reading was thirty-one degrees, Fahrenheit.

"Ah hah!" Mason said.

He had been itching to leave. But they had told him don't be an idiot. Nobody leaves in the middle of the night. Stay in Jim's room until morning and then leave like a civilized person . . . .

Now he stuck his head into the den where Raleigh and Frieda were sitting before the fire sipping Burgundy. They were sitting back-to-back and touching, on a red ottoman, both staring into the fire.

"Ah hah!" Mason said again.

They looked up.

"I'm leaving," he said. "It's misting rain. I think it'll ice up before morning. If that happens, I can't get out."

Frieda and Raleigh got to their feet. They followed Mason outside. His car was already packed.

"I'd better," Mason apologized. "Martha hasn't heard from me since I got here. And I need to see Charlie first thing in the morning."

Outside Frieda folded her arms, clenching them, and toed up and down in the cold. She rocked back on her heels.

"Two things, Mase," she said.

"Okay."

"Tell Vern to go ahead and phase out the experiment. Tell him I'll call him in a week."

"And keep good notes," Mase suggested.

"You don't need to say that. The boy is covered up with numbers."

"The second thing?" Mason asked.

"Dorie Morton wants tickets. When the new team has a schedule. She was emphatic. I have her address."

Mason stared. Raleigh Jones was beginning to shake his hand.

"What will you call the new team?" Raleigh wanted to know. Mason could see Raleigh's breath now in the light from the kitchen door, which was still open.

"I don't know . . . hadn't thought much about it . . . ." Mason paused. Then he said: "How about Light Brigade . . . or Lighthorse Cavalry . . .? We'll work on it, Raleigh!"

"No," Frieda said. She crinkled the corners of her eyes.

"What?"

"They're the Warriors," she told him.

Then Mason and Frieda were embracing, goodbye, faces alongside and upturned. He squeezed her hard, and was aware that her hug in return was from the sides, showing good pressure but keeping him where he was . . . .

He looked at her, at Raleigh.

"No doubt I'll be back," he said.

"No doubt," Frieda said.

Mason was aware of the perfume she had put on earlier that morning. He could not name it. No doubt it would bother him until he figured out what it was.

And maybe after that, he thought.

Robert Winship was born in Iraan, Texas, the son of a high school principal and part-time rancher. A graduate of Rice University, he was a member of the famous 1949 football team and played in that season's Cotton Bowl (January 2, 1950) and East-West Shrine Game and then had a contract with the Philadelphia Eagles. Later he had a career of many years selling oil and gas drilling and production equipment around the world. He now lives and writes at the family's Rockpile Ranch near Junction, Texas. Author of *The Brushlanders*, winner of the 1992 *Texas Review* Press Southern and Southwestern Writers Fiction Breakthrough Award, Winship writes a weekly column for *The Junction Eagle*; his fiction and nonfiction prose have appeared in *Concho River Review*, *Hawaii Review*, *RE Arts and Letters*, and *The Texas Review*.